BLESSED FIRE

A SUPERNATURAL HORROR NOVEL

BY

P.W HILLARD

Contents

Chapter 1

That kind of unique damp breeze only found on rainy boardwalks across Britain drifted in through the thin gap at the top of the car window. Mark adjusted in his seat, clutching the carrier bag to his chest. It was warm and smelled strongly of vinegar. He fished out a package wrapped in white paper which crackled as he handled it.

"Large chips and a sausage in batter." He handed the package to the woman sat in the driver's seat.

"Thanks." Jess unwrapped the package on her lap, resting some of the paper on the steering wheel. "Did you get the curry sauce?"

"Yeah, here you go." Mark passed a small Styrofoam carton in a brown paper bag. "Any sign of him?" He peered forward in his seat. They had parked across the street from a fried chicken takeaway. A cartoon chicken in a baseball hat leered down at them.

"He turned up for work not long after you went in the chippy." Jess dipped her sausage into her curry. She blew on it and took a large bite. "Don't seem to be that many staff in there," she muttered, her words muffled by the mouthful of sausage.

Mark unwrapped his own chips. "Right well plan of attac- "He was interrupted by Jess tapping him on the shoulder. She opened the car door and stepped out into the street. A young man wearing a red and white striped uniform was carrying large black bags around the side of the fried chicken shop. The cartoon chicken grinned on his back. Mark stared at the still hot chips on his lap, sighed and placed them on the driver's seat. He stepped out and began to follow Jess.

The man in the chicken shop uniform lifted the heavy metal lid of the bin and heaved the black bags into his. He was tall, toned and had black hair cut into a fade. He wiped his hands on the blood red apron that covered his front and turned to walk back to the front of the shop. Two figures blocked his way. A man, thick heavy grey woollen coat covering a plane white shirt and beige chinos. His hair was flecked with grey, thin streaks of it running across his temples. Thick glasses framed his piercing blue eyes. A thick stubble covered his jaw. The second figure was a woman, tall with a thin face, her chin and nose pointed. She had fiery red hair tied in a long ponytail. She wore a navy-blue suit underneath a black windbreaker.

"Gregg Harken?" Asked the woman. She opened her jacket. Reaching for something inside.

"Who's asking?" replied Gregg. He shifted nervously.

"Detective Constable Holden, this is my partner Detective Constable Curren." She pulled an identity badge from her jacket pocket.

"We've got a few questions for you," said the man she had identified as Curren. He stepped forward. Gregg took a step back, thought for a moment and then broke into a sprint.

Mark sighed heavily. "And I didn't bring my running shoes," he complained. The two police officers broke into a run, feet pounding after Gregg. They rounded the corner after him as he turned out of sight. The small alleyway behind the fast food outlet opened onto another street. Gregg collided with a portly man carrying a shopping bag, spilling fruit onto the street. He stumbled for a moment, regained his footing and continued to run.

"Stop police!" Jess shouted, stepping over the pedestrian who was scrabbling after an orange.

"One day," Mark chuckled "that will actually work."

As they pursued Gregg down the street, slowly they gained on him. The crowd was being separated by him as he fled like a ships' wake. Unimpeded they gained ground on him little by little. Marks knees ached a dull throbbing pain, Jess' face had gone a shade of red to match her hair. Gregg strode confidently, evidently still having plenty of wind in his sails. He bore to his left, sliding down an embankment into the carpark of the Valueways branch near the end of the street.

"God dammnit," complained Mark has he slowly drudged down the small slope. Slimy wet mud covered his shoes. "These were...new...," he wheezed, his breath ragged. He stopped for a second to shake them off as Jess ran past him. She twisted, dodging past an old woman pushing a trolley. The car park was full, it brimmed with cars. Reaching the first row of them, Gregg crouched briefly onto all fours, before launching himself into the air, clearing four rows of parked cars. His arms flailed as he flew, and his ankle twisted as he landed. He careened into a white Transit, slamming headfirst into the doors before collapsing on the floor.

"They always try to get clever," Jess rolled her eyes as she spoke. She reached to the back of her belt and unclipped a set of handcuffs. "Come on mate," she grabbed Gregg, locking the handcuffs around his wrists. "You're nicked."

Gregg screamed. His skin stretched as his face reshaped itself forming a long snout. Wiry brown hair sprouted from his skin. His nails stretched out become long sharp claws. His gum swelled as a set of razor-sharp teeth dropped in front of his human ones. Then, like an elastic band, his form snapped back into place. He screeched in defiance before attempting the transformation again. He thrashed and kicked on the ground. He tried desperately to wrench his wrists free of the handcuffs. Pale blue runes glowed along them, and his skin let off a faint sizzle each time he tried to shift. Mark stared at his watch counting whilst Jess leant scribbled a note for the owner of the now dented van. Gregg let out a long drawn out breath and sat up. He closed his eyes and took slow controlled breaths.

"Four minutes and nineteen seconds," declared Mark with a flourish of his hand.

"Better than most, congratulations kid," Jess tucked the note beneath the van's wiper blade. "You're part of the elusive sub five-minute club. Normally takes a little longer to work out the cuffs."

"Who are you? What are you?" Gregg asked frantically.

"We told you," Mark crouched next to him. "Police, just ones who deal with things that are, well, like you." Mark gripped his arm and lifted him to his feet. "Let's go with, special."

One on each arm they marched Gregg back the way they had come. Jess had to awkwardly slow her pace to not pull ahead. People drifted out of the way, gossiping to each other as they paraded the handcuffed Gregg across the street.

"So how long?" whispered Jess in his ear.

"How long what?" Gregg barked back.

"Keep your voice down," murmured Jess "How long have you been a, you know?"

"A fry cook?" Gregg said puzzled.

"No," Jess rolled her eyes "a werewolf."

"Oh my god Jess, you can't just ask someone how long they've been a," Mark lowered his voice to match them "werewolf."

"No, it's ok." Gregg shrugged. "I got bit when I was fourteen, one of the other kids in my foster home."

"Sorry to hear that" apologised Jess. "Doesn't excuse a life of crime though, I went through foster care and look at me."

"You haven't even told me what I've done!" protested Gregg.

Mark put the key into the boots lock and popped it open. He gestured at the contents within. His face was twisted into a scowl.

"This is what you have done," Jess crossed her arms. "Care to explain yourself?"

"Trainers?" Gregg said puzzled. "They sent some kind of special police, with magic handcuffs over some trainers?"

"Hey, look, laws the law." Mark stared at him. "Doesn't matter if you're a wolf, or a vamp, or a kappa rules still apply."

"The fuck is a kappa?" asked Gregg.

"It's like a kind of turtle spirt. Actually, it doesn't matter," Jess replied. She reached into the car boot and pulled out one of the several pairs of trainers contained within. "We picked these up from a storage unit under your name. Abbidos? Really? You're going to sell fake trainers on Facebook and you don't even bother to check them."

"I didn't know they were fake!" protested Gregg. "I bought them off a mate! They seemed good to me."

"Wash many hots, rotation accelerate. Those are the wash instructions," Jess was holding one of the trainers in front of her; reading from a label inside. "It lists the shoe size as four hundred and twelve."

Mark drove for the journey back. He had stuffed his bag of chips into one of the plastic pockets in the driver side door. They had long since gone cold be he begrudged wasting the two pound twenty he had paid. Jess was, as usual, scribbling something in her notebook. She wrote down everything, always said it helped with the paperwork later. Mark thought she must have hundreds of the things scattered around her house by now. Gregg had lain down flat on the rear passenger seats. They drove an unmarked black Toyota so there was no partition between the front and back like a normal police car. With the handcuffs on though Gregg was no more threatening than the average twenty something, and he was being co-operative enough now the game was up. *This is always the worst part* thought Mark, swallowing down a cold chip with grim determination. Special investigations was officially part of the Metropolitan Police, but because of its unique nature had dispensation of operate across the country. Most local forces couldn't hold anything supernatural for too long, so long drives back to New Scotland Yard were common. Thankfully Broadstairs was only a two-hour drive from

London. Mark had once been part of a cross cultural exercise with their American counterparts. It was funny, to them a four-hour drive had been "nothing", but four hundred years had been "an eternity".

"Everything ok back there?" Jess broke the silence by asking.

"Sunshine and roses," replied Gregg sarcastically. "Where are we going?

"Specialist holding." Jess turned in his seat to look over the headrest. "Cells for people of... supernatural... capabilities.

Gregg sat up with a start. "So, what, you're going to throw me in some hole and throw away the key?"

"What? No!" Jess looked visibly hurt. "You'll be processed and tried just like anyone else. You'll probably be on the train back to Broadstairs by tomorrow morning. You'll be registered as an S.N and given some stuff to help you."

"What kind of help?" asked Gregg.

"Guides of how to conceal your lycanthropy, what to do if monster hunters get your trail, support groups, that kind of thing."

"Wait, wait," Gregg leant forward close to Jess, enraptured. "Lycanthropy? Monster hunters?"

"Lycanthropy is the technical term for being a werewolf, everyone knows you get bit you turn, but that's what the actual disease that changes you is called. Monster hunters is fairly self-explanatory."

"So, someone out there is trying to kill me?" Greggs asked frantically.

"Well, hopefully not," Mark added, feeling left out of the conversation. "We try and stop people before it gets that far. Movies, telly shows, books, all have done a lot of damage to your public image so to speak. People find out what you are, and it tends to be pitchforks at dawn."

"How did you even know what I was? I've never shown told anyone, shown anyone?"

"Simple detective work," answered Jess. "Rumours about town of a figure leaping buildings in a single bound, sprinting across fields, stuff that gets certain rumour websites excited. Spring-heeled Jack sighted once again! That kind of thing."

"That got us on the trail of something odd in the town," Mark continued "and we liaised with the local constabulary on what cases they were working on."

"What and you got werewolf from dodgy trainers?" Gregg laughed, partly at himself, partly at the leap in logic.

"Well, no," said Jess. "But you were selling on Facebook under a fake name, Gregg Wolfman."

"Not the cleverest in school were you Gregg?" Mark Jabbed.

They had pulled the car into New Scotland Yard's carpark, dragged Gregg from the car and marched him over to a small lift door hidden in the far corner. They stepped inside squeezing up against each other in its tiny space. Mark pressed a button and it began to descend. It opened to a long corridor filled with dripping pipes. Something scuttled in the dark.

"This isn't creepy at all," said Gregg, trying to break the silence.

"Joys of budget cuts." Jess gurned at him. They reached a set of double doors, a pale worn olive green. They swung open as they pushed through. The doors opened onto a large open place office space. Detectives sat at desks starting at monitors tapping out reports with slow single key presses. One was resting their hand on their chin but had forgotten the were holding a sandwich. Immediately behind the double doors was a curved desk where a uniformed officer was sat.

"Shauna," Said Jess, pushing Gregg in front of her "this is Gregg. Say hello Gregg."

"Hello," he murmured.

"Shauna here," Jess continued "will get you processed. Not part of the community. He's going to need the full orientation."

The young woman stepped out from behind the desk. She had dark tanned skin, her black hair tied up in a bun. She held her hands tucked into her uniforms vest.

"Come on then kid, got a long boring PowerPoint to go through." Shauna beckoned to him, and he followed out a set of doors on the right-hand side of the room.

Mark leaned back in his chair staring at the computer screen, typing out the arrest to the best of his recollection. It was slow going. Trying to remember everything from a high-pressure situation after the fact was surprisingly difficult. Jess sat at the desk next to his, nose deep in her notebook. Mark had tried to copy her once, write everything down. It had lasted about fifteen minutes before he had dropped it into a toilet by accident. Now he relied on Jess who kept notes enough for the both of them.

"Think that kid will be alright?" Mark asked.

"Probably," Jess was starting at her notebook in one hand and typing with the other "In theory he could get prison time, but it's more likely community service or a suspended sentence."

"Couple of trainers isn't exactly high crime is it?"

"Not for us to say," Jess shrugged. He closed her note book and clicked save on her report. She passed it over to mark. "At least we might get him some help. Jenkins and Singh got another one last night."

"Shit really?" Mark sat up in his chair. It let out a loud squeak. "That's what, four now?"

"Five including this one." Jess opened a drawer on her desk pulling out an open packet of digestive biscuits. She dunked it into a cup of tea that had gone lukewarm as she had typed. "I was talking to Jenkins when I made the tea. She thinks whoever is doing it is getting bolder. Not stupid either, they keep moving on after each kill. Even if other targets are in town."

"That's not good," Mark sighed. "A competent hunter can do a lot of damage."

"Three victims so far have been werewolves, one particularly hairy ghoul and something called a nagual."

"It's a kind of shapeshifter. Mesoamerican origin," Mark said. His eyes were closed, and he was tapping the sides of his temples.

"Never ceases to amaze me," Jess rolled her eyes "the human encyclopaedia. Should add yourself to the lore books."

Mark shrugged. "Just got one of those memories I guess?"

"You can remember that, but can't remember your own phone number?" Jess raised one eyebrow.

The bustle of the office carried on into the evening. To the casual observer the scene might seem like any other police station across the country. A careful eye might notice things that are off. A small set of runes carved on the handles for the doors. A detective holding a book encased in glass at arm's length. The Sergeant manning the desk opening her lunch box and removing what seems to be a raw chicken breast. To the members of the special investigations division this was a quiet normal day. Normal being of course relative. Across the office floor an older woman wearing a pale blue trouser suit over a pink blouse beckoned to Mark and Jess, who stood up and strode over the office the woman had vanished back into.

"Ma'am," said Mark taking a seat. He shifted nervously. The chair was made of cheap plastic with plain metal legs. It was uncomfortable, but he suspected that was the point. Jess took the seat next to him, pulling at her jacket as she sat.

"I wanted to thank you both for an adequate job earlier," Detective Chief Inspector Florence Weston was not one for praise. "You have both been performing as expected with recent cases, especially as some of them may have been...," she thought for a moment "above your pay grade shall we say, at a more traditional unit."

"We are very grateful ma'am," replied Jess nervously. "I've seen more working than in my entire career before."

"Yes well, pleasantries over," Mark and Jess looked at each other confused at the statement, "I have another case for you."

"With all due respect ma'am, we just got back to London this morning," Mark fidgeted as he held her gaze, "I'm assuming it's another job with travel, otherwise you would have come over to us."

"Very astute of you D.C Curren," the inspector lifted two identical manila folders and passed handed one to each of them. "I'm sending you to somewhere called Pontypridd," she slowly sounded out the towns name, "someone there claims they were attacked by a ghost."

"Unlikely, ghosts very rarely attack people," Mark stated, scanning the contents of the folder.

"We need to check it out either way," Florence got up, walked past them and opened her office door. She stood there impatiently, pushing the handle down. "Take tonight and head out in the morning."

Chapter 2

Claire, lay curled up on her bed. Tears streamed down her face which was red and swollen from her torrential crying. She scrolled through photos on her phone, breaking into an audible sob when she reached a photo of herself with a boy in a dark blue tracksuit. They were outside a cinema, camera held up above them at an angle. In the photo Claire was looking at the camera pursing her lips whilst the boy was looking down at a phone. She scrolled off the picture, it hurt too much to look at. The phone buzzed in her hands, a message sliding down from the top of the screen. *"Slut"* it read. She threw phone off her bed and watched it bounce off a large stuffed bear. She gripped one of her pillows to her chest and let her anguish pour off her.

A few hours passed, the sun had set, and Claire had neither bothered to draw the curtains or switch on the light. The room was washed with a pale moonlight, lightly illuminating it. She rolled over, and stared at it, a perfect milky circle floating in the sky. There was a loud scratching noise as her phone vibrated on the floor. *I'm such an idiot* she thought to herself. *I should never have sent him those photos.* Another loud rattle as her phone shook again. Then another she swung herself upright and rested her feet on the floor. Claire reached down and picked it up. One message. Unknown sender. She swiped her phone to open it. *"I can help."* it said. Claire sat staring at the message. Three dots blinked at the bottom of the screen and a second message appeared. *"We can get revenge."* Claire gripped her phone and typed a reply. *"How?"*

Claire was alone, her parents having gone out for the evening. She enjoyed her own company, she felt powerful on her own, non-one to judge her. It was why she felt comfortable taking those photos. It had been less than an hour before the whole school had seen them. The messenger had left very strange detailed instructions, but Claire had followed them to the letter. First, she had printed every photo of him she had taken, plus the photos she had sent him. The instructions were clear they needed as many as possible, so she had clicked print until her father's printer was printing only scratchy faded images. Next the messages had told her to draw a large circle full of ornate shapes. Claire had taken a large marker and drawn it onto the bottom of the bath, thinking it would have proven easier to clean off. Then the unknown writer had instructed her to gather what it called a sacrifice. Any meat would do, it had clarified, so she had taken some chicken breasts from the fridge. She had placed the pictures and the cold slimy chicken into the circle as instructed and waited. Her phone rumbled on the side of the sink. A new message. "*Burn it*".

Claire pulled out one of her mother's lighters. As far as her dad knew she had quit smoking years ago. Claire felt strangely glad she hadn't. She clicked the wheel to spark it, holding it at arm's length turning her head away. The resulting flame was much smaller than she thought it would be. She reached into the bath and touched one of the photos, it caught alight and began to slowly burn, the papers edges fraying as it melted into embers. "*Now what?*" she text back. The reply was instant. "*Watch.*" Slowly the burning paper sped up its disintegration. The other pictures were catching alight now joining the slowly growing fire. The scattering of images shrank until the burning edge met the wet raw chicken. In an instant the faint glow became a flaming roar. The chicken erupted into a pillar of flame, it lapped at the ceiling. Claire watched transfixed as the pillar stretched and turned, as if were waking from a deep sleep. The fire was bright but let out only a dull heat. No smoke rose from the inferno.

"Thank you, my friend," a bizarre voice like crackling wood slipped out from the flames. They briefly became blue, the heat rising to a searing wave in time with its words. "Ah, I thought I might be trapped forever. Thank you." Claire stepped backwards, falling seated onto the toilet. She stared at the fire transfixed. "Now then," the flames continued "I did promise to help you."

"H-H-How?" stammered Claire. The fire seemed to shrink and expand, as though it were breathing.

"Come closer, let me see you," replied the flames. Claire staggered to her feet and stepped closer to them. "You are very beautiful; those others do not appreciate you. I will help you, all you need to do is say yes."

"Say yes to what?" Claire asked.

"To me," said the flames.

Glyn sat on the swing laughing. Two of his friends were spinning a third on the large metal wheel in the centre of the park. The third was shouting at them to stop. He reached into his tracksuit trousers and pulled out his phone. He laughed to himself, looking at a photo a friend had sent him. They had applied a filter to one of the pictures Claire had sent him, adding dog ears and a lolling tongue. *A right dog!* read the message beneath.

"Hey lads check out this one," he called out. There was no reply. The three boys messing with the merry-go-round had stopped, they stared at a figure strolling across the park. She wore a bright red dress than ended beneath her knee. She was wearing makeup, her hair tied up into an elaborate bun. Her lipstick matched the vibrant dress.

"It's Claire," said one of the boys, "You're in trouble I think." The three of them laughed at him. Claire reached the metal fence that surrounded the play area and pushed open a gate that squealed with years of missed maintenance.

"We need to talk," Claire stared at Glyn, her eyes seemed to shine in the dark.

"Ooooooooo," chanted the other boys.

"Silence," Claire commanded. She looked at them, a righteous anger in her eyes. They stopped. "We need to speak alone. I suggest you leave us."

"Go on lads, I'll see you at school tomorrow," Glyn gave the other boys a thumbs up, and they walked through the open gate into the night. He motioned for Claire to take the swing next to him. She stepped forward, instead standing before him. "Listen babe, I'm sorry, one of the boys got my phone and- "

"Unacceptable." Claire interrupted. "You have taken advantage of this girl. Used her for your own gratification and then slandered her to her social circle. Is this what people have become?"

"What? You swallow a dictionary or something?" Glyn let out a nervous chuckle.

"Still you mock her." Claire crossed her arms and leant forward, bringing her eyes level with his. "Tell me, why do you feel the right to do this?"

"You're being weird," Glyn leant back on the swing, uncomfortable at how close she was. "Why are you always weird."

"I see," said Claire. "I see what we are dealing with now. I'm sorry, I think you may be unredeemable. I would have respected honesty, if you had admitted you simply desired it." Claire closed her eyes and sighed. When she reopened them, her irises glowed a pale gold. They seemed to flicker like flames.

"The fuck are those, you look- "Glyn was cut off, his words becoming a strained gurgling as Claire gripped him by the throat. With one hand she lifted him from the swings seat, his legs dangling as she held him in the air. His phone slipped from his hand, landing in the chipped bark that covered the floor.

"Now, because I am generous, I am going to tell you what happens next." Claire turned still holding him in the air. "I will release you, and you will run. I will chase you, and when I catch you I will inflict torment on you a hundred-fold what you gave this girl." Claire let her grasp go and Glyn crumpled to the floor. He spluttered trying to catch his breath. "Now," Claire said reaching down to pick up Glyn's phone. She snapped it between her hands like a biscuit. "I suggest you start running, I wouldn't want anyone to think I didn't give you a sporting chance." She reached up and with a tug tore the chain that held one of the swings from its frame. Claire pulled the other end free from the chair and tested its weight in her hands. "Well come on then. Get to it."

Glyn ran, the rough bark of the playground giving way to slippery mud of unkempt field. The playground was at the centre of the park, which featured several fields used by the local school to practice cross country. Glyn now wished he has paid attention in those lessons. His breath felt ragged and horrible. He tasted blood from his bruised throat. His knees ached from where he had been thrown to the floor. He pushed through the cluster of trees and bushes that formed the barrier from one field to another. He erupted on the other side in a flurry of leaves and branches. His face was scratched, his tracksuit top torn. Glyn had emerged onto the parks football pitch, he stopped for a second to catch his breath.

"This doesn't inspire my confidence in you." Glyn looked up. Claire was leaning against a goalpost, her bright red dress illuminated by a floodlight. She was spinning the chain around in a wide arc casually.

"Fuck off!" Glyn shouted.

"Charming," said Claire. She flicked her wrist sending the chain lashing across Glyn's chest. The end was sharp, and it cut into his skin, tearing his jacket in a spray of blood. He fell to the ground clutching at his wound. Claire walked over to his screaming, writhing form. "Here, let me help." She touched his chest with her open palm. There was a loud sizzling and faint wisps of smoke. Glyn screamed. "Now, now. That should stop the bleeding." Claire crouched down, placing her mouth next to his ear. "Now I would resume running if I were you."

One foot in front of the other. Glyn held his chest, it pounded in agony from where it had been cauterised. He limped, having twisted his ankle as he had fallen. *One foot in front of the other* he thought to himself, forcing himself slowly away from whatever that thing was. It certainly wasn't Claire anymore. She had been so quiet, so shy. When Glyn had asked her out she had jumped at the chance despite never really talking to him before. So was so easy to tell what to do, to have do his homework or go to the shops for him. The idea that maybe whatever was chasing him was right and he had used her never occurred to Glyn. He simply limped onward with a determination he had never before exhibited. The lights of the football pitch were fading behind him. He could see the entrance, a huge twisted wrought iron thing. Its elaborate design of leaves wrapped around the bars gave it horrible shadow against the street lights outside, a wall of barbed thorns. Escape in sight, he redoubled his efforts, forcing himself to jog, ignoring the pain of his ankle.

"Pretty pathetic attempt really," Claire was leaning on the brick pillar the gate hung from as Glyn stepped from the park onto the street. He stopped awestruck, letting out a slow wheeze as he tried to catch his breath. "I have to say I expected more. I guess that tracksuit is just for show."

"Hel-," Glyn's cry was cut off as Claire held up her hand. A series of rough scratches floated in the air, burning fiery orange.

"That's enough from you I think." Claire lashed out with her foot, striking Glyn in his twisted ankle. He collapsed to one knee, his mouth wide in a silent scream. With a second kick Glyn tumbled backwards into the park side of the entrance. He held his side, there had been a horrific cracking when Claire had struck him. He coughed drizzling blood on the ground. A slow echoing screech rang out as Claire pulled the park gate closed. She winced as she gripped the gate by one of its sculpted leaves. There was a faint smell of burning. She reached down and picked up the swing chain from beneath a bush. "Now, time to keep my promise."

A cheery chime rang out from the phone on the bedside table. Claire reached across and slapped the screen to turn it off. She slipped her feet into a pair of pink slippers she left and her bedside table and adjusted her pyjamas that had become skewed during the night. She yawned, pocketed her phone and shuffled down the stairs.

"Morning love," her mother said half distracted as she packed a laptop into its bag. "There's toast on the side."

"Thanks mum," Claire replied, taking a slice and biting into it hungrily.

"Sandra, take a look at this," said her father striding into the kitchen, his dressing gown uncomfortably open.

"Jesus Mike, cover it up," said her mother, pulling her husband's robe closed as he reached up to the ancient CRT television that had sat in the corner of the kitchen since they moved in. It came on with a flicker.

"Police are asking this morning for anyone who was near the Ynysangharad park in Pontypridd to come forward-"said a news reporter standing in front of an obvious greenscreen.

"How many times did you think he had to practice saying that?" Mike asked.

"Ssh," replied Sandra

"Police discovered the body this morning in what they are describing as a ritual killing. No specifics have been released yet, but several eyewitnesses report the victim had been torn into pieces and strung across a chain tied to the park gate. Police refused to clarify if this was indeed the case."

"Grim isn't it?" Mike said, muting the television.

"And you felt the need to share it why?" Sandra asked disapprovingly.

"Well they said he went to Claire's sixth form. A Glyn Powell?" Mike looked expectedly at Claire.

Claire shrugged. "Don't know him, different classes maybe?"

Claire stood in the bathroom. No trace of her little pyre remained. She had been sure to clean it up. She ran her hand under the tap. A large burn had formed on her left palm, a perfect leaf pattern. She stared in the mirror. Her reflection stared back, grinning wildly at her. Her own face was sullen.

"I told you we would get revenge," said the reflection. "This is just the start of a great partnership."

Chapter 3

Jess stepped down from the bus. The door behind her closed with a hiss and the air was bitter and cold. She zipped up her windbreaker, pulling the zip up to her neck. Jess shivered and tucked her hands into her jacket pockets. Her breath hung in the air, a tiny frozen cloud. She strode down the street; her feet pounding eagerly to get out of the cold.

The sky was dark, streetlights blocking out the stars. Jess often hated having to travel for work, but that was one thing she was grateful for. You very rarely saw the stars in London. Her hand reached out and touched to small metal gate that sat at the entrance to her front garden. She jostled the gate open, the cold made it creak as she did. She stepped down the small gravel path with a rhythmic crunch. She reached for keys, her hands shaking from the cold. They jangled as Jess struggled with the lock. The keys turned with a click and the door slowly swung open. The corridor within was dark. There was a thudding noise, growing closer as she stepped inside.

"Muma!" The thumping became a roar as a small girl burst into the corridor, her tiny legs kicking furiously as she ran. She stopped before Jess and grinned. She produced a sheet of paper from behind her back. The girl had drawn a crude drawing of a house and three stick figures. "I made this!" the girl announced.

"That's wonderful Lana, need to add it to the collection." Jess took the picture in one hand and scooped up the girl in the other. She carried her down the hallway, flicking on the light with her elbow. Lana played with Jess' ponytail as they walked. She pushed down a door handle with the back of her hand carrying the picture and stepped into the kitchen.

"Welcome home love." A blonde woman stood at the kitchen sink scrubbing a dish with a brush. She smiled. Her long hair was held back with a headband, she wore a floor length floral dress. An unlit cigarette hung from her mouth.

"Hannah, I wish you wouldn't smoke around Lana." Jess stepped over and pecked the woman on the check. She set Lana down in a chair by the small table they kept in the kitchen but seldom used.

"It's not lit, I was waiting for you to get home," Hannah said, putting the cigarette down on the kitchen counter. "There's a plate in the fridge for you." She watched Jess open the fridge, attach the picture with a magnet, and pull out a plate. She peeled off the foil and walked over to the microwave. "Speaking of which, you are home now right?"

Jess sighed. "No, I've got another case," she said, pressing buttons on the microwave as she spoke. "I head out in the morning."

"I know what you do is important," Hannah said, putting her hands around Jess' waist. "But I wish you could be home more. Lana is starting to ask questions. She knows her mother isn't home as often as the other children's. Our situation will be...," she thought carefully about her words, "more difficult, for her than most children anyway."

"I know," said Jess blowing steam off the plate. A pair of sausages, a pile of mashed potato and some peas wobbled in tandem with each other as she turned and placed the plate on the counter. Hannah turned with her still hanging on to her waist. "It's just... I can't protect her from bigots. Not all the time. At least doing my job makes everyone, Lana included, safer."

"That includes those bigots," said Hannah, letting go of Jess' waist and putting her hands on her hips.

"I know," admitted Jess opening a cupboard and taking out a small tub of instant gravy. She flicked the kettle on. "We're raising smart girl, one day she'll be able to tell those people to fuck off- "

"Bad word!" shouted Lana, she giggled.

"But, what I see out there," Jess continued. "I could live without her ever knowing about it.

Jess sat on her sofa. The lights were off aside from the faint glow of the television. A trailer for a documentary on a failed festival played on repeat. The sound was off, and Jess was reading through her copy of the report. Hannah lay on the sofa, her head resting on Jess' lap. She was asleep. Jess sighed and tossed the report on the arm of the sofa. She stared down at Hannah and began to stroke her long golden hair. She wished she didn't have to leave. Recently Jess had spent more time on the road than at home. She was certain she saw Mark more often than her own wife and child. She leant back staring at her ceiling. A thick gash had been cut into the artex. Hannah had wanted to remove it, but Jess had refused. It was a reminder.

A year earlier, Jess had been a beat constable. She was good at her job, and well liked in her station. She had returned home after a long shift, her hair messy underneath her hat, sweating profusely under her stab vest. She had stopped at the end of her garden path. The door was wide open the night air. There was a smash from inside and she had run in without a thought.

Inside the house she had found Hannah crouched in the corner of the living room cradling the then even smaller Lana. In the centre of the room was a large gangly creature. Its skin was an ashen grey, its eyes a piercing red. Its arms and legs were long and thin. Its fingers were spindly ending in long sharp points. It hissed through a set of needle like fangs. It was standing on the coffee table, its face flicking around the room. It let out a wail, faintly at first, but building into a terrible screech. It pounced into the air, its talons angled at Hannah. Jess ran forward shoulder first barging into the monster mid-air. It slammed into a side table back first, bending unnaturally. It sloped to the floor hacking a thick green liquid. Jess grasped her baton and struck the creature, bringing it down in great arcs. It squealed and kicked out at her, knocking her backwards. The creature stood up, its viscous green blood pouring from above its eye. It clambered over Jess on all fours, its claw like fingers digging divots into the floor. It hissed bringing its sharp unnatural face close to hers. Slowly she reached down, grasped the small canister of PAVA spray at her belt. With a click she sprayed it into the creature's face. It stood up screaming. Its foul blood sprayed everywhere as it clawed at its own eyes. It stumbled about lashing out wildly. One swing of its arm scratched across the ceiling taking a thin slash from the artex. Sensing her moment Jess grabbed a small side table by the leg, the lamp atop it smashing on the ground. She swung the table smashing it against the monster's head. It broke, the leg she was holding splintering off and the monster tumbled to the ground. She lifted the splinter leg and thrust it downward into the beast's chest, the wood biting deeply into its flesh. It spluttered and shook, before falling still. Jess pulled the table leg free and stood there, weapon in hand, horrible green blood splashed across her.

After, Jess had been whisked away, taken down beneath New Scotland Yard. There she had been given what was referred to as "the talk". There all the secrets of special investigations were laid bare. The nightmares that lurked in the night, the unspeakable things that howled at the edge of reality scratching to get in. She had been sat there as they explained what a changeling was, and how it wanted to steal Lana away. Her family had been lucky, Hannah had a bad habit of waiting up for Jess to get home and was awake when the changeling had expected sleeping parents. She had let out a nervous laugh when she explained she had used her spray to blind it. When the detectives had interviewed her, they had eagerly written it down.

"A lot of what we know is old, real old. Never know when something might be useful we never considered. Good to know PAVA works on one of these," one of the interviewing detectives, a tall dark-skinned man with a well-kept neatly trimmed beard and a black turban, had said.

Then, just like that, Jess had found herself transferred, made a detective faster than she had ever seen. Every member of the department had a similar story. Whisked away from ordinary police work, dragged into the weird and macabre. It made a lot of sense, it wasn't like they could start a recruitment drive, and it was a lot easier to explain to someone who had seen it first-hand. Jess had been taught the basics, how to stop certain kinds of creature, how to handle occult objects, how to use charms to stop any more changelings from breaking into her home. She had taken to the work, her natural fussiness and habit of writing everything down proving useful detective skills. Hannah had been unhappy with it at first, but Jess always just pointed out the thin gash in their ceiling. They kept it, a reminder of what was lurking in the world.

Whilst Jess was sat at home, stroking her wife's hair, Mark was also sat on his couch. He held a plastic cup full of substandard noodles in one hand, whilst propping open a book with the other. It had a red leather cover, cracked with age. He lifted his hand, keeping the book open with his elbow and pulled a greasy forkful of noodles into his mouth. He put the plastic pot down onto a stack of books he had been using as a makeshift table and turned the page. Inside was a large diagram of a creature seemingly made entirely of wings and hands. He nodded sagely to himself. Somewhere beneath him the tell-tale rhythmic thud of his phone vibrating thumped. He closed the book and tapped his pockets looking for it. Mark thought for a moment and reached down between the cushions, producing the phone triumphantly.

He opened the notification to an email from Weston. Mark rolled his eyes; the woman was never off the clock it seemed. He opened it, *"Ghost case. Further details."* Included were all the details of the original file, plus what seemed to be a recording of the interview with the victim. They had already been given a transcript. Their boss was nothing if not thorough. Mark chuckled, he knew that Jess would already probably be printing it to add to the file. She did love a good file. He clicked the video and watched it silently. He could see a young woman, crying heavily, black mascara running down her face. She was wearing a party dress made from what he thought might be shiny purple plastic. She was shaking as she cried, the woman looked terrified. Mark drummed his fingers along his chin as he watched. Ghosts often appeared before people and were largely harmless. Sometimes one would decide to move a cup, or nudge a painting, but the transcript claimed that one had pushed someone clean out the window. Apparently, someone had decided to host an illegal rave in an old abandoned house nestled in the Welsh valleys famous locally for being haunted. Mark threw his phone onto the sofa and sighed. It was probably a wild goose chase, and even if there was a ghost dealing with one was a nightmare. The only reliably way to get rid of one was to help it complete whatever task bound it to the earth and that always required working the coldest of cold cases.

He stood up, stepping over to the overloaded bookcase that bent under the weight of the tomes held within. He ran his finger across spines as he searched for a specific book. Mark regularly claimed they were kept in a specific order. This was a lie.

"Ah there you are," he said to no one in particular, grabbing a book from the shelf. "Right, time to brush up on ghosts I guess."

Chapter 4

Mark heaved the heavy tan case onto the train's luggage rack, his arms straining as he did. The case, an old leather thing with a brass clasp and worn corners, hit the rack with a rattle. Mark tested the shelf, adjusted the case, and satisfied, walked down the aisle towards his seat. Stuffing his own small black suitcase in the overhead rack, he slipped down into his chair. A tatty thing, its upholstery pink and pale green dots on a dark blue background. Nestling himself in Mark looked at his watch in worry, leaning out into the aisle to try and spot Jess. Through the window he caught her running across the platform, red hair flying behind her. She was clutching her own suitcase to her chest, stumbling as she tried to slow herself stepping onto the train. Jess crashed through door into the carriage panting. She hastily stuffed her suitcase onto the rack and collapsed into her seat next to Mark

"Morning sunshine," said Mark, reaching into a small carrier bag that had been hanging at his elbow.

"Sorry, sorry," Jess apologised, unzipping her jacket. "Lana wanted me to take her to school, and we've been on the road so much I haven't been home much recently. I couldn't say no, you know?"

"Yeah I get it," Mark answered. "Family is important, or so I'm told." He pulled a thin object from the bag, wrapped loosely in paper. He handed it to Jess.

"Oh, thank god," she said, unwrapping it to reveal a sandwich baguette, freshly fried bacon glistened within. "You know me so well."

"Eat up, it's going to be a long day. Figure we should deal with the body first, probably more urgent." Mark pulled his own sandwich from the bag. He produced a can of cola, which he handed to Jess.

"Wait what body?" Jess asked, taking the can from Mark's hand.

"Not read your emails this morning then?" He replied.

Constable Aasif Rhaman had been on his early morning jog. Every day he ran through the park, he found the cold morning air invigorating. That particular morning it had rained briefly, and he had considered not going out, before strapping on his trainers and heading out the door before he could convince himself otherwise. Dawn had just broken, and as usual Aasif had been the first person to the park. He entered through the smaller side entrance near his home and ran along the patch that encircled the perimeter, splashes of water striking his legs as he ran through the shallow puddles that had settled on the concrete. Somewhere deeper in the park a bird was calling out, its tweets forming a haunting melody. Aasif rounded the corner, coming around to the main gate. He nearly tripped as he stopped dead. The main gates were closed, tied shut by a chain that seemed to have been knotted by hand. A set of arms and legs hung from the chain, they had slid down on it until they reached the knot, splaying out like a macabre necklace. The body they belonged to was impaled on one of the decorative spikes that ran across the top of the gate. The head had been slammed onto one, it jutted bent from the corpses mouth. A thick pool of blood had formed, sticky red running across the ornate leaf patterns on the iron gate.

"Aw shit," said Aasif, unplugging his headphone and taking his phone from the holder on his arm. "Knew I should have stayed in today."

"Ok so," started Mark, as the train began to slide out of the station. "Apparently this morning a body was found in the same town our victim of the supposed ghost attack is from. Grisly thing apparently, initial reports indicated the body had been taken apart and strung up across a gate by chain."

"Graphic, but not necessarily our thing. Could just be a regular mundane psychopath?" Jess shrugged.

"Possibly, but it's a hell of a coincidence if it is." Marks thumb slid across his phone, bringing up a recent email to the screen. "Boss wants us to check it out either way, hopefully rule out a connection."

"Know of anything in our wheelhouse that does something like this?" Jess asked, taking a bite from her sandwich.

"Nothing I know of that does this on the regular. Still doesn't rule us out, plenty of weird to go around." Mark chomped into his own baguette, leaking butter across his fingers. He wiped his hand on the paper and continued. "There was that Selkie who was collecting human skin and hanging that up that we had in the Shetlands once. Maybe it's something similar? That was an ironic vengeance thing right because someone stole her sealskin."

"I don't know," Jess had taken out a notebook, flipped down the shelf from behind the chair in front and was scribbling in it with one hand and trying to hold her sandwich with the other "Most supers try and keep a low profile. Nothing about this is low profile."

"We'll find out in about oh," Mark look at his watch, through the window behind him the countryside flew past, a green blur "two and a half hours? Give or take."

Mark and Jess dropped the heavy leather case onto the platform. The air was cold and damp, a thin veneer of rain covered the platform. The station was old, brown stone set into the valley side. The platform carried on far past the station itself, a long winding gash into the hillside. A large digital sign announced the train had arrived, modern technology screwed into old Victorian brickwork. The train they had stepped out of was a small single carriage. Pale green paint flaked off the side. The seats within had been hard and uncomfortable, horrid plastic things that flipped down from the wall. Getting here had required they change from the outdated but at least relatively comfortable train they had boarded, swapping for the ancient rattling thing once they had reached Cardiff. Thankfully the local service had been regular, as they had missed the planned connection trying to carry the heavy case down a set of steep stairs and up another to change platforms.

"Used to be the biggest train platform in the world this did," Mark said, stretching his arms.

"What a useless piece of trivia," Jess complained, he own arm ached from lugging the heavy case around.

"Trivia is never useless!" Mark declared. "Might come up in a pub quiz or something."

"If I'm ever on a quiz show you can sit in the audience and cough for me then." Jess grabbed the handle on one side of the case. "Let's get a move on, grab your side."

Slowly they eased the case down a huge flight of stairs that connected the station to the town. The station had been built into the side of the valley, easily two stories above the town itself. The great archway leading into the station looked like a baroque gateway into the heart of the mountain. The station had a small carpark, a portion of which seemed to be permanently in use by the local police, several cars and a van had been parked in the far corner. A particularly annoyed looking uniform officer leant against one of the cars. She was damp from the wet air, her face a scowl. Thin curls of mousey hair leaked from beneath her hat.

"Must be our ride," said Jess waving at the policewoman. She glared back at her.

"Doesn't look very happy about having to wait for us," stated Mark. "Come one, better go say hi."

The constable hadn't been very welcoming, and Mark was now sat in the back, squashed up against the case, which hadn't fitted in the boot. Its corners dug into him uncomfortably as the car bounced down the streets, winding its way toward the park. The constable driving them was muttering something disparaging against Londoners under her breath, whilst Jess stared out the window. Mark wasn't surprised, it was the common response from other police forces. Special Investigations was based in London, beneath New Scotland Yard even, but officially had country wide jurisdiction. No-one was happy when as far as they were concerned, some people from some fancy unit they had never even heard of until now turned up and started poking around. Mark had felt the same way when he was a newly qualified detective, and someone had turned up at his crime scene to take over. Arrogant he had worked the case anyway, finding himself at the wrong end of a ghula. Afterwards he had been whisked away, given details on Special Investigations, and now he was the one turning up at crime scenes. The transition had suited him well, Mark had always been a bit of a bookworm and able to recall vast amounts of normally useless information. Traits it turned out were useful for dealing with the occult. Some of his colleagues jokingly called him the human grimoire.

Jess stepped out from the car with a splash, its driver seemingly choosing to stop where the puddle was deepest. She leant into the back through the window.

"You check this out, I'll drop this," Mark said tapping the case "at the hotel. We'll meet there once you're done here."

"Right, I'll see you later," replied Jess, giving a thumbs up. She stepped away, ducking under a line of tape that had been strung across the street. The entire park and the street around the entrance had been closed. Uniformed officers were scattered around keeping watch. Jess flashed her I.D. to one as she walked towards the large white tent that had been set up over the gate. Several people in white paper suits were milling around outside it, scribbling on clipboards. A large bull of a man, thick broad shoulders and arms barely held in by his uniform was talking to one. A series of diamonds on his epaulets marked him as a Chief Inspector. "Detective Constable Jessica Holden, special investigations."

"Chief Inspector Harold White," replied the Man, holding out his hand. Jess shook it. "Don't normally get D. C's to investigate murders, but the orders come from the top."

"We have a little more... leeway, with our unit sir. We think this might fall under our specialism," Jess replied.

"And what exactly is your specialism?" Harold asked.

"Honestly sir, weird things," said Jess, shrugging her shoulders.

"Yes well," Harold said, "I think this might qualify."

Jess stood inside the tent that had been erected around the gate. It was an old wrought iron thing, long thing bars with an elaborate decoration in the form of leaves and vines wrapping around the bars. It curved upwards across each of the sides so when the gate was closed it formed a curved hill encrusted with short sharp points. A short length of chain had been wrapped around both sides and tied off into a knot originally, but the crime scene techs had removed it to remove the body. Two silver tables with wheels had been placed inside the tent, the length of chain lay on one whist the body parts sat on the other. Jess crouched down to get a good look. The body had been torn into five parts, each arm and leg separated from the body. Slipping on a pair of white latex gloves Jess picked up one of the arms. It was still clad in tracksuit that was torn and flopped loosely. The arm had not been cut cleanly, instead the wound was jagged and uneven, and though it had been torn clean off. A rough hole, about the size of one of the gates top spikes was punctured through it. Placing the arm down she turned her attention to the chain. It was a few feet long and fairly thin. Parts of the chain were coated in a thick clear rubber, that reminded her of the swing set in the local park she sometimes took Lana too.

"Is there a playground in this park?" Jess asked.

"Yes, on the other side," replied Harold, who was stood in the entrance to the tent watching her.

"Has anyone checked it? This chain had to come from somewhere, I think it's from a swing." Jess examined the chain in her hands. "Yeah look." She held one end of the chain, it ended in a small bolt encased in thick black plastic. "This is where it attaches to the seat. Looks like it was ripped off."

"Someone ripped a chain from a swing set and carried it across the park to use in a murder? Seems unlikely?" Harold questioned.

"Unlikely is what I deal with, can you send an officer over to check for me?" Jess placed the chain down on the table. Harold walked out of the tent, pointing at officers and shouting incomprehensibly. Jess went back to the body parts, the other arms and legs were the same, all torn not cut. She looked at the torso. Its jacket was torn across the font. She unzipped it carefully, revealing a large burn across the chest of the young man. It was roughly the same size as the tear in the jacket. There was a loud flap as the Chief Inspector returned to the tent, his face bright red.

"Looks like, you're right. The playground swing is missing a chain. Can't believe we missed that," he said, embarrassed.

"Don't worry about it, like I said, this is specialist stuff. Did your officers find anything that could be used to burn someone?" Jess asked.

"I'm not sure I follow?" Harold said, puzzled.

"Look at this, a cut right across his chest, but the skin underneath is burnt. I think whoever did this cut him, but then cauterised the wound." Jess pointed to the exposed torso on the table.

"Why?" Why do that?" asked Harold.

"Stop the victim bleeding out is my guess. Prolong the pain a bit further. I think this boy was tortured before he died." Jess turned and stared at it, her eyes scanning it for clues.

"You mean like this here?" said Harold pointing to one of the iron leaves. It was charred, difficult to see to see against the black of the iron.

"Yeah, just like that," Jess smiled. She began to scrawl into a notebook she produced from her top pocket.

"Ok so," said Mark, waving around a piece of steak on his fork wildly as he spoke "someone tore him apart. "He stopped, realising that he was getting funny looks from the other diners in the hotel's restaurant. "Tore him apart," he continued in a whisper. "Not cut, torn, like by hand?"

"Yeah, something strong," Jess agreed, cutting into her own steak. She picked up a small gravy boat filled with peppercorn sauce and poured it over her plate.

"Right. And you say they tortured him?"

"Big burn on his chest, looks like they cut him and cauterised him. Whatever they used left a burn mark on part of the gate." She took a bite from her meal, staring at the table thoughtfully as she chewed. "Think it's one of ours, has to be. The strength needed to do that kind of thing."

"Not necessarily. Could have used a car or something. They did have a chain, tied him up and pulled." Mark leant back in his chair.

"Chain was from a swing though, I'm not sure it's actually strong enough to do that. Plus, I think the chain was torn off too," Jess said. "We'll need to look into a that bit more.

Interview the victim's friends, family, find out if they knew where he was that night. You got anything?"

"Yeah actually." Mark slid his phone over to Jess. "Lots of sightings of ghosts over the years at that house." He swiped the phone, flicking through old news articles he had collected from the internet. "Most of them talk about a woman in what seems to be a maid's outfit, seen primarily standing behind windows."

"Victim says in her interview that the ghost tried to push her through a window."

"Right exactly, I think maybe there might be something to this," Mark admitted.

"Any ideas on who the ghost is, any deaths at the house or anything?" Jess asked, taking a long sip from her glass as she did.

"Nothing yet, house is just outside of town, farmhouse for years before being abandoned. Apparently, the last owner was wealthy in the late eighteen hundreds, so a maid makes sense. Nothing I can find on any deaths though." Mark took his phone back, sliding it into his pocket. "Of course, that would be too easy."

"Plan of action for tomorrow then," said Jess. "I'll go interview the murder victims' friends, you'll check out the house."

"Seems good to me, notice I get the more dangerous task thought," said Mark dubiously.

"More dangerous!" Jess laughed. "Did you never go to high school?"

Claire stood before the mirror in the bathroom. The last day had been a haze, everything seemed pale and colourless. She stared at her hand, the burn had not gone away, the perfect shape of a leaf on her palm. She knew Glyn was dead, she got flashes from the night, brief moments of violence and gore. She didn't care. She knew she should feel guilty, sad, angry, and a million other things but she felt only hollow. Like the thing inside her was pushing out all emotion, leaving no space to feel.

"Are you ready Claire?" asked the voice inside her. Her reflection speaking the words.

"Nearly done!" Claire pressed her lips together, making sure her lipstick wasn't smudged. A vivid red to match her dress.

"Tonight, we take a big step my dear!" said her reflection.

"I guess you're right," Claire replied. She could feel the entity building up, a raging fire within, ready to take over. She felt its energy fill her limbs, her mind. A warmth that filled her body, erasing all else. "Tonight Claire," she said to herself, her own lips moving with the reflection. "We start to make some friends."

Chapter 5

Nestled in the welsh valleys, high up on the hillside, is a house. Once it was vibrant, full of life, children playing in the yard whilst the adults tended the flocks on the hills. The house had seen a handful of generations to fruition when the farm fell on hard times and it was sold to the head of a wealthy mining family. This coal baron set about building his own grander home, adding and expanding until the modest house was merely the foyer to a much larger home, its insides gutted, and its hearth blocked. This new more imposing home that had swallowed the first like a snake, becoming an over designed baroque thing, gradually adding to its mass and size until it too was abandoned, it's owners mine running dry. Sat, disused in the cold wet welsh weather it had become an infrequent haunt for teens looking to prove their bravery to largely disinterested girlfriends. Legends grew how the house too was haunted, the spectre of a maid stalking the halls. The homes once stately Victorian exterior was now an explosion of colour, thick with spray paint, the marks of teenage exploration and rebellion.

Mark stood before the house, holding his coat closed against the fine mist of rain that blew sideways, the winds caught by the valley and amplified. He opened the back of a large van he had rented from a company in the town and crouched down. Producing a large brass key from his pocket he placed it into the lock of the imposing leather case that he had heaved into the back the night before. The thing shuddered as he swung the lid open, its weight shaking the case as it fell on its hinges. Inside was a trove of books, dusty tomes with hardbound leather covers. A selection of smaller boxes were squeezed between the books. In a pouch sewn to the lid were several curious objects, various types of handcuffs, small stuffed dolls and unlabelled silk bags. Mark reached within, taking a small box, the kind of snap-shut cheap ring box that was the purview of deluded men the world over. He opened it, a small blue crystal rested inside, tied to a thin cord. He took the crystal, closed the box, and slammed shut the trunk.

Still trying to keep his coat closed with one hand, Mark started his walk towards the house. In his other hand he held the small crystal, its cord looped around his fingers. He cursed the wind, it would make the amulet useless outside. The door to the house was a heavy wooden door, its white lead paint flaking from exposure to the elements. It swung slightly in the wind, its latch long since broken. He pushed it open and stepped inside. Rubbish lay strewn everywhere, remnants of the rave that had been held there a few nights before. A leaflet scatted past, caught up in the wind from the door. *"Rave at the haunted house on the hill!"* it read. Mark closed the door as best he could behind him. He needed at little wind as possible. He stretched out his right arm crystal held within, and tipped it out, hanging it by its thread from his finger. He waited for the crystal to stop its swing on the cord, to expend the inertia from the drop. Slowly is came to a stop. It held there motionless for a moment, before slowly the crystal began to move. It formed a small perfect circle, the repeated, going around and around in a rhythmic motion. Carefully, Mark stepped forward, and the crystal span ever so slightly faster.

Jess sat, legs crossed, hands gripping her notepad, flicking back and forth between pages, as she waited. She took out her pencil and drew a large question mark next to a note about "*friends of the victim*" before sliding the notebook back into her suit jacket pocket. Jess reached down and lifted a mug from the small desk beside her. A faded picture of cat was emblazoned on the side. The image had faded apart from two disembodied paws floating eerily against the white ceramic. She took a sip; the tea was lukewarm and had far too much milk. A beige drink for a dull beige police station. Jess was sat in the reception of the small station, waiting for her interviewee to turn up. The slightly dotty receptionist had asked her if she wanted a cup of tea six times in the last fifteen minutes, so she had taken it to primarily stop her asking. The station was old, everything was the kind of odd tan and beige colour that was popular in the seventies. The reception had the kind of blue plastic chairs you could find stacked in village halls and school gyms across the country. The ceiling was the same kind Jess had seen when she was in school. Thick polystyrene tiles with a weird brown speckling. The kids in Jess' school had a played a game they called "knives" wherein they stole knives from the cafeteria and would throw them directly up, digging deep into the soft tile. The idea was to see whose knife lasted the longest. Jess had not gone to a good school.

"Sorry, sorry!" apologised a uniformed officer, swinging open the station's door. His brown skin damp from the thin rain that seemed to cloak the town in a permanent mist. His eyes were a rich dark hazel, his beard trim and well kept. He walked over to Jess, his bright yellow jacket crackling as he walked. "Constable Rahman," he said, hand outstretched

"D.C Holden," Jess answered, shaking his hand. "Glad I could take some of your time."

"It's about the murder, right? Figured as much, well come on in, happy to help." The man nodded to the lady behind the counter, and a thin door opened with a buzz.

"Ok, so Constable Rahman-," began Jess.

"You can call me Aasif, want a cup of tea?" He gestured to a cheap white kettle. The two of them had taken a seat in a small break area. Aasif had called it the kitchen, but Jess had seen larger "kitchens" in caravans.

"I've got one thanks," replied Jess, holding up the disembodied cat mug.

"Hah! If Janet made it what you've got there is a mug of milk. I'll make you a proper one." Aasif opened a small cupboard beneath a sink that could be more accurately described as a water fountain. He placed them on the counter and pressed the button on the kettle.

"So," said Jess, placing the notebook on the table, sliding it open to a blank page, "you found the body correct?"

"Yeah," Aasif said. He turned and leant his back against the counter. The kettle behind him started to rumble slowly. "I go for a run every morning, park is near my house."

"About what time was this?" asked Jess, scribbling away in her notebook.

"Oh, about five thirty-ish?" Aasif reached back under the sink producing a worn red biscuit tin. The lid came off with a pop and he removed two teabags from the treasure trove within.

"Anyone else in the park at the time?"

"Not that I saw, I'm normally the first one there each morning anyway," he admitted. The kettles rumble had grown louder, and it was now roaring furiously. "Didn't see anyone between when I called it in and the cavalry arriving neither."

He lifted the kettle, pouring water into the mugs. Steam rose from them alluringly.

"Notice anything…weird whilst you were there?" enquired Jess.

"Weirder than a body strung up like one of my aunts prized necklaces you mean?" Aasif stopped dipping the teabags by their string and shook his head. "Sorry, that came out wrong. It's tricky, I'm not sure how your supposed to cope with seeing something like that, you know?" He stood there for a moment, silent, teabag string in hand.

"Haven't you had any support? Any kind of trauma counselling?" Jess asked, the pencil scratching as she wrote on her notepad.

"Hah, fat chance. I'm on a waiting list I suppose, but not much money to go around here. Sometimes it's like living a few decades in the past. We have to make do with what we have." He pulled the teabags from the cups, throwing them into a small green bin that rested on the counter.

"Trust me, it's important," Jess stated.

"That the voice of experience is it?"

"Something like that."

"Well," continued Aasif, opening a small fridge, the kind popular with teenage boys to store weak beers in their bedrooms. He produced a small glass bottle of milk. "Depends what you mean by weird?"

"Any abnormal temperatures. Odd smells, noises, did you feel an overwhelming sense of dread?" she asked.

"Can I class your questions as weird? Nothing springs to mind. Aside from the murder." Aasif placed a tray onto the table. It carried the two mugs and the milk bottle.

"I haven't seen one of these since I was a kid, think my Nan used to have them," Jess smiled, as she poured the milk into her tea.

"There are some perks to living in the past," said Aasif, clinking his mug against hers.

Mark stepped warily through the house. He had hoped being inside would protect him from the odd, almost sticky rain but the building leaked heavily in several places. He held his hand outstretched as he walked from room to room, kicking his way through plastic cups and discarded cans. The crystals spin varied by room, twirling slower the further he walked away from the hallway. Stepping back, he walked towards the narrow staircase that dominated the back half of the corridor. The crystal began a faster, wider arc as he moved up the first few steps. Mark sighed, for once he would like to not go upstairs in a creepy run-down house.

A few hours earlier Mark had stopped to interview the victim of the ghost attack at her home. A young woman by the name of Chelsea Jones. He had been greeted by her and Chelsea's sister Mercedes who he had been assured was younger, but it was difficult to tell under a frankly frightening layer of fake tan.

"It was a ghost, for sure!" Chelsea had said excitedly, apparently over the trauma she had shown in the video.

"It was, for sure!" echoed her sister, who, as far as Mark knew, hadn't even been at the rave.

"It was a woman, floating off the ground," continued Chelsea.

"Floating!" added her sister.

"And she had, like an old-fashioned maids' outfit, like the one your Darren wanted you to wear," Chelsea said looking at Mercedes, "her face was all, I dunno, mushy?"

"Mushy?" quizzed Mark.

"Like, out of shape, like drooping," Mercedes clarified.

"No that's not right," said Chelsea, pointing her finger at her sister as she thought, "you know how when your dreaming, and it's so real, like you could reach out and touch it. Then you wake, but there's the moment when your dreams fall away, everything melting into the real world. Like that." Chelsea just stared at her sister, dumbstruck.

"So how did it attack you exactly?" Mark shifted uncomfortably in his chair.

"I was on the top floor, looking for Jack, my boyfriend. He said he wasn't going to be there, but I swore I saw him with Tina Moston," said Chelsea, her demeanour switching in an instant.

"Ugh, Tina is such a bitch!" Mercedes said, crossing her arms.

"That's when it appeared, floating in the doorway. It reached out at me and I felt a, pressure, like it was pushing me. I tried to move, and it just opened its mouth wide. Too wide. The pressure pushed me, like hard, I flew into the window. Lucky it was open and that Mikey, it was Mikey's gig, had parked his van there. I landed on that, still got a bruise though, want to see?"

"No no! Its fine!" exclaimed Mark, desperately trying to stop the young woman who was mid lifting her top. "Thank you, this is great!"

Jess sat in the passenger side of the police car, and clicked her seatbelt in.

"You sure you want me with you?" asked Aasif, who clutched the drivers wheel nervously.

"Yeah, I need a ride, and you need to...not be alone," Said Jess.

"I'm fine honestly!" he protested. "Where are we headed anyway?"

"This address," said Jess passing him her notebook. "I spoke to the victim's teacher, apparently he hung around these same two lads constantly, brothers, a Daffyd and David Greenwood."

"Ouch!" Aasif laughed.

"What's funny?" Jess asked, perplexed.

"Daffyd is just David in welsh. Guess their parents aren't too creative."

The two of them drove, slowly through the streets of Pontypridd, the roads were wet with a sheen of water. Jess noticed it always seemed to be not quite raining. Enough to get you wet but not enough that you notice it before you stepped out. She preferred good old-fashioned London rain which at least knew what it was doing. Not as high up in the valleys as other welsh towns, Pontypridd was still a winding town, a maze of turns and hills, of council estates stacked one on top of the other like beer mats at a boring pub. People went about their daily business, stepping in and out of shops, smoking on bus stops and using crossings much more slowly than Jess would have liked. The rain didn't seem to bother anyone, who simply ignored it as though the town was populated by ducks. Everything seemed slower here. Born and raised in London Jess was used to the mindless swam or people that seemed to fill every street. She had been quietly amazed the first time she had left London to see that people used a whole escalator. She assumed keeping the left side open for people to run past was a perfectly normal thing to do. Apparently, the rest of Britain vigorously disagreed.

"Here we are," Said Aasif, pulling the car to a stop. The house was part of a long terrace, the outside of each covered in thick layers of pebble dashing. A small metal gate swung open lazily in the breeze. "Ready?"

"We aren't going to wait a minute, see if the rain clears?" Asked Jess.

Aasif laughed. "If you wait for the rain to stop in Wales, you'll be here a long time. Besides its only spitting."

"What a horrible way of phrasing that."

"Hello! Police! Anyone home?" Jess stepped inside, the door to the house was ajar. "Hello?"

"Maybe no-one's home?" Aasif asked.

"Hello?" Jess stepped down the entrance passage and pushed open a door to another room. "Ah, Aasif, you better call this in."

"Call in wh- "He stopped as he turned to look at the now open living room. "Yeah, I'll call it in."

The building was a slaughter house. An older man, who Jess assumed was Mr Greenwood the senior, was impaled onto the living room wall. The metal curtain rail had been pulled from above the window and forced straight through his stomach and into the plasterboard. The rail had bent from his weight and his body was now slumped half supported by a coffee table, the finial of the curtain rail resting on his stomach. Mrs Greenwood was in the kitchen. Her head had been slammed into the oven door repeatedly until both the glass and her skull had cracked open. Jess found the two boys upstairs in their shared bedroom. Each lay on their beds, chests ripped open, ribs arching outwards like great wings. Their organs had been pulled out and hooked onto their ribs like a grotesque washing line. Entrails dripping onto the floor. Jess was leaning over the older boy, Daffyd when Aasif knocked on the door.

"I called it in, backups on the way. Holy shit. This is fucked up." He stepped into the room, careful not to step in any of the blood. "This has to be linked right?"

"Must be," said Jess, she had slipped on a pair of gloves from the pocket inside her jacket and was rummaging in the pocket of the body. "Aha!"

"What are you doing?" asked Aasif.

"Found a phone. You're right, these boys knew the first victim, could be something on here." Jess tried to swipe on the phone's touchscreen, it was locked. "You're taking this rather well."

"My dad was a halal butcher, wanted me to follow in his footsteps. Seen more than my share of blood and organs," answered Aasif.

"It's a bit different when it's a person." Jess was leaning carefully over the body, phone in hand.

"Yeah, but I'm grateful for the stronger stomach right now. What are you doing?" asked Aasif puzzled.

"One downside to modern phone, ah there we go, facial recognition. All unlocked. Doesn't matter if you're alive or dead." She held the phone to her face and began opening apps and reading messages.

"I'm not sure I want to know how you realised that. Didn't look like that was a first for you," said Aasif.

"I wish I could say it was," Jess admitted, "Oh these have been some naughty boys indeed. Looks like they were spreading some err, rather intimate, photos of a girl. It seems like she sent them to Glyn, the first victim, who wasted no time showing everyone."

"So, a motive then, but that girl would be what, sixth form? Sixteen or seventeen like these two? How could she do all of this!" asked Aasif, his face twisted in shock.

"Well, once backup arrives, let's say we go find out."

Mark hit the floor hard, knocking the wind out of him. The spectre drifted slowly towards him. He had been in the room where Chelsea had been attacked but a few moments, crystal spinning madly in reaction to the spirit when it had appeared. With a gesture it had thrown him into the hallway. Scrambling to stand Mark was thankful it hadn't chosen the window again. There was no ratty second-hand van belonging to a wannabe DJ to save him. As the spirit advanced Mark could feel it exerting an overwhelming pressure, its force squeezing him uncomfortably. The thing was pale grey, as though all colour was anathema to it. Her face was stretched its sunken features stretching into contorted shapes as though it were clay. It wore a maid's outfit its skirt drifting as it floated. The entity reached out, running its hand along the wall, its nails were sharp curved talons that cut thin slashes into the peeling wallpaper.

"Ah shit," said Mark as the ghost wailed. "He reached into his coat pocket, producing a small black bag, his hands trembled as he struggled to open the drawstring that kept it close. The pressure from the spirit grew as it loomed over him, terrible claws bared. Reaching into the bag Mark took a pinch of powder onto his palm and blew. The spirit shrieked as the dust touched it, each mote turning into a tiny spark as it burnt. Mark saw his chance, sprinting down the stairs, the front door slamming behind him, bouncing off the doorframe. Opening the van door, he leapt into the seat. Having had to flee far too many times than he would have liked, the keys had been left in the ignition. He switched the engine on and peeled off with a squeal of his tires.

"Fuck voicemail," swore Mark down the phone, he drove quickly, eager to get distance between himself and the house. "Jess when you get this, we got a problem, fucking things not a normal ghost. Our angry female spirit has a physical form, claws, I'm pretty sure that it's a fucking onryo. Good thing I had iron filings with me or I would have been fucked. Call me when you get this."

Jess could feel her phone buzzing in her pocket. As she stood with Aasif by the door. She knocked again ignoring her phone. They had gotten the address from the school, the boys having cruelly included the girls full name with the pictures. The door opened ajar with a squeak, stopping on its chain.

"Hello?" said the girl inside, no more than seventeen. She wore pale blue pyjamas and a pair of slippers that seemed to be entirely fluff.

"Claire Payne? I'm D.C Holden, this is constable Rahman, can we have a word?"

Chapter 6

Mark looked at his phone. There was still no reply from Jess, but he wasn't concerned. Jess was notoriously terrible at returning calls, texting or just using phones in general. Mark had never not seen her screen smashed. He placed the phone onto the small bedside table in his hotel room and resumed his task. Picking up a large can of orange spray paint from beside the phone, he began to paint large ornate glyphs onto the walls.

He stood back when he was done, fingers orange from the paint. A bewildering array of symbols covered the wall. Kanji, Babylonian sigils, hieroglyphs, pentagrams, and arcane runes of every conceivable kind. Satisfied, Mark opened the small black silken pouch he had used in the house and slowly poured a thin line around the perimeter of the room. When the first bag was empty he took another from his case, having dragged it back into the room. Once he had completely lined the outside of the room, using a third bag as he did this, he took the remainder of the iron filings within and sprinkled them across the carpet, taking care to reach under the bed. The whole floor now covered in a thin scattering of iron, Mark grabbed the spray can and stood on the bed.

"For fucks sake," he cursed, as he tried to spray the ceiling, having to jump repeatedly on the bed to get enough height. With great difficulty he sprayed a large a large snowflake symbol, an eight-pointed star, the ends of each crossed with a curve, pairs of straight lines drawn through each spoke of the star. An old Norse rune of protection. Panting, Mark sat down on the bed, leant over into his case, and removed a book. The cover read *"Wraiths and Revenants: An encyclopaedia"*.

Flicking through the book, Mark found the page for an onryo. The picture included was an old Japanese print, a grotesque female form in a white burial robe, long black hair and curving talons. He read through the passages, trying to pry useful information from the pages like a miner would dig for gold. The book was a mass market widely available book, nothing about it was particularly occult, instead being a recounting of folklore. In Marks experience folklore was passed down from generation to generation for a reason. It worked. It normally transpired that traditional methods were overkill, stabbing a vampire with anything worked just as well as a wooden stake, but it was a great starting point.

"Typical, just my shitting luck," Mark swore at no-one in particular. The only example the book listed of stopping one was by a legendary Buddhist monk, not something Mark could easily get on tap. Curious he picked up his phone and searched quickly on the web. There was a group of Buddhist monks in nearby Cardiff! Unfortunately, it seemed they were on an annual retreat and so out of the country. Mark let out a loud sigh, rolled his eyes and placed his phone back down. "Ok Mark," he said to himself, "it's still a kind of ghost. There has to be a way to get rid of it". He glanced back down at the page. Vengeful female spirt, betrayed in life, seeks revenge, prone to jealousy. It seemed too familiar to him. He thought for a moment and flicked the book to another page. *"The Woman in White"* it read. There he was presented with a familiar image. A spectral woman, white gown flowing, driving by revenge, created by a betrayal in life. "Right so onryo and women in white," Mark said as though talking to the book, "they seem so similar they must at least be related. Different interpretations of the same kind of spirit maybe?" Thinking for a moment,

Mark picked up his phone, scrolled for a moment on his contacts and then dialled.

"D.S Singh," answered a voice.

"Rajan, hey, it's Mark, that woman in white you dealt with a few years ago, how did you sort it?"

Rajan Singh stood on the parapet, looking over into the courtyard, slowly following the line as it shuffled onwards. He adjusted his turban slightly; the wind was blowing a gale and being this high up had exacerbated it. In front of him a group of American tourists were excitedly taking pictures and leaning worryingly over the ancient stone.

"In the twelfth century," continued the tour guide to a chorus of impressed murmurs from the tourists, "the original wooden motte and bailey was replaced with the first stone castle at this site." She stopped and stared at the glazed looks in front of her. "A motte and bailey is a kind of castle, with the keep on a hill in the middle and an enclosed courtyard around it." She was met with several nods to signify that of course, they had known that all along. "Once the castle would have had several more buildings – "continued the guide as she descended the stairs, the tour following her.

Rajan, waited patiently for the tour to pass the destination he needed for his place. A small fire exit located just off the gift shop. Slipping silently from the crowd, he approached the dark green door. As he had hoped it was the older kind, its alarm tied to the great metal bar that ran across the door. The end of the bar was connected to the alarm, when it was straight it connected the circuit, pushing the bar to open the door broke it, triggering the alarm. Rajan pulled out a small flat sheet of metal from his pocket. One of his less scrupulous contacts had provided him with the tiny conductive magnetic card. Pushing it flat against the bar, Rajan very carefully and slowly pushed the handle down, card pressed hard against it. Inch by inch he pushed the door open, ensuring the small card completed the circuit in its place. The small black sheet stuck to the mechanism, preventing the alarm. Leaving the door ever so slightly ajar he returned to the tour who were busily stripping the gift shop of overpriced tea towels and calendars.

Carefully approaching the castle, torch in hand but switched off to hide him from the dark, Rajan was relived to find the door still open. He pulled it just wide enough for him to squeeze through, stepping inside. He stood before the entrance to the gift shop, a large metal shutter having been rolled down to cover it. He shivered, pulling his jacket zip up as a chill breeze drifted through the hall. Flicking on his torch, he lifted a small blue crystal suspended on a cord from his pocket, dangling out in front of him. It began to swing slowly in a circle. Cautiously, and quietly, he began to walk, the breeze growing into a faint whistling wind as he did.

He stepped out into the courtyard, the wind having reached an angry bluster. The crystal was spinning furiously, despite the elements arrayed against it. Rajan stopped, before him was the small stone alcove responsible for the last sighting of what he sought. A civilian had taken a photograph of a woman, pale grey almost white, a faded apparition weeping by the stone. The crystal was pulling against its cord in anger, threating to tear form Rajan's hand, so he slipped it into his pocket. He shone the torch into the archway, the darkness within swallowing even its light. That when he heard it. Faint as first he almost mistook it for the wind. It grew in volume become clearly the sound of a woman sobbing angry painful tears.

"Hello?" said Rajan in a whisper.

"Hello, hello? Is someone there?" came a meek reply.

"Can I help you at all, I'm here to help you?" He stepped forward, closer to the arch. The shadow seemed to slither towards him, forming into the shape of a woman, her dress ragged. Her skin was ashen grey, her eyes sunken dark pits.

"They took my child! They took him!" screamed the spectre, drifting towards Rajan a few inches from the ground. "They took him! They took him!" the ghost became more and more angry as she repeated it, changing in moments from meek girl to furious demoness. She seemed to stretch and distort, her limbs becoming thin distended branches, swinging wildly. She shrieked a bellowing noise, somehow high and low pitched at once and flew screaming at Rajan. Then she was gone.

"I didn't," said Rajan down the phone. "It was harmless. Scary as shit but no threat to anyone. We left it there, good for local tourism."

"Yeah somehow that's not much help to me. The thing I'm dealing with is horrible. Just being near it is like this weight pressing on you. You like can feel its grief physically. Plus, its able to take some kind of physical form, scratched up the walls pretty good. I'm thinking it's an onryo," replied Mark.

"What's one of those when it's at home?" Rajan asked curiously.

"Ever seen a Japanese horror film? One of them. They seemed pretty like your classic woman in white ghost, figured they might be the same thing. Doesn't seem like though, can't mark this one down in the tourism column." Mark shrugged his shoulders even though he was on the phone.

"Doesn't mean it's not. There ever been any other attacks from it you know of?"

"No, first recorded one recently." Mark listened intently, intrigued where Rajan was going.

"There are stories about ghosts at your location, local legends and stuff?" Rajan enquired.

"Yeah, going back at least a hundred years."

"Well maybe your movie ghost is something a woman in white can become? Like if they get supercharged or something makes them really angry. Maybe whatever happened to her has happened again, or maybe something else is amping up ghosts in the area," said Rajan. "

"You are a genius, next thing is working out how to stop it," said Mark. The door to his hotel room knocked. "I got to go, think that's Jess. Thanks man."

"Didn't feel like answering your- "Mark stopped as he opened the door. It wasn't Jess, but a young woman. She was smiling up at him rosy checked. She was wearing a maid's uniform. "Oh, I'm sorry, don't need any housekeeping, I forgot to put the do not disturb up." The woman stood there silent, smiling an eerie grin. "That's a pretty old-fashioned uniform they... oh shit." The woman let out a slow hiss, like air escaping from a tire. She lunged forward at Mark and smashed into an invisible force with a thud. She stood up, her form had become paler, her skin lighter. Her eyes had become piercing black. She lashed out, swinging at the doorway. As she did great orange sparks burst from the air. Mark stepped back into the centre of the room. The wards he had set up were holding for now.

"You're mine" hissed the ghost, drawing out each word. She leaned against the open doorway like it was a glass pane. Sparks flew as she pushed her face against it. "You're mine. Do not run from me my sweetheart. Don't be like the other men, they all leave me. Incited by whores!" Her whisper had turned into a shout. "You won't do that to me my love?" Slowly but surely, she began to push through the door, orange sparks flaring from her limbs, stepping through a waterfall of fire. Mark stepped up onto the bed, directly beneath the rune he had drawn on the ceiling. "Every man has let me down." Her colour had faded completely now, becoming an almost shimmering white cloud, dark specs of grey where her skin was showing. She flexed her fingers, which had sprouted long talons menacingly. She grimaced and let out a hiss of pain as she stepped onto the carpet, the iron filings burning her skin.

"Let you down how?" asked Mark. The ghost stopped, apparently puzzled at the question.

"Promises broken, my first love promised to take me as his bride, make me mistress of the house not some servant," Mark could hear the disdain as she spoke. "Spent all his money on sluts and whores! Ran his business into the ground. Had the audacity to blame me! So, I took what was mine! I trapped him in the cellar and set him ablaze!" The spirt laughed.

"Is that how you died too? There isn't even a cellar on the plans. Are you still down there?"

"It doesn't matter! The house is mine! Mine! I awaken and find what again! More whores!" The ghost waved her arms in the air angrily. Sparks continued to burn at her feet, her anger cancelling out any pain it caused her. "But no matter, now I have a handsome gentleman caller, a respectable man to build my respectable family." She stepped forward, closing on the bed.

"So, err, what exactly do you want from me?" Mark said.

"To be my one and only my love, to forsake all others!"

"I can do that!" Mark replied panicked. "In fact, you know what, why don't you go home, and I'll be right along. We can start our new lives together."

"You mean it my dear?" The spirit smiled, revealing mangled stump like teeth.

"Of course, just have some other business to tend to first" Mark said, hoping his idea would work.

"Don't be long!" said the ghost. Colour returned to, first her clothing and then her skin. She stood there looking the perfect picture of a happy young woman, and then vanished.

Mark stepped to his hotel room window, opening it wide in the vain hope the fresh air would help remove the oppressive force the ghost had projected. He leant his head out, willing the winds to blow it away. He look down at the black van he had rented his heart dropped. Great gashes had been torn into the sides, his tires ripped to shreds.

"I get my first girlfriend in months and not only is she a ghost, but she fucking keys my car. Fucking typical."

Chapter 7

Claire unhooked the chain from the door and pulled it open. She beckoned Jess and Aasif inside, yawning loudly as she shuffled down the corridor in her fluffy slippers. The house was much like the others Jess had seen in the area. Terrace houses squashed against each other like sardines and cover with a thick grey layer of pebble dashing. The inside wasn't much better, the hallway was narrow, the bulk of it taken up by ill placed stairs. They walked single file, following the girl as she pushed open a cheap plywood door and stepped into the kitchen. Grey plastic worktops with a faux marble effect stacked atop weary cupboards whose better days were past them. There was a small white table with two chairs in the centre, it struck Jess as wildly impractical in what was quite a small space. A portly man, thins wisps of grey hair sprouting from his mostly bald head, stomach hanging slightly over his trousers stood in the corner, staring at a battered old television. It wasn't on.

"Dad, police are here," droned Claire, taking a seat at the small table and taking a bite from a sandwich. The crusts had been cut off, but the bread bulged with something Jess couldn't quite make out.

"How may I assist you officers?" said the man, turning on the spot from where he stood. Turning to face them, he looked tired, his face drooping with exhaustion. He was wearing a black suit, his collar buttoned tight and sealed with a jet-black tie.

"Oh, are we interrupting anything?" asked Jess.

"Not at all," replied the man in a boring monotone.

"It's just the suit, dressed a bit formal for a Friday lunchtime," said Jess, pulling her notebook and pencil from her top pocket. She began to write something down. Aasif rocked on his heels behind her, intrigued by what was happening. He had only ever seen a detective interview someone on television. "Going anywhere?"

"No," intoned the man, "this is just how I dressed today." He stood there silent for a moment as if forgetting where he was. "I'm Mike Payne, this is my daughter Claire." Mike pointed at Claire slowly and deliberately, like a child repeating stage instruction at a nativity play.

"That's what we're here for actually, we wanted to talk to Claire. Do you mind if I take a seat?" asked Jess, gesturing to the small plastic chair opposite Claire at the table. Claire looked at her father and shrugged.

"That is acceptable," he droned. Jess slipped into the seat, motioning for Aasif to stand behind her. She leant forwards on the table, her arms held underneath.

"So, Claire, do you know a Glyn Powell at all?" asked Jess. There was a faint, almost inaudible tearing sound.

"Not really, I know he went to the same sixth form as me. That's about it." Claire didn't look up, her gaze not moving from the sandwich in her hands. Something inside it dripped. Aasif felt a touch on his hand, he glanced down to see Jess trying to surreptitiously pass him a page she had torn from her notebook. He grabbed it and glanced at the page. The top read *"put this in your pocket"* and underneath were a bunch of odd symbols and shapes Aasif had never seen before. Carefully he slipped the page into his pocket. Peering over Jess' shoulder he could see her drawing another set of identical symbols onto a blank page.

"Are you sure that's true Claire? You know you shouldn't lie to the police?" said Jess.

Claire's head shot up, her fingers squeezing into the bread. "I'm not a child," she shouted, flecks of food spraying into Jess' face.

"Maybe then," said Jess, brushing bread and flecks of what she assumed was jam off herself. "Maybe you can explain the messages we found on his friend's phone. They were very clear you were in a relationship with him. Seems he shared some very compromising photographs you might not want released." Mike stepped forward, halting when Claire raised her hand.

"How did you get that phone?" Claire asked. Her previously meek voice had gotten stronger, more direct. She sat up straight in her chair placing the sandwich flat on its plate.

"Two brothers, Dafyyd and David Greenwood were found dead this morning. I think maybe you knew that?" accused Jess, pointing her pencil like a finger.

"I don't know what you mean?"

"Three young men responsible for spreading around your dirty pictures all found dead, hell of a coincidence. I think maybe you decided you wanted to get some revenge?" Jess flicked the page on her notebook, holding it so Aasif could clearly see. "*Dangerous,*" she wrote.

"Even if I did, doesn't mean I could kill them. I've been here the past few days. Caught sick with a cold I'm afraid," said

Claire, coughing weakly for dramatic effect. "Maybe someone else found out and decided to teach them a lesson for me?"

"What like daddy dearest there? Don't think so, he's not all there at the moment, is he? Befuddlement spell maybe?" Jess asked, shaking her head in Mikes direction. Aasif's face was a mask of confusion, Claire leaned forward, narrowing her eyes.

"I'm not sure what you're trying to insinuate?" Claire hissed.

"Come on, five victims, all torn apart, not cut apart. Burn marks on one torso. One was nailed to the wall with a curtain rail. You would need abnormal strength to do that, and unless you've been really packing in the protein shakes you would need some kind of magical assistance. So, what, you find an old book with your friends, try some of the spells, realise it works and it spiralled out of control? Re-enacting The Craft were you?" She looked over her shoulder to face Aasif. "Actually, I think that films before her time."

"Probably," Aasif replied, still bewildered.

"This is absurd," protested Claire, raising her hands. Revealing a burn in the shape of a leaf.

"Then can you explain that then?" Said Jess, pointing at the burn.

The next few moments happened as a blur for Aasif, before he knew it Claire's father had barrelled across the room at him, hands outstretched. He crashed into Aasif slamming him to the ground, gripping tightly around his neck. Aasif spluttered as he tried to pry the man's hands free. As her father had dashed across the room, Claire had flipped the table high over Jess' head sending it crashing into the kitchen wall, the cheap wood splintering on collision. She stood in a semi-crouch, her arms outstretched, fingers flexing menacingly. Jess had ducked as the table had flown into the air and in one smooth motion stood back up grabbing the plastic chair she had been sat on, swinging it in a wide arc which struck Claire on the side, seeing her tumble to the ground. Quickly turning she brought her foot up sharply, her black boots digging deep into Mikes stomach. He roared, a mixture of defiance and pain but held on tightly. Frantic, his breath becoming ragged Aasif reached to grab one the tables legs, half splintered and split. He brought his hand up sharply striking his assailant in the temple with the foot of the leg. Mike grunted, momentarily stumbling and falling backwards as Jess heaved on his shoulders. They fell together, the heavy-set man landing on Jess winding her. He rolled off, scrambling to get his feet. Still half dazed Aasif reacted on instinct, leaping on the man as he stumbled clasping one of Mikes wrists with his handcuffs. Mike swung around hollering with bestial rage, the arm Aasif had gripped twisted unnaturally, a loud popping sound signifying it had dislocated. He raised his free arm to strike as Jess grabbed it. The two struggled against the man, each wrestling an arm as he thrashed and raged.

"Come on big fella calm dawn," said Jess through gritted teeth. Mike screamed at her in response, specks of spittle cascading from his open maw. She pushed against his arm as Aasif did the same, locking the handcuffs behind Mike. He immediately began lashing out with his feet, kicking with rage. Aasif swung his leg in a kick as Mike lashed at Jess, knocking him off balance. He fell backwards, slamming into the kitchens fridge before toppling forward. The fridge door bounced open, blood and organs from within splattering onto the floor. The severed head of a woman slid off the top shelf and bounced across the linoleum. Training kicked in and Aasif was on him, placing his knee into the small of his back. Mike bucked like a bull, roaring with contempt.

"Hold him still!" Jess shouted over the constant screaming.

"Yeah!" Aasif replied. "Trying to." Quickly taking her notebook from her pocket, Jess looked around for a moment, snatching up the front half of her pencil, seemingly smashed in the scuffle. She scrawled on the page frantically, her rune work loose and sloppy. She tore the page free and rolled it up. Crouching she gripped Mark by the jaw, forcing the page into his open mouth.

"Hope this works," she said to herself. Mike continued to rage for a moment, before slowly petering out, and collapsing in exhaustion, a baby with its dummy. "Right, we better cuff the girl before, oh-, "she turned to face Claire. The girl had worked her way upright and was standing in the doorway. Her face was torn badly on its right side where the chair had hit her. Blood stained her pyjamas. Her right hand was raised, before it floated the shape of several odd scratches, the air a burning bright orange. "I wouldn't if I were yo- "

"Silence!" screeched Claire. The burning lines flashed bright blue erupting into flames. There was a moment of quiet and then they exploded, a blast of force knocking Claire from her feet sending her careening down the hallway. A sudden painful heat touched Aasif's leg. He reached into his pocket and pulled out the slip of paper Jess had given him. It was slowly burning to ash. There was a clatter of metal as the front door handle was pulled. Claire lifted herself to her feet, arms resting on the handle. She pulled the door, chain bolt snapping tearing paper. She turned, looked at the two battered police, standing in a slowly growing pool of blood from the fridge. Then, she was gone sprinting through the doorway with unnatural speed.

"Ok...so...," said Aasif, bent over, hands on his knees as he tried to catch his breath. "What...the fuck...is going on?"

"Good question," answered Jess.

Aasif rubbed his neck. A large bruise had formed on it, remnants of Mikes attempted strangling. "So, monsters, magic, all of its real?" he asked.

"Yep, whole lot of other weirder stuff too," Jess said, her latex gloved hand prodding the raw meat in the refrigerator with a wooden spoon she had fished out of a drawer. "I'm pretty sure this," she waved the spoon in a circle, "is Mrs Payne."

"What happened to him?" Aasif said, nodding his head towards the sleeping man on the floor.

"Some kind of control spell, pretty powerful one for him to fly into a rage like that. Normally you just get the weird zombie thing on its own. Don't worry, I'm guessing he'll sleep like that for a while. I imagine it took it pretty much out of him."

"Out of him! He nearly took it out of us!" protested Aasif. "What did you do to stop him? And what do you mean you guess?"

Jess shrugged. "A whole bunch of what I do is guesswork."

"No manual for this kind of thing?" chuckled Aasif nervously.

"The opposite, whole bunch of manuals, books, tomes, scrolls, problem is the fifty fifty true to bullshit ratio. We got lucky, I put down the few runes of dispelling I knew and popped them in his mouth. Thankfully one of them seemed to do the trick. That's what saved us two. Seen the signs of a control spell once or twice, figured having some budget charms might come in handy. You see the blowback on her spell? Didn't think she expected that." Jess bent down and picked up the sandwich Claire had been eaten. She opened it, inside was a half-eaten human tongue.

"What was she? You seemed to think she was a teen dabbling with spells?" Aasif said, stepping over to Claire, careful not to step on the pool of blood and defrosted refrigerator ice.

"Maybe at first, but I'm pretty sure I was dead wrong. You see how fast and strong she was, and that magic, those marks, only seen one thing like that before and it was old primeval magic. You notice she went down pretty easy when I hit her with the chair. Sure, sign of possession."

"Like the exorcist possession?" said Aasif shocked.

"Could be, it's not like in the movies. The spirit riding your body doesn't look after it, that's why they're so fast and strong. You know like how people get super strong from adrenaline and lift cars in emergencies and stuff? They do that all the time. Still a fragile human body though. The Exorcist might have been a different film if that priest knew he could just punch it in the face. The two don't mix though, eventually the body will give out running hot like that." Jess had placed the sandwich back on the ground and stepped towards the doorway, away from the blood. "At that point the spirit might puppet around the corpse for a bit, which is its own frankly grim thing, or look for a new host."

Claire ran, blood pouring from her face, limping on one leg. She stopped, looked at the row of terrace houses before her and chose one at random. Walking up and knocking on the door she waited, wiping at her cheek with her sleeve. The entity was in full control now, meek timid real Claire taking a backseat when the police had arrived. The door creaked open to reveal a young woman in her early twenties.

"Oh my god what happened to yo- "she began, unable to finish her sentence as the top half of her body dissolved into ash, hit at that instant by an incredible heat. The woman's legs toppled backwards, the embers of her body floating slowly into the air like fireflies. Claire stood, her hand outstretched, glowing orange scratches fading from the air, vanishing to nothingness.

"Well, that still works," said Claire to herself.

She stood in the woman's bedroom, before a full-length mirror. Her clothes sodden with her own blood. She reached up and ran two fingers down the gash on her face. There was a horrid smell of burning meat as she seared the wound closed. Satisfied it was shut, she opened the woman's wardrobe sliding outfits past one after the other.

"Ah, this will do," she said, pulling a bright red maxi-dress from its hanger. She turned back to face the mirror, holding the dress against her chest.

"Maybe we've gone too far, maybe this was a mistake?" asked her reflection. It looked tired, large bags around its eyes, its posture sloped.

"Don't worry my dear," said the physical Claire. "Go back to sleep, I'll handle everything from now on."

Chapter 8

"What the hell happened to you?" asked Jess. She stood in the doorway to Marks hotel room, blood stains soaked onto her trousers past the ankle, suit misshapen and creased. Behind her stood a similarly bedraggled uniformed officer, bruises beneath his meticulous trimmed beard. He smiled nervously.

"I could ask you the same question?" Mark stood, his hand resting on the door handle. The room was a mess. Strange spray-painted sigils adorned the walls, a thin dusting of something dark brown was sprinkled liberally across the floor. Footprints were burned onto the carpet at odd places.

"Found our murderer," said Jess. Her voice thick with exhaustion.

"Found our ghost," replied Mark, equally tired. "See you found a friend. Good for you." Mark smiled at Aasif, who was still trying to take in the mess in the room beyond the threshold.

"I better go first," Jess said, stepping inside the room.

"So, fast, strong, knows some magic, but can't take a beating?" Mark said, pulling the paper lid from a wrinkled silver carton. Inside glistened, meat suspended in a thick orange sauce. He breathed deeply from the curry, before setting down on the bed beside him. He was sitting cross legged, his top shirt button undone, tie loosened. Jess was sat on the floor after carefully laying out several of the hotel towels, eager not to get iron filings in her lamb bhuna. Aasif was sat on a small bucket chair in the corner of the room, the kind of hard uncomfortable chair that seemed to exist only in hotel rooms. He was staring into his own tray, fork held mid-air, chicken tikka slowly dropping into back into the container. "Maybe some kind of possession? Is he alright?"

Jess turned to head to look at Aasif before resuming eating her meal. She took a large bite, chewed for a moment and then spoke. "I think so, he did well. Could of froze up but he was pretty quick to act. Gave him the brief version of the talk."

"You ok over there buddy?" Mark asked, waving his fork sprinkling the hotel sheets with curry. "Ah shit," exclaimed Mark, "well guess we're getting charged for cleaning anyway."

"That girl?" Aasif spoke, his voice a near whisper. "Can we help her? If she's possessed like you said can you do, I don't know? An exorcism?"

"Maybe," said Jess. "Not our field of expertise though."

"I thought all this was your field of expertise?" said Aasif puzzled.

"Even through all this weirdness," Mark gestured to the room around him, "we're still coppers. Our job is to catch the criminals and lock them up. Courts deal with the rest."

"Criminals?" Aasif sounded shocked. "That's what you would class this as?"

"Sure, why not?" said Jess. "This thing is a murderer. Look, that's the best way to treat this. The law is the law, if you're a werewolf but you never hurt anyone, why should we treat you any different? You'll tie yourself in knots trying to puzzle it out otherwise."

"Look if we can help the girl, we will, but honestly-," Mark paused for a moment, "people possessed tend not to last. They get run too hard by the thing riding them. You need to prepare yourself for the worst." They sat there for a moment, silently eating. There was a loud crack as Mark snapped a poppadum. He shrugged in apology.

Aasif chuckled. "You know, my father was pretty devout. Not me, turned my back on his faith, teenage rebellion and all that. Now a demon has possessed a girl, and he was right all along."

"It's a bit less clear cut than that." Mark said, inhaling deep from a carton of onion bhajis he had opened. "You're right, it's probably a demon. A ghost could possess someone but they're a lot less coherent. Supers are a bit like humans-,"

"Supers?" asked Aasif, crossing Mark.

"Supernatural creatures. Supers. They're like humans. Lots of conflicting religions and beliefs, who knows what's true? A demon might threaten you with the pits of hell, but a Wight might scream about Valhalla. Some of the weirder stuff doesn't line up with any religion. Look at this room, these symbols are proof of how mixed up things are." Mark pointed at a glyph on the wall, "That's Greek," he pointed at another, "that's Japanese, that one is Aramaic." Mark pointed at the single marking on the ceiling, "That's Norse. They all work. Who's to say any of them is wrong."

"What is with all the wards anyway?" asked Jess.

"Oh right, yeah, we've been so wrapped up in the other thing. Yeah, so I promised myself to an onryo," Mark said.

"Promised yourself? And to a what?" Aasif said, intrigued.

"I think we're betrothed, maybe? It's a kind of ghost, really angry, really dangerous. Generally, ghosts are harmless, this one can be pretty deadly, big claws." Mark mimed a clawing motion. "It's up at the old house outside town."

"The Davies house. A Maids ghost," declared Aasif.

"Yeah, that's right." Mark narrowed his eyes.

"It's a local legend, kind of a rite of passage around here."

The three of them moved closer as Aasif told his tale. Spinning his story like they were around a campfire. "Legend says the house was owned by Merfyn Davies, a terrible man. He ran a coal mine, shipping great loads of it through Pontypridd. The story goes that he was an arrogant man, thought himself the Lord of the town. He had a maid who followed him everywhere, a girl who loved him. He had a reputation around the town as a ladies man but this girl was blind." He leant in closer. "When you go to the house, you're supposed to knock three times on the cellar door at the back. It's said that the mine hit hard times and he crossed some people he shouldn't, so they killed him and his maid and put the bodies in the cellar. If you know, you're supposed to hear them knocking back. Every teenage boy goes there at some point, normally to impress some girl who couldn't care less. Lots of people claim they have seen a ghostly maid staring at them through a window."

"Actually, makes sense, the ghost claimed she had died in the cellar," Mark said, leaning back.

"It spoke to you?" Jess asked.

"Yeah, it was remarkably chatty. Makes sense the way it acted. It pushed that girl out the window because it was jealous, and it latched on to me because it's replacing this Davies with any man I guess?" Mark grabbed his phone from the small table next to the bed. "So, question is why now? Seems like she was harmless enough up until recently?"

"Six bodies!" screamed Florence. "Six!" Jess winced, holding the phone away from her ear from the noise. "Do you know how hard it is to spin one supernatural death as something normal for the media? And you've got six! At least tell me you have leads."

Jess leant back in the hotel room chair. She was alone, Mark and Aasif had left to work on the onryo problem, leaving Jess to report back in with the office. "Yes Ma'am," she replied. "The girl is definitely possessed. She was much too coherent for it to be a spirit, and it was using magic to control the girl's father. At least we managed to save him."

"The man is in a coma from what I gather, hardly saved is he?" said Florence her voice thick with disappointment.

"Better than dead Ma'am. He was a lot luckier than his wife. We've circulated the girl's description around the local police, they have strict instructions not to approach. Ma'am I think we might need to tap our sources on this one." Jess held her breath, knowing what she was asking for was considered extremely dangerous.

"Agreed." Jess let herself breath. "I'll send D.S Singh and D.S Cooper. What about this ghost thing?" asked Florence.

"An onryo Ma'am, very dangerous kind of spirit. Curren is on his way to the house currently. It came to his hotel room, so it's not bound to the location, but it seems content enough to stay there unless provoked." Jess carefully left Aasif unmentioned. Any mention of him and he would quickly find himself transferred to London. Jess wasn't sure she could drag another person into the kind of life she led.

"Knock it on the head for now then. If it's localised it's much less important than the possession. Try and wrap this up quickly, we can't afford any more deaths and the local brass are already spooked. We do not want any locals trying to take this into their own hands. That never ends well," said Florence, a sternness in her voice telling Jess that this wasn't a suggestion.

"Understood Ma'am."

Mark and Aasif stood at the back of the decrepit house. It was early afternoon but darker than Mark expected, thick grey clouds blotting out the sun. Thankfully it wasn't raining, a first from Marks experience of South Wales so far. In front of them was a set of cellar doors, heavy wooden things, surprisingly intact despite their age. Mark bent down to grab a small metal handle on the left-hand door and pulled. It didn't move. He tugged on the right handle one and again it didn't budge. He put both hands on the two doors and heaved, losing his grip and falling backwards onto the ground. Sitting on the ground he brushed he hands on his coat and looked up. Above him in the top window was a pale figure, it waved its talon like nails in an oddly friendly manner.

"Holy shit did you see that?" Asked Aasif.

"Yeah, don't worry, I think you're safe. She seems to have latched onto me and she kind of runs on jealousy. If I had brought Jess think it might have been a different story," said Mark, pulling himself to his feet. There was a clatter and the cellar doors burst open, untouched by either man. A faint cold breeze wafted from inside. "Think she's inviting us in."

The inside of the cellar stank of damp and mould. The stone walls coated in thick black. Here and there were handprints from adventurous teenagers. Mark reached into his pocket, pulling out the small blue crystal he had used earlier.

"What's that?" enquired Aasif.

"The crystal reacts to a ghost's energy. The ghost itself, the places it haunts, the things it touched all have a sort of aura." Mark dangled the crystal on its string, it began to move, circling around in larger and larger circles. "The closer you are to one of those auras the bigger the reaction. See?"

"So, it's like one of those electromagnetic things they use on ghost hunting shows?" Aasif asked.

"Except this one works. Those things are junk. If ghosts gave off electromagnetic radiation how would you know? Everything electronic gives it off. Hell, in our society it would be like looking for, well, not so much a needle in a haystack but a specific strand of hay in a haystack. Forest through the tree's kind of thing." Mark stepped forward a little, then back, trying to judge the twirling of the crystal. "Problem with this thing is it doesn't tell you which way to go, just need to try different directions and see how it reacts. Like playing hot and cold as a kid." He took one step to the side, and then stepped back to his original position. He repeated the motion the other direction.

"You look ridiculous," chuckled Aasif.

"It's not a glamorous job," shrugged Mark in agreement. He turned, and seemingly sure of where he needed to go, strode onwards, crystal spinning as he went. "Here," he said. "The black on the walls seem to be scorch marks, this looks like the start of it, look how the floor is darker here."

"So, what do we do? How's this help us?" Aasif said.

"It doesn't. Best way to get rid of a ghost is to resolve its unfinished business. That's a lot harder than it sounds. Hoped maybe we would find the bodies or something, was a shot in the dark really. Looks like the stone walls contained the fire, but it would have gotten real hot. Guess everything was destroyed." Mark pocketed the crystal. "At least we know now she was telling the truth."

Claire sat in the empty living room of the home she had invaded. The legs of the homes previous owner had been placed onto a large recliner in the corner of the room. Claire had taken the time to bend them as though they were sitting. She was leaning back in the centre of a three-seater sofa, arms stretched across the top, red dress trailing on the floor. She had found a supply of makeup and had tried, poorly, to cover the large burn on left side of her face with makeup. Claire drummed her fingers impatiently. She stood up, began to pace across the room, hands behind her back. She cleared the room twice, then stopped, spotting a tablet on the black flat pack coffee table under the window. She grabbed it, slid it open and brought up the internet browser. Slowly, using one finger, she typed into the search bar. She opened her search, revealing a map of the town.

Claire wandered around the house, collecting the things that she needed. Dirt from the garden, a collection of salt and herbs from the kitchen, a pair of old tights from a bedroom upstairs. Taking her ingredients back into the living room he placed the dirt and herbs into a small plastic bowl, a cartoon builder beaming back at her from inside it. Claire turned to the dismembered legs and with a horrible wet tearing ripped free a chunk of its thigh. She squeezed the wobbling flesh, filling the bowl with blood. Taking the old tights, she tore out a rough square. Pouring the mixture of blood and dirt into the tights she squeezed. The blood trickled through the material, splattering onto the tablet and its open map. At first the blood splattered randomly, but within moments it began to stretch out across the map, the droplets pooling into distinct points. Seven distinct locations each marked by a splash of gore. Taking a photo of the tablet with her phone, Claire stood up, walked to the front door and out into the street. She smiled, a plan forming in her mind.

Chapter 9

In the Soho part of London, hidden down an alleyway squeezed tight between two buildings are a small set of stairs. On the wall above them are a set of neon letters, glowing bright pink illuminating the alleyway. "*Lucille's*" it says. Behind the letters a devil sits in a martini glass, its neon legs flashing back and forth in a kicking motion. In front of the stairs stand two detectives, their faces flashing pink in time with kicking legs.

"I hate this place," said Dale Cooper, dropping a cigarette to the floor and stubbing it out with his foot. He turned to Rajan. "You think they made it as dodgy as possible on purpose?"

"Almost without question," said Rajan. "You ready to head in?"

"Guess so?" replied Dale. "We sure this is necessary?"

"Boss thinks so," Rajan answered. "Right, let's go in."

The small metal door swung open with a creak. Inside was the riotous sound of laughter. People stood around drinking craft beers from bottles. The jukebox blared Weezer's Buddy Holly. A man in a flannel shirt with a bun brushed passed the detectives. A ratty bar sat at one side of the room, worn metal stools at its edge, strange bottles neither detective had heard of stacked slapdash behind it. A woman was wiping down the bars dark wooden top. She wore a white blouse tucked into black denim jeans ripped at the knees. Her hair was tied up with a red and white spotted handkerchief. Her lipstick a vibrant red.

"Evening Lucille," said Rajan stepping over to the bar. "Got a minute?"

"All I have are minutes. All day every day, tending this bar. Just this and nothing else. Certainly not done anything recently that would warrant a visit," said Lucille. She smiled sarcastically. "Oh, and D.S Cooper is with you?" She grinned, authentically this time. "Can I get you a drink honey?"

"Uh, no thanks, I'm good." Dale nodded nervously as he spoke.

"We need some info, for a case." Rajan pulled up one of the stools, making a horrible screeching noise as it dragged across the hard tile floor. He sat on it.

"It's always for a case. You know," Lucille reached across the bar and touched Dale on his arm, "you can always come by anytime, you're always welcome." She smiled and stepped back, picking up a glass that she began to wipe with a cloth. "You know, you can't just," she glanced at the bar to check she wasn't being listened too, and then leant forward anyway, "you can't keep coming around asking questions. This is supposed to be you know, incognito."

Dale shrugged. "You know the terms of your agreement, you're on taps for info when we need it."

"Well, if it's for you." She batted her eyes at Dale in an over exaggerated manner. "You can tap me anytime." Dale blushed profusely.

"Yes well, is there anywhere we can talk more privately?" asked Rajan

"Not even going to get a drink first? Support a small local business?" replied Lucille. The look on Rajan's face answered for him. "Fine," she said. "Hey Abbie!" Lucille called out across the dingy bar, waving at a woman wearing a short black shiny dress, thick heavy spiked boots and dark eyeliner. She was carrying empty glasses on a flat black plastic tray. The woman nodded in reply. "Cover the bar for me for a min? Need to take care of something." Abbie's face was a dour sullen sulk. She shrugged. "That's a yes, come on follow me." Lucille beckoned to the two detectives.

Lucille led them through the crowd, across the dingy bar. Out from behind the bar the men could see she her jeans were three quarter length. She wore plan black ankle boots, revealing a tattoo of what appeared to be an apple with a bite taken out. She pushed easily though the crowd without effort, people subconsciously moving just enough to avoid her. They did not do the same for the two detectives, who crashed their way through the crowd, bouncing from shoulder to shoulder. Lucille stepped through a line of women waiting to use the bathroom, the line silently opening for a moment. Not a single woman looked up from their phones as they did.

"Sorry ladies, sorry!" apologised Dale as he squeezed through. Just beyond the line was an old wooden fire door, pale green paint flaking off it. It was covered in bright neon posters for bands Dale had never heard of. They were all handmade, the slight fade from photocopying a dead giveaway. Dale had been in a band in his university days, and it brought back memories of sneaking into the library with a stack of multicoloured paper to make band posters without being caught. He pushed the door open. Beyond was a dark stairway leading upwards, dark brown tiles with metal runners at the end of each step. The two men walked the stairs, boots thumping on the tile. At the top of the stairs a door stood open, light pouring out from within.

"Welcome to my earthly abode!" laughed Lucille. She was stood just beyond the door way, leaning on an old blue sofa, its leather torn and resewn in spots. They were stood in a small bedsit directly above the bar. A tiny thing with a single room. Open plan kitchen moved straight into living room. A thin transparent pink cloth had been tacked to the ceiling to separate the living space into separate sleeping and living areas. Each was dominated by a double bed and sofa respectively. The walls were covered in cheap flat pack shelving to try and maximise space. Above the bed was a large framed poster of Elvis. "Well, it's something at least. A lot better than my last place. Moved somewhere hot and somehow found the only cold spot somehow. Imagine that!"

"Yeah, I'm err, imagining it. So, you going to help us?" said Dale.

"Sure sugar, don't mind me, always had a flair for the dramatic." She winked awkwardly.

"We've got some things to show you," Rajan declared, pulling a tan paper folder from his jacket. "Is there anywhere we can, sit, I guess?"

"Take a seat boys!" laughed Lucille, swinging her legs over the sofa and sliding down into the middle seat. Awkwardly Dale and Rajan sat down on either side of her. Rajan passed the folder to his right, into the waiting hands of Lucille. "So, what can I do you for?"

"There's a possessed girl. It's not spirit possession, so it must be demonic. You know anything about that?" asked Dale.

"Not a sausage." Lucille leant over to Dale, resting her hand on his thigh. "I don't live that life anymore. I'm a good girl now, well, most of the time."

Dale coughed nervously, brushing off her hand. "Well, you are the preeminent expert in them. You did make them after all."

"Did I?" Lucille dragged out the last syllable, her voice turning high pitched. "I mean supposedly, but honestly I don't remember. There's a lot of things I apparently did or didn't do, it's all a bit fuzzy. Memory does that. Sometimes I forget what I had for lunch the same day, things from that long ago are a bit of a jumble." She raised her hands in protest. "Besides, that was the old me. You're asking the new me. New life, new identity. That's the point of witness protection. That is, if policemen didn't turn up every other week or so. Answer this Lucille, answer that Lucille. I'm not demonic google." She grabbed Dales hand and held it with both of hers. "You're always welcome here of course Dale. You're ever off the clock and want to just pop down…"

"Focus Lucille," said Rajan with the tone of a school teacher. "You going to help us or not."

"Sure fine, but because Dale asked, not you." She opened the folder and thumbed through the pictures inside. She let out a long whistle. "This is a doozy. This is what six different bodies?"

"There's a seventh victim currently in a coma. Some kind of mind control magic," answered Dale.

"Mind control magic? That's not terribly common. Is this one stuffed into a fridge?"

"They were eating that one. In a sandwich apparently," said Dale. "We actually think that one might have been the second victim, tough to tell with it being kept in the fridge like that."

"I guess that's one way to dispose of a body. Bit Hannibal Lector for my liking, but better than digging an obvious grave I guess. Still, can't help you. Not a demon." She slammed the photos back into the folder with more force than she needed and held it out before Rajan.

"What do you mean not a demon?" he said, he crossed his arms leaving her holding the folder out awkwardly.

"What I said not a demon. Not their style." Lucille tossed the folder onto the floor in front of her.

"Wanton murder, possession, over the top violence, weird magic. Sounds pretty demon like to me," Dale said, leaning down to pick the folder up.

"Dale, I expected better of you. For shame." Lucille crossed her arms pouting. "Possession yes, murder well of course, violence goes without saying. This is all too sloppy. You see, the thing with demons is that they're just like angels."

"Angels?" asked Dale disbelievingly.

"Yeah angels. You know, hunky bastards, flappy wings, keen on blowing their own trumpets so to speak," said Lucille sarcastically.

"I know what angels are."

"Do you though? The male model with a trombone look is just the human idea of them. Most angels are a lot weirder, multiple headed lions, there was one I used to date that was a series of wheels spinning around each other. I mean, technically I'm an angel and I can do this." Lucille touched her hands to her temples. Lifting her hands from her head two black gnarled goat like horns grew, their tips touching the palms of her hands. There was a scratching noise from the leather behind her and a thin tail with a sharp single talon had popped up from between her jeans and her blouse. Her skin took on a dark red colour.

"Get to the point," Rajan said, his patience clearly running out.

The horns and tail vanished with a puff of grey smoke. Lucille's skin took on its prior alabaster tone. "You're no fun." She poked her tongue out at Rajan. It was pierced with a silver stud. "My point is angels aren't these glorious saviours that humans think they are. They are creatures of order. The same goes with demons. Evil bastards yes, but ultimately, they want the same thing as angels. Order. That's what they do, angels and demons, try and keep the universe in some semblance of balance. Things get a little too goody-goody demons nudge it back the other way with a well-placed whisper or deal. Things get a little too dark the angels bump up the charity or something. Back and forth for all eternity. Two sides of the same coin. This is all chaotic, it's born of rage and the joy of violence." She waved at the folder. "Not a demon's style."

"Right, so any idea what did do it?" questioned Dale.

"Sure, it's obvious." Lucille smirked smugly.

"Mind telling us?" Dale sighed.

"Say please."

"Mind telling us, please?" repeated Dale

"It's a Jinn," declared Lucille, pleased with herself.

"That's just another word for demon," Rajan interjected.

"Well, I would love to say you were right. That's a lie. I actually love how wrong you are. Jinn are not demons. They aren't some magic wish granting cartoon either. Jinn are a kind of, middle ground between angels and demons. Not quite either. Very dangerous. Very rare." She leant back onto the sofa stretching her arm across the back behind Dale. "Jinn means concealed, or more commonly beings concealed from the senses. Way back when, in the fuzzy memories, they caused a whole heap of trouble. Unlike angels and demons, they only exist for themselves. Couldn't give a hoot about order. Quite the opposite. They love chaos, causing it, being around it. They got the boot from the universe a long time ago. Too much trouble."

"What the hell does that mean?" asked Rajan

"Hey! Language, I don't go around making digs at Britain. It means what it means. They got ousted, into the in-between space between this dimension and the next, supposedly where they couldn't make any trouble. Every so often, when the barriers between realities are already weak they can hop a ride on that metaphorical train and come over. Still don't have a form here though, might appear as a kind of smokeless fire. That's why it took the girl, ride her body around town like a fleshy uber." Lucille leapt up from the sofa, startling the two men. "Tea?" she asked.

"No thanks. What does it want?" Dale said, twisting in the sofa as Lucille walked over to the small counter.

"It's got to have permission to use the host, so it will probably do whatever it promised the girl first. That will probably explain the bodies. Then, once it's done that it will probably do whatever it wants really. That's kind of the problem. It might want a cup of tea from a café, and then midway through decide it wants to murder everyone in the café. One thing it will want is some friends. It's going to try and bring others here."

"How did it get here, you said reality needed to be weak?" Rajan was holding up his phone, recording Lucille's rambling explanation.

"Yeah, all kinds of reasons. Could be someone deliberately doing it, could just be naturally occurring. Plenty of things lurking around the Earth that started somewhere else. Some angels think that might include us. Damned if any of us can remember clearly though. That would throw a loop in your holy books huh?" Lucille laughed to herself as she slowly dipped a teabag. "Anything else weird in the area?"

"Yeah, there is." Rajan nodded. "So how do we stop it?"

"Beats me?" Lucille held her hands up.

"Beats you?" said Dale, "You know all this, but you don't know how to stop one?"

"I was on ice when they got kicked out." She took a long sip of tea. "On your own with that one lads. Now I've enjoyed our chat, especially with you Dale, but I need to get back to work. Anything else?"

"Think she's telling the truth?" said Dale as they went through the door back into the bar.

"No way. Not in a million years." Rajan stroked his beard. "I think she's probably telling the truth on what this Jinn thing, but she knows how to stop them. There's no way she doesn't. Plus, she isn't exactly known for honesty."

"Well, our job here is done anyway. Let's get out of here, she gives me the creeps," admitted Dale.

"I know what you mean, being so close to... that is a bit disconcerting." Rajan started walking across the bar and Dale followed. They opened the front door and started up the steps into the alleyway.

"It's not that, it's the flirting, it's a bit full on," Dale said.

"That's what creeps you out? Not the whole, you know, the Devil thing?" Rajan turned around on the stairs to face Dale, shocked at his statement.

"That doesn't bother me. Shauna is a ghulah, my mate Gaz is a werewolf. I once played chess with a ghost. Nice fella. It's the heavy flirting. Feels weird coming from a woman. Does that make me sexist?" Dales eyes looked up as though he was trying to puzzle it out.

"Probably." Rajan sighed. "Really, that's your hang up?"

"It's probably unprofessional as well, witness protection and all that."

"Yeah, that's it. That's the worst thing. The worst thing about going out with Satan."

Lucille walked down the stairs a few minutes after the detectives, still clutching her warm mug of tea. She looked out across the bar. When she had agreed to the protection arrangement she had asked specifically for this. She wasn't allowed to leave, having exchanged one prison for another, but at least this one was alive. People laughing, cheering, enjoying themselves. An eternity of boredom meant Lucille was eager to at least experience a small slice of life. It also amused her no end people's tendency to ask barkeepers for advice, not realising who they were asking.

"Hey Luci" said one of her regulars as he walked past beer in hand. She smiled. It was a small cooped up life, but it was a life, and Lucille was eager not to lose it.

"Abbie!" shouted Lucille as she stepped up to the bar. She pulled up a stool and sat down.

"Yes boss," said Abbie, leaning her elbows onto the bars counter.

"Can you get a hold of one of your contacts from the old crew?" Lucille pointed to a bottle of whisky she kept behind the bar. Abbie understood she wanted a glass of it with the unspoken bond of people forced to live long hours with each other.

"Not allowed boss, no contact with our old lives remember. My flat around the corner and here. Only places I can go. Not eager to break our agreement."

"Don't bullshit me, I know you keep in touch with some of the old gang. I know there's that incubi who sends you new albums." Lucille stared at Abbie sternly.

"We do have the best music," admitted Abbie, handing Lucille a finger of whisky and pouring one for herself.

"Damn right we do," said Lucille clinking her glass against Abbie's. "Look we need to let people know about what those bobbies just showed me. It needs to be dealt with properly."

"Got it boss." Abbie downed her whisky in one and set the glass down. "I'll see what I can do. You know, it's a bit mean to tease that one copper like that."

"Tease?" protested Lucille. "You've got me wrong there, I actually think he is cute as hell."

Chapter 10

Brian sat in the single chair in his living room. A worn creaky leather thing that used to recline but had long ago gotten stuck. He was slouched down, can of cheap lager in one hand, television remote in the other. He was wearing a pair of elasticated lounge pants, his worn white shirt left on from his work day, the top few buttons left open. He had opened a streaming app on his television and was scrolling idly through documentaries on serial killers. Outside it was dark, night haven fallen adding dark to the rainy and drab descriptors normally applied to the town. Brian had just chosen a particularly grim looking documentary about a cannibal who ate only faces when there was a frantic knocking on his door.

"Uh, hello?" Brian said, holding his front door open. In front of him was a young girl, bedraggled from the rain. She was crying, her makeup running a jagged pattern down the large burn on the side of her face. "Are you ok?" he asked.

"These guys, these guys..." spluttered the girl.

"It's ok, its ok," said Brian "come in. We'll call the police I guess?" He stepped aside his arm outstretched, beckoning the girl into the house. Claire cracked a smile and stepped past him leaving a trail of wet on the carpet as her dress dragged across the floor. "Through there, the living room is just on the left. Do you need a towel or something?"

"No, No, I just..." Claire was stood by the recliner, tears pouring forth. "I was walking him and these men they just came out of nowhere and they- "she stopped as Brian placed his hand on her arm.

"It's ok, you're safe now," said Brian.

"You aren't," said Claire.

Claire struck him in the centre of his chest with her palm. Brian toppled backwards from the force spluttering. He stumbled tripping over a small side table landing onto his back. He lay there, stunned from the blow as Claire stood over him.

"Up you get," she said grabbing Brian by the arms and pulling him forward. She made the right hand into a fist still gripping Brian with her left and punched him hard in the face. His lip split, and he spat blood.

"Please don't," begged Brian, "stop."

"Oh, I don't think so," growled Claire punching him again. "I know what you are." She struck him a third time.

"You don't understand!" cried Brian.

"Oh, I do." Claire grabbed him by the shoulders and slammed him backwards, his head crashing into the floor. "Show me." She smashed his head onto the ground again. A bloodstain was forming on the carpet. "Show me!" Claire shouted.

Brian closed his eyes for a moment, when he opened them again they were bloodshot. His pupils open like black pits. He released an unnatural screech and pushed Claire, sending her flying into the opposite wall. He climbed to his feet and let out a slow rumbling growl that was rhythmic, an almost ticking noise. He seemed to grow by at least a foot, his form growing lithe and thin. Slowly his tongue slithered from his mouth, revealing rows of sharp teeth erupting from his gums. The end of his tongue, now at least three feet long opened into its own sharp mouth, a hideous writhing lamprey.

"An aswang, lurking here in the arse-crack of the world!" laughed Claire. "Can't be many of you left."

"Fuck you!" hissed Brian, the smaller mouth on his tongue moving in time to his speech. "I told you to stop, now you'll pay you bitch!"

"And you were so nice before," said Claire brushing plaster off her dress. "Sorry but I need to borrow some blood, I'll just need hmm, maybe four or five litres." She held out her hands palms up, pale blue flames crackled on her fingers. She brought her fingers together forming two small balls of fire which she rolled through her knuckles like a pair of coins.

"Don't say you weren't warned," spluttered Brian. He crouched, resting one hand on the carpet.

"So predictable," Claire sighed, she rolled the flames back into each palm. Brian leapt into the air, screaming a terrible high-pitched wail as he did. Claire gently blew onto her palms, they blossomed into terrible gouts of raging fire. Brian's cry of defiance became an agonising cry of pain as he was engulfed in the inferno. Claire stepped to one side as Brian crashed down, losing control as he struggled to put out his burning form. Claire reached down, unhurt by the flames, grabbing Brian on the back of the neck. She struck him with her other hand. "This could- "she hit him again, "of- "she continued to hit him, "been so easy." Confident she had at least momentarily stunned him, she lifted one leg, slipping off the black pump she had stolen with the rest of her outfit. She brought her heel down hard on Brian's thick slithering tongue. His body smouldered, the room stank of burning flesh. Claire bent down and gripped the tongue with one hand. Keeping it pinned with her foot she tore it free in a spray of blood. Brian's still smoking form let out a feeble groan of pain. "Stay here a moment," said Claire as she strolled off, tongue dangling limply from her hand.

She returned a few minutes later. Meat cleaver in one hand, mop and bucket in the other. She tossed the mop side and lifted Brian's charred body, unconscious but still alive. She rested his neck on the lip of the bucket.

"We could have done this without all this unpleasantness," said Claire in an oddly upbeat tone. "Oh, who am I kidding? This is the fun part." With a great arcing swing she brought the cleaver down onto the back of Brian's neck. Severing a head is a messy slow thing. Each strike cut deeper into the flesh. There was a loud clicking noise as she struck down and it took several fearsome blows to cut through the spine. Eventually, Brian's head dropped into the bucket, bobbing the in the blood that had nearly filled it to overflowing. Claire reached into her dress pocket, stopping momentarily to inspect a section that had become torn in the scuffle. She produced her phone and opened it to the picture she had taken earlier. She crossed off one of the blood spots using the phones image editing tool. "That's one down," she said to no one in particular.

Jess lay in the bed of her own hotel room. She held her phone above her head. On it her wife's face smiled gently. On the sofa behind her Lana was asleep, curled up with a large white stuffed bear.

"Sounds like you have your hands full," said Hannah, her voice scratchy over the phone's speaker. A Large crack ran down the glass. Jess was notorious for breaking her phone constantly. "Please promise me you'll be careful."

"I always am!" protested Jess. "We'll wrap this up and be home before you know it." Jess had told Hannah about having to deal with two cases at once. She had neglected to mention the bodies piling up. The office worked tirelessly to try and downplay deaths in its cases, the last thing they needed was the press rushing to capitalise on a new serial killer like flocking vultures, but Jess always tried to screen Hannah from the worst of the things she saw. "How's your work going?"

"Got an article going up later today, the editor was impressed, says more work might come my way soon." Hannah's face beamed with a grin.

"Wow that's wonderful love, things are really coming along for you." Hannah was a freelance journalist. It worked wonders for their home-life, allowing her to look after Lana at the same time, but getting jobs was sporadic and unpredictable. They had talked about Jess leaving the force if Hannah could find a full-time position at a magazine or paper, but Jess knew that would never likely happen. She had seen too many horrific things, privately Jess had resolved to keep working for as long as she could, to protect as many families like hers as possible. It was moments like this, where all she wanted to do was sit down on the sofa next to the sleeping Lana and wrap her arms around her that truly made the job difficult. "Any idea what they might ask you to do?"

"Probably something like this one. We guess what cheese you like from your choice of celebrity photos. Hardly making good use of my degree, but it pays our bills. Plus, you never know, might stumble across something worthwhile. Maybe some kind of camembert conspiracy?" Hannah laughed at her own joke, her giggling was infections and before she could stop herself Jess was laughing along with her.

"Jars, pots anything? Come on man, you have to have something." Claire was talking to herself as she slammed cupboards and pulled out drawers. She opened a door to a small utility room sending the jacket that had been hooked on its corner tumbling across the floor. An identity card clattered from a pocket. *"Brian McKenzie Vale Fertility Centre"* it read. Inside the small room was a handful of appliances, an old battered washing machine, a tumble dryer with a wobbly door, and a large fridge. It's white plastic yellowing with age. Claire pulled the door open and stared at the contents within. Rows upon rows of jars, just what she was after. She picked up one of the jars and stared at it. A thick red mucousy liquid swirled within. Claire could make out a tiny, almost imperceptible hand shape in the cloud within. "Oh, you are a naughty boy then," Claire said. Slowly she carried each jar to the sink, pouring the foetal slurry into the sink. She hummed to herself as she rinsed each jar in the sink, before dunking them into the bucket, filling them to the brim with Brian's blood.

Mark was finally alone. He had gone through a cover story for Aasif over and over until they had all the details straight. He had just upped and vanished with Jess and been present at a major incident. Mark didn't envy the man. He had just learnt the worst thing imaginable walked among mankind, but now faced something even worse. Police paperwork. Mark had briefly considered simply putting in a call with Weston, get the requisite forms filled to have everything classified and save Aasif a bunch of hassle. He had noticed that Jess had left him out when she had submitted her report though and guessed that she wasn't keen on dragging someone else into their world. Eventually they would have to mention him, and once that was done Aasif would find himself transferred to London, trained to be a detective and roped into the department. It's how they were all recruited, and it was inevitable, but Mark had no intention of going behind his partners back. He slipped off his shoes and lay on his bed, still clothed, staring at the runes on his walls. He pulled out his phone and stared at that instead. No calls, no messages. He opened his emails. Nothing there either. He refreshed everything impatiently, waiting for something from the London office and their information gathering visit. Hopefully they had something because Mark was out of ideas.

"Excuse me?" said the voice behind Brenda. She jumped startled, dropping her car keys. She had finished her late shift and was climbing from her car on her driveway when the voice had spoken. She turned to see a girl in a red dress bringing down a meat cleaver into her skull. It stuck at a forty-five-degree angle in her forehead. She stumbled backwards.

"Ow, what the fuck?" said Brenda confused. The girl stood there, intrigued at the woman still standing from what would be a lethal blow on anyone else.

"So, what are you then? Revenant? Wight? Ghula? Dragur maybe? Something along those lines." Clare stepped forwards toward Brenda slowly, one deliberate step at a time.

Brenda tugged at the cleaver, which rocked back and forth as she did so. "What in the shitting hell do you want? What are you some crazy hunter bitch?" A trickle of blood ran down from her wound. It was thick and dark crimson, almost half coagulated already.

"Nothing so crass!" said Claire, her face a mocking display of fake incredulity. The charade dropped as her face became sullen. She thrust her hand forward, Brenda's chest collapsing as Claire's arm dug deep into half rotten flesh. Claire cracked a twisted smile and the two stood there staring at each other for a brief second before Brenda burst into flames. The smell was horrendous, her already dead skin quickly burning into a layer of thick dark ash. Claire skipped over to a large black bag that had been left at the entrance to the drive way. She pulled out an empty jar and skipped back over to the burning corpse. Brenda had made no noise, released no panicked screams. She had burnt like kindling and was already slowly collapsing into dust. Clare bent down and scraped some of it into an empty jar, before walking back and tossing it into a black bag. She lifted the bag over one shoulder and walked off down the street.

Aasif rubbed his eyes as he stepped out into street. He was glad to breathe in the fresh night air, after spending so long in the stuffy station. Over and over he had been asked the same questions, and over and over he had answered them. Mark had been careful to advise him to leave out the weirder parts of the last day and the rest of the questions had been easy as he had simply told the truth. He had given a lift to a detective and had assisted in the arrest of a man attempting to assault two officers. His superiors were clearly frantic, they seemed to be treating both him and the detectives as suspects. Mark had stated this was normal, and that whilst they would have clear orders not to interfere local forces apparently always got jittery. It made sense, if Aasif didn't know the truth he would probably be involved in the station gossip himself. There was probably already plenty of nonsense stories about what had happened to him floating between every constable in town. His supervising Sargent had told him to take a few days off, which was an obvious a sign they didn't trust him as he could get. He leant his hands onto the metal railing which lined the ramp up to the station doors and took another deep breath of night air.

Claire stood in the middle of a field. Before her further down the valley was the town of Pontypridd, a cluster of lights nestled together in the dark. A galaxy held between two mountains. Her dress was torn, another burn covered her arm where one of her targets had slashed her. She was covered in mud where she had dug a hole into the field. In this hole she had poured the contents of the jars, blood, viscera and in one case, ash. Remains of all the supernatural beings she could find. Around the hole she had dug lines into the ground, a series of scratchy runes slashed into the field. She held out a finger, a tiny flame flickering from the end. Reaching over the pit she shook her finger and the flame fell like a water droplet. It gently landed on the gory mixture which burst into a roaring flame. The world itself seemed to bend for a moment and the flames seemed to freeze in place, a horrid red hole in reality.

"Come on brothers and sisters I don't have all day!" A burst of flame shot from the frozen fire, flying off into the sky like a firework. "Next, next keep it moving." Another bolt shot forth, followed by another, soon they sprayed forth like a roman candle. "There we go! Welcome! Welcome!" cried Claire, bursting into a manic laughter.

Ethel sat in her chair. She was waiting, impatiently staring at the clock. Her daughter was supposed to pick her up an hour ago. Ethel knew she wasn't coming, but she clung on to that hope anyway. She was wrinkled and frail, it had taken her hours to put on her best cardigan and beige trousers on her own. On the side table her phone buzzed. She picked it up, lifted her glasses from the beaded cord that held them around her neck, and moved her arm back and forth in an attempt to see. Once she hit the magic distance of close enough to read but not too close to be blurry, that seems to be common for everyone of a particular age, she squinted to read it. "*Sorry mum can't make it tonight. I'll take you out next week I promise.*" She put the phone down, leant back into her chair and picked up the television remote. She slammed the buttons angrily, as she changed the channel to a soap opera. A man was tending the bar, he turned and looked directly into the camera.

"Ethel" said the man through the television. She ignored him. "Ethel!" he shouted.

She stared at the screen in disbelief. "He-Hello?" she said.

"Alone again Ethel? She doesn't care about you anymore. A burden that's what she thinks you are." The man walked out behind the bar and towards the camera until he blocked out the rest of the image.

"No, no she's just busy," protested Ethel.

"You and I both know that's rubbish. Broken promises, lies, deceit. She doesn't care about you."

"I don't know what else to do." Tears had formed in Ethel's eyes. "What do I do?"

"Oh, I know what to do, you just need to do a few things first. Get a pen, we'll need a list."

Chapter 11

Chief Inspector Harold White stood in the street staring up. The houses in Pontypridd town centre were tall things, much older than the rows of terraced houses that ran like veins through the valley. Faint mist was forming on his glasses from the ever-present cloud of rain that covered the town. Around him officers buzzed hurriedly, cutting off the street with tape and keeping away gawping bystanders. Even at this early time in the morning a crowd has materialised from buildings like dust settling on a table.

"Grim isn't it?" Asked Sergeant Jack Hayes, a man who had known Harold for nearly as long as Harold had been in the police. No matter what promotions had come his way, Jack had refused, choosing to instead stay where he considered himself most useful. "This is what, the eighth body now?"

"Eight we know of," clarified Harold, "I'm getting really sick of cleaning up after these so-called specialists."

"I know what you mean. They turn up somewhere and not five minutes later they call us in to clean up the mess. And they sent Detective Constables! To deal with murders! They didn't even send us people with the appropriate ranks," said Jack.

"Sounds about normal around here. We are low on the order of priority. Funding, equipment, investigators," Harold gestured at the scene above him, "always bottom of the pile."

"Still, think we should take a crack at this ourselves." Jack rubbed his chin for effect. "Can't do any worse than they are. Get anything from that bobby who spent time with them?"

"Nothing. He is either keeping his mouth shut or really does know nothing. Not that it matters, you should see the names that have signed their paperwork. I couldn't touch this even if I wanted to." Harold's gaze remained fixed upwards as the two had spoken. Above them, in the second story of the building. A small beauty studio was situated directly above a low-end pawnbroker. Both stood directly opposite the great hungry maw of the train station stairs. The window had been thrown open, its long stained beige curtains hung out into the breeze. The curtains had been twisted into a line of two knots. Each knot had been tied around a woman's limb, an arm and a leg on each curtain. The swung in the wind like a morbid set of wind chimes. "I better call them," sighed Harold.

Jess stood in her living room. A Changeling, its strange elongated limbs, its terrible foot long talons hissed. At its feet Hannah lay dead, her throat torn open with a flick of the changeling's wrist. In front of it sat a trembling Lana. Her eyes streamed with tears, too terrified to move.

"Come on, come to mum!" shouted Jess, beckoning to the toddler. She sat still shaking as she sobbed. The entire room suddenly vibrated, and a loud unpleasant buzzing filled Jess' ears. The creature cried with pain and snatched up Lana into its arms. "No stop!" The buzzing started up again and the creature began to stride towards the window. Jess tried to follow, but her legs refused to move. The buzzing returned, shaking plaster loose from the walls. The changeling began to climb through the open window. Jess fought against her stationary body. Slowly her legs began to move, she stepped forward, brought her foot down to the ground, and woke with a start. She tumbled onto the hotel floor, her duvet collapsing atop her. Her side throbbed from the impact. On the side table, her phone buzzed incessantly.

"Hello?" said a weary Jess. She blew her red hair out of her face and held the duvet wrapped tight around herself.

"D.C Holden?" asked a voice at the other end.

"Speaking," Jess replied. The words felt strange in her tired mouth and she rolled her jaw around trying to wake it.

"This is Chief Inspector White. Sorry to wake you so early, but we have another one for you." He sounded more annoyed than truly sorry.

"Ok, I'll wake my partner and we will be right down."

Marks door creaked open. He stood there, bleary eyed. He was wearing only his boxers yet had somehow acquired a bag of iron filings. He held it in one hand expectedly.

"Jess? What time is it?" He asked.

"Just gone four a.m. Expecting company, were you? Not going to ask where you were keeping that?" Jess pointed at the small black cloth bag in Mark's hand.

"Under my pillow if you must know. And yeah, could have had another visit from our ghostly friend. I wasn't taking any chances." Mark turned and walked back towards his bed. "Ow, Ow Ow," he said as his bare feet walked across the carpet still covered in sharp iron dust. He sat on his bed and picked up his glasses. He wiped them on his bedsheets and then slid them onto his face. "Guessing you aren't here for a glass of milk and a bedtime story?"

"Get your clothes. There's another body. Call just came in."

"Jesus Christ," said Mark. He stood inside the beauty salon. The limb laden curtains had been pulled inside and the windows shut so as not to provide a bizarre puppet show to the nosy locals below. The victim's torso had been leant against the windowsill. It had no clothing on and had large thin oval burn Marks covering its body.

"Right so," Jess said, walking back into the salon, staring directly at her note book. "Victim is a Gillian Mason, owner of the salon. It's only a rough estimate but they think time of death was about ten p.m. last night."

"So, she's been out there for hours an no-one noticed? Poor woman. Any idea what these burn marks are?"

"You really are such a man sometimes. Those are from hair straighteners. The first victim in the park had burns as well," Jess noted.

"That makes sense, I checked my email, got some intel from Raj last night. I'll go over it once we're away from prying ears." Mark cocked his head.

"That bad huh?" asked Jess.

"Yeah that bad. We know anything else about this victim?"

"Not too much. Single, no children, late forties. Has one relative we know of, an Ethel Mason, lives in a care home outside of town." Jess flipped her notebook closed. "Why this woman then?"

"What do you mean?" replied Mark.

"Well, so far the victims have all been linked to that girl the uh," she opened her notebook for a moment, "Claire Powell. How is a salon owner linked to her? Bad haircut maybe?"

"Could very well be, look, meet me outside I'll go over what we know."

"So Rajan says it's a Jinn." Mark lifted a mug to his lips. The warm coffee within releasing a cloud of pleasant-smelling steam. He took a sip.

"The fuck is a Jinn? Like a genie, right? Big, blue grants wishes." Jess wrapped her hands around her own cup, a hot milky tea. The two of them were sat in a small café someway away from the crime scene. The small Welsh town was starting to stir, rousing slowly from its slumber like its nation's great dragon symbol.

"No, It's some kind of spiritual entity. Apparently, something in the middle between an angel and a demon."

"Coming down more on the demon side so far." Jess dipped a biscuit into her tea.

"So, Demons, whist evil little shits, do everything they do for a reason. It's not wild random plans. Jinn apparently lack a certain, moral compass. In a way that is much more dangerous." Mark took another drink from his coffee slurping loudly as he did.

"So, the torture, eating people, gruesome over the top murders, that's because they felt like it. Why were the first murders so personal to Claire? The real Claire. Ah shit." Jess swore as the biscuit she had held too long in her tea collapsed as she pulled it out. She picked up a small spoon and began trying to fish out the soggy paste from her cup.

"They need permission to possess someone it says here," said Mark, looking at his phone. "Guess that's the deal? Let me possess you and I'll help you get vengeance. Maybe you were right, and she did get a bad haircut once. Maybe it really is that petty?"

"That's a scary thought," said Jess putting down the spoon, evidently happy her tea was now biscuit free. "A teenage girl has a lot of petty grudges. So, what's the plan."

"No idea. We're out of leads a little. Until she resurfaces we are a little stuck," admitted Mark.

"We can't sit here on our arses twiddling our thumbs. There is already far too many victims here. Hell, one is too many. We need to do something. What about the burns?" Jess took drink from her cup and then coughed, having not gotten as much of the biscuit out as she had hoped.

"Oh right. Apparently, Jinn take the form of smokeless flames naturally. Explains the obsession with burning stuff I think," replied Mark.

"Burns...burns..." Jess snapped he fingers excitedly. "Claire had a burn on her hand. A leaf shape, real distinctive. In the park there was signs of burning on part of the gate. That was also a leaf shape. The gate burnt her somehow."

"What was the gate made of?" said Mark intrigued.

"It was this old wrought iron thing. Must be some kind of reaction, like with the ghost."

"Makes sense. Iron has a bunch of symbolism, its tied strongly to the earth itself. Its why it works on things like ghosts and faeries. They aren't of this world so it's like kryptonite to them. Report says Jinn exist normally, uh, between realities it says here, so must be a similar effect." Mark thought about it, opened a note on his phone and wrote the fact down.

"Ok well, let's go," said Jess putting down her cup with a loud clink. "Can't sit here all day."

"Where are we going?" asked Mark, following her out of the café, sliding on his woollen coat as he did.

"To get some backup."

"Oh," said Aasif. "It's you." He stood in the doorway to his home, wearing a black tracksuit. His arms were crossed.

"Morning, we got your address from the station. Hope you don't mind," said Jess waving from behind Mark, who was stood directly in front of her.

"What do you want? I'm on forced leave because of you. For hours they questioned me. Hours!"

"We are really sorry about that," apologised Mark. "Look, we need someone who knows the local area. We're a bit stuck and honestly, it's a lot easier than having to explain what's going on to someone else."

"I'll get in trouble," objected Aasif.

"You'll be fine," said Mark dragging out the last syllable to an almost obnoxious length. "You'll be amazed what a letter from our boss can clear up. Ow!" He turned to face Jess who had jabbed him in the small of his back with a pointed finger. She cocked her head and gave him a disappointed look.

"Fine, come in," Aasif rolled his eyes and walked deeper into the home beckoning them to follow.

"That sounds pretty nasty," said Aasif after they explained that mornings discoveries. "How am I supposed to help though?"

"Well first we need a lift," admitted Mark candidly, "can't keep getting taxis everywhere. Expenses only go so far."

"More importantly!" interrupted Jess. "We don't know the area. Like where would a teenage girl hide around here?"

"It's not a teenage girl though is it, it's a Jinn you said?" Aasif shook his head. "You know my old man was pretty devout, always telling I needed to beware of Jinn and their influences. Never thought he would be right."

"You are right," interjected Mark, "but possessing beings can normally tap into the mind of their host. Know what they do. It's going to seek out the same kind of places."

"Well around here there is plenty of places to hide. It's a poverty-stricken area in some parts. More than its fair share of squats and drug dens." Aasif shrugged.

"We start there then, need to do something. At least," said Jess standing up. "Get your keys."

Jess sat on a small brick wall outside a run-down house. Its windows covered with metal sheets. Mark was scraping his shoe on the same wall having stepped on something unidentified inside.

"This is the fourth one now. How many more are left in this town?" asked Mark angrily.

"Squats or dens?" asked Aasif. "Because the answer is too many either way."

"This is a waste of time," said Mark putting his leg down.

"Compared to what, doing nothing?" asked Jess. "I would rather be doing this, even if it is a goose chase."

"It's a pity we can't use like, a tracking spell or something to find her. Some kind of divination maybe? See when she arrived and when she left." Mark lifted his coat and sat down on the wall next to Jess.

"Didn't the cameras tell you that?" asked Aasif.

"Cameras?" Jess asked back.

"Yeah, that hairdresser is right opposite the train station, right?"

"Yes," said Mark, curious where Aasif was going.

"There's a closed pub next door, used to get all kinds of trouble with it before it got shut down. There are cameras across the outside of the station because of that." Aasif said.

"Cameras Mark," Jess said, turning her head to stare right at him.

"Cameras," Mark sighed.

The three of them sat in Aasifs car, an old Ford KA. Mark had lost that particular game of rock paper scissors so had to squeeze into the back of the tiny car, accessible only by moving the front seats forward. Jess stared out of the window, arm resting on her hand. She lifted her head as she noticed a small patch of black up the mountain before her.

"What's that?" she asked.

"Oh that?" said Aasif, his vision glancing quickly at the scorched earth. "Kids around here love to start fires in the fields. Gets to be a real problem in the summer, the valley sides can dry out and we get some nasty brushfires."

"Sounds about right for kids," chimed in Mark from the back seats.

Dale swivelled in his chair, holding a sandwich in one hand. He pointed it aggressively at Rajan.

"I'm just saying, everyone deserves a second chance," said Dale, jabbing the corner of the sandwich in Rajan's direction. Loose ham flapped about as he did.

"Some people really don't deserve them," objected Rajan.

"Yeah well, I'm a firm believer in it. People in witness protection are supposed to be on our side after all. It's the professional ramifications I'm more worried about," admitted Dale.

"What professional ramifications?" Asked D.C.I Weston. She was stood behind Dale, she leered at him. She had a large trolley with her, covered in thick leather-bound books.

"Oh, it's nothing really Ma'am," said Dale quickly, trying to cover his tracks. "What you got there?"

"I'm so glad you asked D.S Cooper!" replied Florence, clapping her hands together in faux excitement. "Seeing as you two are without a case for the moment, I thought you could help out Mark and Jess. This," she said lifting a heavy book with a heave; it shook the desk as she dropped it in front of him, "is one of the books the archives guys says mention Jinn."

She wheeled the trolley closer with a loud squeak. They each had opposite cubicles, theirs backs facing each other. She placed it in the gap between them. "These are just some of them. There are two more trolleys on the way. So," she tapped a shoulder on each man simultaneously, "get reading."

The car door closed with a slam as the three stepped out of Aasif's car. Across the road the street was still blocked with police tap, though the curtains had been taken down. Before them was the imposing train station, its dark stone rising on the hillside. A man-made wound carved into the mountain. Several large white cameras were bolted onto the rock, a curious mix of the modern strapped to the old.

"Right, let's go then, time to spy on the populace," declared Mark.

"Do you not do that anyway in your super-secret society police squad? You know unseeing eye and all that?" asked Aasif.

"Uh, what?" said Mark bewildered.

"Well I've been thinking, if monsters are real- "

"We don't use the term monster," interrupted Jess. "It's considered offensive. Supernatural minorities is the accepted term. Sometimes just supers but that can be a bit dicey with some people."

"Right well if...supernatural minorities, are real," continued Aasif, "I figured maybe other things were. You guys are covering this up aren't you."

"I guess? Never really thought of it like that," said Mark.

"So what else is true? Flat earth? Illuminati? Lizard people?" asked Aasif, he seemed genuinely concerned.

"So, no, Earth is still round," said Jess.

"Yeah and the Illuminati? Not a thing. You think if there was one world controlling organisation they would be doing a better job," added Mark.

"Lizard people I'll give you. Never met one myself but I suppose it's possible," continued Jess.

"Yeah that could be a thing," confirmed Mark.

"Great, thanks. Not sure my world could use any more revelations. Let's get this over with so I can go back to sitting in my house watching daytime TV and eating cereal for lunch," said Aasif, striding towards the seemingly endless staircase of the station.

Chapter 12

At the end of the platform was a metal gate, it had seen better days, its chain rusted and broken. One of its hinges held limply to the wall. The station security guard grunted as he turned a key in the gates padlock, the slow turn of a lock unused creaked forward. He held the key triumphantly when the lock opened with a satisfying pop, his moment of elation broken when he realised it had bent. He sighed, put the key back into his pocket and beckoned for his three shadows to follow him onwards.

Mark, Jess and Aasif followed the guard. Past the collapsing gate, far under the wooden pavilion its colours faded and dull compared to the still in use section. Plants were starting to spring up from between the stones beneath them. They walked for what seemed like an age, until lights of the newsagents attached to the station disappeared around the gentle bend of the valley.

"Right here we are!" declared the guard, arms stretched wide before a green metal door that looked oddly out of place set into the Victorian stone. A small keypad jutted from the brickwork next to it. The guard tapped in a number and swung the door open.

Mark whistled. "Wow," he said, "this is a doozy." Rows of monitors covered the room. Cameras had been fitted down the length of the line, covering a huge swath of the town.

"Don't use it much," shrugged the guard. "Used to get a bunch of trouble with the pub opposite. Right dive it was. Since it shut down most of the vandalism stopped. Personally,

I think one camera would have done, just over the entrance you know. Figure maybe the company could write it off their tax or something. Went a bit mental."

"Kind of out of the way isn't it?" asked Aasif.

"Ah primo real estate is a station. Plenty of places looking to sell expensive coffees and damp pasties to people who haven't got anything to do but wait. Stuck it down here so it's out of the way." The guard checked his watch as he spoke. "Look, I know I'm not supposed to show you this without the forms. Data protection and all that, but I'll leave you to it. Caught a glimpse of that horror show on my way in this morning. You do what you have to do." He nodded at the three of them and took his leave.

"I'm pretty sure if Orwell was alive this would kill him. Literally," said Mark

"Literarily?" questioned Jess.

"No literally. I guess literarily too. Literally literarily," pondered Mark confusingly.

"The fuck are you two on about?" interjected Aasif. "We going to check these cameras or not." He pulled out a small plastic chair with castor wheels and sat down. "Ok so, when should we start looking?"

"Ten P.M or there about. This camera has a direct view of the salon," said Mark, tapping a screen which wobbled worryingly. "You know how to work this?"

"If my six-year-old nephew can work YouTube I got this," answered Aasif. "Ok so this is nine o'clock."

"Someone's leaving. Right there's the victim," said Jess. On the video the woman they had seen earlier, limbs still attached, was waving another woman good bye as she exited through the ground floor door that led to the long stairs up. "Keep going. Scroll forward a little. Stop!" Jess pointed at the screen. A figure was walking towards the salon's door. A short woman wearing a pastel pink coat and a what looked like a separate clear plastic hood. Her white hair was up in rollers, thick milk bottle glasses rested on her nose. "Is that an old woman?"

The three of them watched transfixed as the old woman entered the salon, the victim letting her in but clearly confused. They sat slack jawed as they saw a few minutes later the windows thrown open, the old woman starting to knot the limbs into the curtains. The woman stood for a few moments to admire her handy work then vanished, appear a few minutes later at the door on the ground level. Calmly she walked off into the night.

Mark broke the silence. "Ok. So, it's something else to add to our shit list."

"Might be. Might not. Could be our Jinn has swapped bodies?" Jess reached inside her black windbreaker and pulled out a police notebook, flipping its pages over the ring binding.

"Could be there is more than one," pointed out Mark. Jess put away the note book and reached into her suit jackets top pocket producing another.

"That's a chilling thought," added Aasif. He stared in disbelief as Jess put away the second notebook and slipped one out of her trouser pocket. "Got enough notebooks there?"

"That's kind of her thing," said Mark

"I got it," Jess said triumphantly. "Ethel Mason. The victim, she had an elderly mother in a care home."

"What and you think this is her?" asked Aasif.

"Sure, why not. Same Jinn, different Jinn, we've got no idea. What we do know is that when Claire was possessed the first thing the Jinn did was go after people she had grudges with." Jess waved her notebook like a fan. "Maybe Ethel here wasn't too happy with being put into a home."

"Think she would go back to the care home?" Mark said as he leant over a monitor. He had startled scrolling through the video feed.

"It's where we found Claire," replied Aasif.

"Harder to hide there though. The Jinn we came across killed one parent and controlled the other. If it could control both why didn't it? A whole care home might be beyond it." Jess had put all three notebooks on the small table before the cameras and was trying to find a blank page in one.

"Fucking sneaky little shit!" exclaimed Mark. The others turned to face him startled. "Sorry. Could be Jinn-Claire just felt like killing one of the parents by the way. Look at this." Mark pointed at a monitor. He had scrolled the time all the way to the police cordoning off the area. "Here." He drew an imaginary circle around one of the onlookers in the early morning crowd. It was mostly drunks and people wearing high visibility jackets on their way to or from night shifts. Stood near the back of the crowd, clutching a small maroon handbag was a familiar old lady.

"Little fucker was watching the whole time!" shouted Jess.

Aasif took control of scrolling through the footage, the two detectives standing behind him, watching impatiently over his shoulder. Together they watched the old woman fade in and out of the crowd over time, moving away and then coming back to try and keep attention off her. Mark and Jess watched themselves arrive at the scene and an hour or so later leave, uneasy that they were so close to the killer. The coroner arrived around nine A.M to collect the body, the crowd dispersing as it did. The woman finally walked away. She stepped into a shop, hand in her handbag, and then vanished.

"Nothing on any of the cameras on the station past this point that anyone has seen?" asked Mark.

"Nothing, she up and vanishes after she enters that shop," Aasif said. He leant back in the chair, stretching his arms.

"Time to leave this then," said Jess gesturing to the room around them, "and do so old-fashioned boots on the ground police work."

"Did you know about this before we got here?" accused Mark.

"Not at all!" Jess had her face pressed against the window. Behind the glass was an array of pens, notebooks and several other pieces of high-end stationary. She pulled free from the glass and excitedly pulled the door open, dashing inside.

"Is it really appropriate to be excited at a time like this?" asked Aasif, the two men still standing in the street. The door to the shop was still swinging with the force Jess had opened it.

"You need to find the fun where you can doing something like this. You let it get to you, really get to you, and it will grind you into dust," Mark said. He shrugged and followed Jess inside. Aasif stood there for a second, collected his thoughts and followed.

Aasif had never seen so many pens. He had walked past the store on his beat on occasion, but never had cause to go inside. Aisles upon aisles of pens, big plastic bins of the things. On the far wall was a glass cabinet, it was heavily locked and the pens within were held on separate metal stands. Aasif thought it wouldn't have looked out of place in a museum. Jess was stood staring into it. Somehow, she had already filled a basket with great flowery note pads, handfuls of pens and at least two sets of coloured pencils.

"Best leave her to it," said Mark turning to look over his shoulder at Aasif. "Come on, let's go see what we kind find out."

"I'm Detective Constable Mark Curren, this is Constable Aasif uh- "Mark paused.

"Rhaman," said Aasif.

"A fancy London policeman. Not enough stop and searches there so you branching out?" said the young woman behind the counter. She had hair that was buzz cut on the sides with a faux mohawk sticking from centre of her head. She was wearing a plain white blouse and black trousers. A deep burgundy apron covered her front, the name of the store sewn into the top right of it. *Pen and Ink,* it read. She hadn't even looked up at Mark, instead staring at her phone. The woman was chewing something, her nose ring bobbing in time with her jaw.

"How would you know, didn't even look at my identity. Want to pay a little attention maybe." Mark had taken on a sterner tone.

"First of all," said the woman putting her phone into a pocket on the apron. "The sixties gangster film level accent gives it away. Laahndon," she said in an exaggerated accent. "Secondly you have the aura of a copper."

"You kinda do," agreed Aasif.

"Was there a woman in here earlier," continued Mark undeterred. "Old lady, pink coat, red handbag. Hair still in curlers."

"Oh yeah, weird as fuck. Bought red markers. Tons of them. Spent like sixty quid," said the cashier.

"How long was she here?" chimed in Aasif.

"Ten minutes tops, in and out." The woman began to tidy some pens in a display on the counter. "Picking on little old ladies now are you?"

"Something like that," answered Mark. "Which way did she go when she left?"

"She took the side door, there's a second entrance over there." She pointed across the store.

"Do you have any cameras on that door?" asked Aasif.

The three of them walked the streets of Pontypridd following the trail of Ethel. They bounced from shop to shop, following her progress across the town. After buying the stack of pens she had stopped in a nearby Chinese medicine store and bought a collection of mixed supplies. From there they tracked her to an antiques place where she had picked up a silver candlestick.

"I don't like this," said Mark as they walked down the street.

"Sometimes you just need to hit the beat and- "started Jess.

"No, not this," Mark continued. "I mean the stuff. Herbs, candlesticks, enough pens to draw the contents of the Louvre. Everything about this scream's ritual. Where's the next location?"

"Camera from the antiques place shows her wandering up this street and stopping in that butchers up ahead."

"Oh, come on!" shouted Mark.

"This is bad?" asked Aasif.

"Yeah," Jess answered, "meat and blood are common ritual components. She's up to something, and it can't be good."

The butchers was a bust, unlike the other shops it didn't have a camera, so the trail went cold there. The three of them had taken seats on a street bench just outside. Mark was taking bites from a pie he had bought inside.

"So, this was a colossal waste of time," said Aasif.

"Still worth a try, better than waiting for trouble to come to us," said Jess, trying one of her new pens in a police notebook.

"It's a pity we can't just find out where everyone is all the time," Mark added, his mouth still half full of pie.

"No that is something Orwell really wouldn't approve of," laughed Jess, "right to room one oh one for that." She stopped herself and sat there for a moment staring downward. "Room. Room." Jess pulled out her phone and flicked open the internet, taking multiple attempts for her smashed screen to register her inputs. She typed in some search details and then held the phone to her ear. "Hello? Is that Glyn Cork care home? Did I pronounce that right?" There was a murmuring from the phone. "Yeah I would never have gotten that right. I'm looking for an Ethel Mason is she there?" More murmurs emerged. "She is? Great. No don't have her come to the phone, I want to surprise her with my visit. Thanks." Jess put the phone back into her pocket.

"She was at the home this whole time?" asked Mark.

"Yeah, she was at the home this whole time," admitted Jess.

"So, I was right, this really was a waste then?" Aasif said.

"Not quite." Mark held up his finger as if he was about to make a point. "Forewarned is forearmed after all."

"Lift your end!" shouted Mark

"I am lifting!" Aasif shouted back at him. Jess stood watching the two men trying to force the unwieldly case into the back of Aasif's tiny car. "Do we even need this?"

"Yes!" came the shout from Mark. They struggled for a moment more and the case dropped into the car boot, barely fitting. "This is our specialist gear. We'll need it." Mark opened the case revealing its contents. Stacks of books sat next to assorted cloth bags. Mark reached in and removed a small black bag tied with a drawstring and a small white square pouch. He passed them to Aasif.

"What is this?" he said, sliding the bag open a little.

"Iron filings," said Jess. "Think of it like PAVA for spirits." She watched Aasif open the small white pouch, sliding out two squares, one dark black, the other a shiny silver on the back and white on the front.

"Business cards?" asked Aasif. "They're weirdly heavy."

"The black one is Iron, the other one is silver on the back" replied Jess. "Good way to check if someone is on the level. No one refuses a business card."

"God damn it," grumbled Mark from within the car boot. "Just got the one pair of Iron cuffs." He stood up, dangling an antique looking pair of old-style handcuffs, the kind connected by a chain.

"To be fair, how often do we need them?" Jess gave him a disapproving look.

"That's fair," conceded Mark. "Right." Mark threw a pouch to Jess. "Let's go then."

"Do we even have a plan?" asked Aasif.

"We rarely do," said Jess, holding her hands up in admission.

Dale let out a long groan, closing the tome in front of him with a thud. He grabbed another one from the cart beside him. He struggled as he turned back in his chair, his arms trembling from the weight.

"Anything?" Rajan asked from across the way.

"Nothing. A whole bunch of nothing, with a side order of, uh, yeah, nothing." Dale swung his chair back around again to face Rajan. "A whole bunch of stuff confuses them with demons, or just contradicts itself. I feel like I'm going mad reading all these books."

"Hey, some of the stuff in the archives will do that to you. Or so I hear." Rajan had leaned in like he was revealing a big secret.

"Not cool, that's not a thought I particularly want." Dale leant back in his chair. "You got anything?"

"Maybe? I don't know. There's some things here I don't understand. This book here." Rajan tapped the top of a dark green book. "Talks about this scroll." He held up an old faded sheet of scrollwork. Both men were wearing white cotton gloves to protect the books. "But I'm pretty sure this is in Arabic maybe? You know on a handful of occasions I've had a racist asshole scream abuse at me because I wear a turban. One once assumed I spoke Arabic. I kind of wish they were correct right now."

"That's a dark thought, what kind of dickhead does that." Dale was shocked.

"I'm lucky, they quickly change their tune when I show them my police ID. Good to get a bit of karmic retribution every now and again. Either way I think we might need to get this translated. Hopefully it has something."

Chapter 13

The drive to the care home was oddly serene. The Welsh hillside rolling past, lush green fields set against a sky whose clouds had finally cleared to reveal a vivid blue sky. It reminded Mark of a similar beauty he had seen once, on a school trip as a boy to the lake districts. It brought into stark contrast the closed in streets and blocked out sky of London. The car trundled onwards, struggling with the climb towards the home. It loomed ominously further up the valleys side. An old repurposed farmhouse, it had grown like a cancer beyond its original form. Extensions and new wings added over the years creating an odd hodgepodge of building styles and ages. Mark thought that had the haunted house they had visited not been abandoned it might have grown in the same way eventually. He felt like it was almost an insult to attach the bland white outgrowths to the old handcrafted stonework, parasites overgrowing the house. A sign blazed past them as they pulled into the gravel driveway. *Glyncoch House: Care and Respite* it read.

Jess stepped out of the car first, her sensible black pumps crunching the gravel underneath them. Mark followed behind her, tipping the passenger side chair forward so he could squeeze out through the door. Aasif put the key into the lock and turned it. He pocketed the keys with a jangle.

"Right, I'll do a once around, check the perimeter. Jess you prep Aasif," Mark said. He nodded, put his hands into his coat pocket, and walked off around the back of the house.

"Ok, so," started Jess, "me and Mark will take the lead. Just follow us and do what we do. Keys." She held her hand out before Aasif expectedly. He fished around in his pocket before dropping them into Jess' outstretched palm. She bent down and opened the boot. "Still got your filings?"

"Yeah," replied Aasif tapping his coat pocket.

"Ok, take these as well." Jess pulled out a handful of tiny scrolls from the trunk in the boot. They looked like a novelty you might buy in a museum. "Put them in your pockets. Not the same ones though."

"What are they?" Aasif enquired, staring at the tiny paper tubs Jess had passed into his hand.

"Remember the notepad paper I gave you?" Aasif nodded at her. "These are more high-end versions of those. Remember to put them back once we're done here. Not something you want to be carrying around with you."

"Why not?" said Aasif, looking at the scrolls anxiously. "Do I need to be worried?"

"It should be fine," Jess' voice was not reassuring. "Sometimes a scroll can dispel another scroll and you don't really want that. It's a bit like magnets but uh, more explosioney."

Behind the house was a large open field bordered by a low hedge. The grass had been kept cut short, leading up to the back of the house in neat striped lines. The one exception was in the centre of the grass, a perfect square of unkempt greenery. The square lay at the foot of an old well, the gardener having avoided it. Mark peered over into the thing. It wasn't particularly deep, and clearly out of use. He could see the bottom, covered in a thick layer of discarded sweet wrappers and cigarette packets. Clearly it was the dumping ground for the resident's secret treats. The cover of the well was a set of metal bars attached to a circular out band. Mark gripped them, feeling them come lose. These were old, the orange rust staining his hands. They were iron. Mark removed the circular set of bars from the top of the well and left them leaning against the side of the well. He looked back over at the house, scanning the back windows, before walking back towards the front.

"Hey," said Mark as he met the waiting pair. "You uh, seen anyone else around?"

"Now that you mention it no," Jess said stroking her chin. "Haven't seen any movement inside either."

"It is a care home. Wouldn't be that much movement I would think," added Aasif.

"Still, its unsettling," Jess replied, "come on, time to see what's what I guess."

Jess pressed an intercom button mounted to the wall. It let out an obnoxious buzz. She tapped her foot impatiently. There was no reply. He lifted the brass knocker and slammed it against the door.

"Coming!" came a shrill voice from beyond the door. A minute later it swung open. Clutching the door stood an old woman. She was squinting at them through thick glasses. Her shoulder length grey hair was curled. She wore a thin dress that was clearly intended to be a nightgown. Jess was sure it was Ethel, the woman they were after.

"Evening madam are any of the staff about?" asked Jess without missing a beat.

"Everyone is busy in the rec room my dear," replied Ethel. "Can you come back later?"

"I'm afraid not," said Jess exaggerating her apology. "I'm D.C Holden, this is D.C Curren and Constable Rahman. Here, take my card." Jess pulled a business card from her coat pocket, handing it over.

"Well, I'm sorry officers but...Aahh!" Ethel burst into a piercing scream. Smoke drifted from her finger tips where she had grabbed the business card. There was a horrid smell of burning flesh. Ethel stared down at the iron card that had hit the stone step before the door with a ringing noise. She looked up, and ran into the building, the old woman breaking into a sprint. Jess ran after her, shows clattering on the hard tile floor. Mark and Aasif followed behind, arms pumping in time with their legs.

They crashed down a corridor, chasing the fleeing Ethel. The old woman was easily outpacing them. She tipped a large silver trolley carrying a tray of pills as she ran. Tiny chunks of medicinal debris scattering onto the ground. It skidded across the floor coming to a rest with its wheels touching the opposite wall from where it began, allowing the pursuing police to squeeze past to its right. Ethel continued to run, her legs a furious blaze of speed. With one swift movement she grabbed an I.V. stand that had been abandoned next to a closed door and spun around, flinging it like a javelin. Jess ducked, and Mark twisted his body to the side. Aasif, wasn't so lucky, the wheeled bottom of the stand hitting him square in the chest. He collapsed to the ground, the air knocked from his lungs.

"Go...Go..." he spluttered, waving his comrades on. They nodded together and continued the chase. Their target darted around a corner at the end of the corridor. Mark and Jess followed their footsteps matching the sound of the heavy rain which had begun to fall outside. The clear blue skies from the journey up had rapidly been consumed by voracious dark grey clouds bursting forth from behind the valley sides.

Mark nearly tripped over Jess as she came to an abrupt stop. They had reached a large set of double doors, before which Ethel stood. She had her hands on the handles, her back facing the detectives. She was letting out a weird slow guttural laugh. It was discomforting, like she was a cat trying to cough up a hairball.

"Oh dearies," she said, "I really wish you hadn't come unannounced."

"Don't move," said Mark, stepping forward slowly, iron handcuffs dangling from his right hand.

"It's still got some time in the oven," Ethel's head turned, looking over her shoulder. "Not quite fully baked yet." She pushed the doors open revealing the nightmare within.

The doorway opened to a large recreation area. Normally full of chairs of resting grandparents, tables arranged in chess games that never really ended and televisions permanently set to a golden oldies' movie channel, the furniture had been almost tossed aside to leave a large open space. Across the floor a large circle had been drawn in blood. Several strange arcane runes neither detective had seen before were scrawled haphazardly in the circle in the same blood. The air had a strange heady aroma of several different burnt herbs, electricity and burnt hair. In the centre of the circle, writhed an unfathomable beast.

It was huge, a pink undulating mass of flesh. The thing was a mess of skin, overlapping folds pulsing as if breathing. Emerging from the mass at four distinct points were long trails of exposed muscle, red and wet. Covering each morbid cylinder were human limbs. Each limb seemed to be stretching over the exposed viscera, slowly sinking in, the human skin pulled to cover the creature. The limbs were clustered in matching clumps. Left legs with other left legs, right arms with right arms. Each had a small circular rune, drawn with red marker pen. Several of the body parts were clearly from older people. They had found the staff and residents. The flesh beast shivered as Ethel strode towards it. Mark and Jess stood still, transfixed by terror.

"What the flying fuck?" shouted Aasif as he limped around the corner behind them.

"Ah my pet," cooed Ethel stroking the monstrosity. "These people are here to cause a ruckus. You weren't ready yet, need a little longer to bake." The thing moaned from some unseen orifice. It attempted to stand, its new born limbs ending with clusters of feet and hands. Stood up the thing was huge, easily ten feet tall. It struggled to move, knocking plaster from the ceiling. Across the cursed thing sections of its skin tore open, revealing human mouths, the ripped skin flapping as each mouth screamed in unison. It lumbered forward, scraping across the ceiling as it moved. Mark and Jess snapped from their stupor as one, stepping quickly backwards.

"What do we do?" asked a frantic Aasif.

"Fucked If I know!" said Mark, much louder than he had intended.

"I've got an idea!" said Jess triumphantly. "Come on." She ran off, the two men following. The entity lumbered forward slowly, Ethel chuckling madly to herself.

The three of them ran back the way they had come, fleeing half panicked down the corridor. Behind them they could hear the slow rhythmic rumbling of the monster. There was a loud creaking and a terrible screaming booming from behind them. The noise of a doorframe slowly being torn from the wall, a slow deep cracking noise, filled the air ominously. Jess slowed herself, crouching to pick up the IV stand that had struck Aasif earlier. She turned to face the door they had passed.

"So, what's the plan?" asked Mark.

"The door, look," Jess pointed at it with the stand. *Oxygen Cylinder Storage* read the sign on the door. *Danger Flammable* read a smaller sign directly below. Jess tried the handle just to be sure. It was locked as she expected. "Ever see Jaws?" she asked striking the door with the stand.

Inch by agonising inch the unspeakable thing eked its way down the corridor. The monstrosity could barely fit, forcing itself to drag itself along with just one arm. Its mouths chattered excitedly, the clacking teeth echoing. The police officers waited, cylinders hastily stacked before them.

"Come on you fucker," muttered Jess under her breath.

"Hope you have a step two in this plan?" said Mark leaning his head towards her, his eyes transfixed on the thing before them.

"Sure do. You got any dispel scrolls?"

"Yeah, right I see where you're going with this." Mark patted down his pockets. "I got three."

"Still got yours Aasif?" Jess asked.

"Yeah, one in each pocket like you said," Aasif answered.

"Ok hand them over boys," she held out her palm expectedly. They reached into their various pockets, dropping the scrolls into her open hand one by one. They seemed to be glowing faintly, the light getting brighter with every scroll added to the pile. Jess bent down and placed them next to the tanks. A pale blue light blossomed from beneath them.

"Ok. So, what now?" enquired Aasif.

"Now we run," said Jess.

Crouched down, rain pouring onto them, they lurked behind Aasif's car. They waited, willing something to happen. The horrid flesh construct still came onwards, a loud thud followed by a rocky scraping noise as it pulled itself onwards.

"Nothing's happening," said Aasif, shouting through the torrent.

"Yeah this is taking longer than I expe-," Jess was interrupted by a loud explosion. A gout of fire erupted from the doorway. They ducked as stone shrapnel blasted loose from the front of the house. A chunk the size of a fist lodged itself in Aasif's windscreen. The house still stood, but was engulfed in fire, the oxygen tanks feeding the hungry flames. The unspeakable horror within screamed an eerie chorus, its many human voices screeching in agony. The screams morphed into a pained gurgle and then stopped. "Holy shit, I can't believe that worked!"

Ethel limped across the field that formed the garden of the care home. Her nightie was covered in splotchy black burn marks. A shard of masonry jutted from her leg like an ancient spearhead. Half her curled hair had burnt away. She spat as she walked, cursing the humans who had come here.

"Going somewhere?" said Mark. Ethel turned to face him. The two other humans flanked him. Each draggled from the pouring rain. Faint smoke drifted from the house behind them, the deluge quickly putting out the budding fire.

"Fuck you!" shouted the injured old woman.

"Such Language! Need to be careful we could arrest you for a breach of the peace under the public order act. Aren't that right constable?" said Jess.

"It certainly is D.C Holden. D.C Curren would you do the honours?" answered Aasif. Mark stepped forward. He held one iron cuff in his hand, swinging the other cuff on the chain for dramatic effect.

"Stay back or you'll be sorry!" cried Ethel.

"Like the people in there were sorry!" Mark stepped forward, his anger obvious in his face. Ethel stepped backwards.

"I will end you!" The woman's threat was shrill. She held up a hand and glowing orange scratches appeared in the air. There was a flash and an unseen force knocked her backward. Stumbling she crashed backwards into the exposed well, toppling over the edge. She hit the ground with a loud crack. Mark stood up, the force having knocked him over. He pulled out a small scroll from his coat pocket, it was slowly collapsing into ash like a cigarette.

"Glad we had spares in the car," Mark said stepping over to the well. He bent down and picked up the iron grate he had moved earlier. He slid it back over the well opening. "You can stew down there for a bit."

"Christ," said Jess peering over. "What do we do with her?"

Chapter 14

Rajan's leg bounced impatiently as he waited. He was sat in a waiting area on one of the higher floors of New Scotland Yard. A small cluster of chairs that seemed to be nearly all cushion yet oddly uncomfortable, the kind that populate hospital waiting rooms everywhere. The waiting area was hastily assembled, its walls were simply cubicle dividers, placed to separate it from the rest of the office. Around him the handful of translators the Metropolitan Police kept on permanent staff went about their business. He slipped down lower in his chair and reached across to a small table, picking up a magazine that was simply called *Words*. He opened it to a random article. *The Etymology of Bolivian Slang* was the title. He sighed and tossed the magazine back onto the table.

"D.S Singh?" A young woman knocked on the divider as she spoke. She wore a light blue blouse and a black pencil skirt. Her hair was mousey brown, cut into a short bob. She was holding a large brown envelope in one hand.

"Yes?" replied Rajan, trying to slide himself into a more professional posture in the chair. The material was oddly slippery, causing him to struggle awkwardly.

"I'm done with the translation, sorry it took a while." The woman smiled awkwardly. "I've never had to translate something so old before, it was a little tricky." She held out the envelope. Rajan stood up and took it from her.

"Thank you, I know it's a little unusual." He opened the envelope and peered inside. A typed translation was nestled in with the photographs he had given her of the scroll.

"You're telling me. Normally I just get emails, texts, whats app messages, you know standard boring stuff. This was pretty interesting. Also, pretty weird. Where did you get it?" enquired the woman.

"Found it searching the flat of a guy we arrested for burglary. Must have taken it assuming it was valuable. Hard to find the original owner when we don't know what it says," lied Rajan. "Thanks Miss...err sorry I didn't catch you name earlier."

"Mina," she replied. "I hope it helps, but that translation is pretty bizarre. It's instructions on fighting Jinn, which is a kind of demon."

"It's not a demon" corrected Rajan before he could stop himself. "Uh, I read a lot of horror books, it's a slightly different thing. I think." He tripped over his tongue trying to reverse his mistake. Mina giggled.

"You don't look the sort," she said. "I love a good Horror. Maybe we can chat about them over a coffee or something?"

"Oh, yeah, I would like that" replied Rajan, blushing. "I'll email you, let you know when I'm free," he said, tapping the work email she had written on the envelope.

"Please do," said Mina. She winked and walked off across the office.

"Fuck," muttered Rajan to himself, "better go the library. I've got some reading to do."

Martin sat at his desk, staring at the monitor screen. Through his headset his customer was screaming the word fraud over and over because his company had dared to send her a bill for product she had received and used.

"I was one hundred and fifty pounds in credit!" she shrieked down the line, "this bill you've sent me is for three hundred pounds! I never used that much, and I never got my credit! Where is my money, you stole it from me! Theft! Fraud!"

"As I explained, you were one hundred and fifty pounds in credit, but you used four hundre- "Martin was cut off as the woman resumed her rant.

"Where are you getting four hundred from, this bill is for three hundred! And you still owe me money!" Her voice was high pitched, causing the phoneline to buzz slightly.

"You used four hundred and fifty pounds, minus your credit that leaves a bill of three hundred pounds to pay. Four fifty, minus one fifty is of course three hundred," Martin explained.

"Are you calling me stupid!" The woman screamed. Martin desperately wanted to reply in the affirmative but held his tongue. "I can do maths!" the customer asserted, despite all evidence to the contrary. "You've taken my money and used it without my consent! That's theft!"

"We've just deducted the credit off the bill. Why would we refund you one fifty only to send you a bill for four fifty, that doesn't make sense?" questioned Martin.

"I'll tell you what doesn't make sense! Four hundred and fifty pounds. I never used that much! How could I possible use that much! It's not right. Who told you I used that much?" There was a loud thud audible down the phone line as the woman had clearly slammed something on a table.

"You did?" said Martin slightly confused. "You requested that much, submitted the order forms, signed for the delivery and then signed when the driver came to collect the empty pallet. That and it's been three weeks. What we sent you only had a shelf life of five days. And I can see a new order form has been submitted for another delivery. You know how much it costs per unit, you know how much you ordered, this isn't a surprise, you knew how much you order would be when you submitted it."

"It's theft I tell you! You'll be hearing from my solicitor!" the woman slammed the phone down with a loud click. Martin sighed. He took off his headset, typed a quick note and then leaned back in his seat. Around him his co-workers were talking to their own headsets, taking orders and discussing bills for the fruit and vegetables the company delivered across the country. Across the office his boss shot him a disapproving glare. Martin sighed and placed his headset back on. There was no respite, no time to rest. Call after call after call, nonstop. Martin often thought that working in a call centre was just the coal mine of his day. Instead of chipping away at the rock face, they chipped at "customer satisfaction" and what sometimes felt like Martins own soul. He gripped his mouse and clicked the button to take another call.

"Hello Martin" said the voice at the end of the line.

"Uh, hello?" said Martin confused, the horrid high-pitched beep that signified an incoming call was missing. "You're through to Vale Produce how can I help you?"

"It's about how I can help you Martin," replied the voice.

"I'm sorry, who is this? How did you know my name?" Martin asked. The voice coming from the phone line was oddly soothing.

"No-one cares about you here. Just a cog in a machine designed to take abuse and turn it into money. Nobody worries about you. Not the bosses, not your co-workers and certainly not the customers. I think they quite like unloading abuse on someone they are safe from. It's sick really," said the voice.

"They don't mean it, they're just upset," asserted Martin.

"You don't really believe that. Humans will take any excuse to be monstrous to each other," came the reply. The word humans struck Martin as an odd choice, but he couldn't help listening to voice, somehow, he knew it was speaking to what he truly felt. "I can help you. Follow these instructions I can help find a more... meaningful existence."

"We hit the jackpot Dale," declare Rajan as he strode from the elevator across the office. He was holding a brown envelope over his head triumphantly. He stepped over to the desk and threw it down with a slap.

"Something good?" asked Dale, picking up the envelope and sliding out the paper inside.

"Yeah, something really good," he pulled out his phone from his pocket. "Mark will love this."

"Not a clue," replied Mark looking down at their captive. "Whatever we do, we need to be quick about it." There was a loud ringing emanating from the house behind them. "We need to do it quick, fire brigade can't be long." A melodic tune played in Marks pocket. He pulled out his phone and answered it. "Hello? Raj, excellent timing mate. Oh, fucking fantastic."

"What is it?" asked Jess.

"Raj I'm going to put you on speakerphone mate," stated Mark.

"Morning all!" said Raj, his voice scratchy and faint through the speaker. Rain splashed off the phone screen as Mark held it out. "We found a recipe on a scroll. Supposedly it can cleanse a person of a Jinn."

"Great, well we happen to have one on hand at the moment. What do we need?" Jess said.

"Ok so you need some honey that's the easy part. You also need black seed oil, apparently, it's pretty popular with new age types so I would start there. Last thing is you need some water over which something called an ayah has been spoken," said Raj.

"That's from the Quran. I guess a bible verse is the closest thing I could compare it to," answered Aasif. Jess shot Mark a disappointed stare.

"Yeah, uh, thanks whoever that is. Otherwise it seems like you just mix them all up and apply to the possessed person," continued Raj.

"Right got it, thanks Raj, we'll let you know how it goes." Mark ended the phone call. "Right so we probably haven't got long, how the hell do we put these together?"

"We go back inside," said Jess gesturing to the still smoking building. "There has to be honey in the kitchen. Maybe one of the residents was into alternative medicine? "

"What about the water?" asked Aasif. Mark pulled out a small brass key from his coat pocket and tossed it to him.

"The trunk in the boot has a Quran, left hand side at the top. Try not to touch anything else," Mark grinned as he spoke.

"Is that going to work? I'm not practicing, not since my dad passed."

"With these kinds of things, the intent is more important than the specifics. It won't matter," answered Jess. She tore a strip from the bottom of her blouse and held the cloth out flat with both hands, letting the rain soak it. "Right, quicker we do this, quicker we can get out of this shitshow." She placed the soaked cloth to her mouth and jogged off towards the building.

The back door had been left open when Ethel had tried to make her escape. Jess stalked the back smoke-filled corridors. Her eyes stinging, she tried to work her way to the kitchen. Mark followed behind her trying to cover his own mouth with his coat. They reached a branch in the corridor. A sign was screw to the wall. The recreational room was to the right whilst the kitchen was to the left. Jess nodded to mark before taking the left-hand path. Mark set off the other direction. Jess continued her walk. The joins between the older and newer sections of the building were obvious, the walls uneven despite the tepid beige paint that had been laid over them. She pushed open the double doors to the recreational room releasing a cloud of smoke that caused her to double over coughing. Catching her breath, she stepped into the room.

The circle of blood had been broken by the creature as it had lumbered after them leaving a long smear of blood across the floor. The room was cracked, its plaster coating torn from it, dust covering the ground. Jess looked around, stepping slowly forward, eager not to meet any surprises. She stopped when she saw a stack of small plastic bags and bottles that had been stacked up against one of the chairs pushed to the wall. The ingredients Ethel had bought from the Chinese medicine store. She picked the bottles up one by one. She let out a loud laugh as she found one that read *Black Seed Oil*. Their luck was turning. Pocketing the oil, she continued onward to the other exit and peered round. She looked over her handy work. The walls of the corridor were cracked and warped from the blast. Several metal chunks were imbedded into the brick. There was a large pile of black ash, the remains of that nightmare thing. The fire had consumed it entirely. Her morbid curiosity satisfied, Jess turned around and began her journey back outside.

"Anything?" asked Mark as she emerged from the house.

"Yeah," she held the small glass bottle between two fingers. "Got the oil."

"Holy shit!" exclaimed Mark, "I figured that would be the sticking point. Where the hell did you get it?"

"Our friend actually had it. It was one of the ingredients for their ritual." Jess placed the bottle back into her pocket.

"Guess that makes sense, if they use it in their magic maybe that's why it works against them?" Mark tapped his chin as he considered it. There was a loud thud as Aasif walked up to them, dropping a large plant pot at their feet. It was full of water.

"Closest I could get to a bucket. Filled it with a hose by the patio." Aasif said. "I just read the first ayah. I did it in Arabic, I wasn't sure, so I just went with that."

"You did good," said Jess, patting him on the shoulder. "Just need to see if this works. I assume you got honey from the kitchen."

"Yep, so how much of each do we use?" asked Mark.

"All of it I guess? Kind of an all or nothing thing," replied Jess.

"Right ok, well here we go." Mark pulled a half used squeezy bottle of honey from his pocket. He held it over the bucket and squeezed, a golden streak of honey splashing into the water below. Raindrops bounced off the surface of the mixture.

"Hey, you awake down there!" Mark shouted down the well.

"I'll kill you!" came the reply from within. Ethel was leaning against the bottom of the well. Her legs were broken, twisted spurs of blood and bone. Her stomach had split, intestines spilling out from under her night gown. The real Ethel was dead, now just a flesh puppet for some twisted entity.

"Eh, well something will get me eventually," admitted Mark. "Don't think it will be you today. What did you do with Claire's body?"

"Who?" asked Ethel.

"Young girl murdered a bunch of people, first one was in the park?"

"Hah, not me! I'm not the only one here. I'm thinking you're after the one who opened the door for us." The Ethel corpse grinned manically.

"Right. So, I'm guessing you aren't going to tell me how many of you there are and where they are?" questioned Mark.

"Fuck you!"

"Didn't think so. Ok guys, time to test this stuff." Mark beckoned to someone Ethel couldn't see. A dark shape appeared at the lip of the well. It tipped slightly water splashing onto her. Ethel screamed. The water hissed as it hit her skin, as though she was incredibly hot. The scream became shrill and unnatural. It stopped abruptly, the now silent form of Ethel sitting perfectly still, mouth still agape. There was a faint glow and then a jet of flame burst forth. It twisted mid-flight hitting the floor of the well. The flame stretched upwards, its flicked in an odd way. Mark could have sworn it looked humanoid for just a second.

"You will pay for that!" said the flame, pulsing from orange to blue in time with the words.

"Ok, dump the rest!" said Mark. The pot on the lip of the well tipped again, the water crashing into the flames. There was a loud high-pitched shriek and then nothing. The fire died down and went out. No smoke drifted from it.

"Is it gone?" asked Aasif, peering over the wells edge.

"Seems like it," answered Mark. He gripped the iron grate, sliding it off the top of the well.

"What are you doing?" Aasif said.

"Making it look like the well was open, so she fell in. I know, don't give me that look. Doing this job means bending the truth a little." Mark thought for a moment. "Ok well, a lot.

Imagine if people knew what was out there. We already have problems with people finding out and deciding to take things into their own hands. If everyone knew, we would have neighbours killing each other out of paranoia in the streets. There are plenty of supers who are upstanding citizens, doing something like this protects thousands. It's not nice, but it is right."

"I guess..." replied Aasif, clearly unsure. "We better get moving then. Before the fire brigade shows."

Aasif sat at the end of Jess' hotel room bed. She was taking out small bottles from a plastic carrier bag and was stacking them onto the small table in the corner of the room. Mark was outside, on the phone to his superior.

"How do you do it?" asked Aasif?

"Sorry, do what?" replied Jess.

"This," he said stretching his arms to indicate he meant everything. "The lies, the death, the nightmares."

"I have a daughter. Something came for her once. Something called a changeling. I stopped it, but that's how I got into this. Honestly, I keep doing it for her. The thought of some other mother losing her child to some other thing, I can't bear it." Jess put the bag down and stepped over the bed sitting down next to Aasif. "My wife wants me to stop. I don't see either of them as much as I would like. But every time we finish a case, I just know I've made the world a safer place for the both of them. At least that's what I tell myself. I have to, otherwise you're right, the world would just be too dark." She patted Aasif's hand.

"I have no-one. Been on my own for the last few years. What do I do? How can I carry on knowing all this." Aasif said, tears forming in his eyes.

"I think, if you can help people, you have to at least try. Yes, people died today, but think of how many we potentially saved. Think of them, and that's how you get through."

Chapter 15

Bill sat in a black folding chair, his legs resting on a metal barrel in front of him. Light danced from his phone, projecting the video onto his face in the dark.

"Police continue their hunt for a suspected serial killer in the South Wales area after a second body was discovered early this morning. Eyewitness accounts say the victim was displayed in a gruesome manner similar to the earlier victim a-" "Bill's attention dropped from the news he was watching as he was interrupted by tall imposing man.

"You actually going to help or just play with your phone?" asked the Man. Like Bill he was wearing a black suit, white shirt and black tie. His head was shaved, a thick stubble covering his head. His suit barely fit him, his muscular frame causing it to stretch precariously as he spoke.

"This is research innit," Bill waved the phone as he spoke. "Need to keep an eye to what's going on."

"In other news," said the newsreader on the phone, "a fire at a care home claims the lives of eight staff and fifteen residents in what is being said to be a freak accident with the homes oxygen supplies."

"Like that!" said Bill raising his voice. "Isn't no way these fuckers aren't responsible for this Aaron."

"Maybe so," replied Aaron. He was carrying a tin of red paint and a paintbrush. Whilst they were around the same height he dwarfed the much thinner spindly Bill. "I've started, you can finish." He held out the paint can and brush.

"Fine." Bill took the painting supplies from him begrudgingly. "You always do it wrong anyway." He dropped his legs from the barrel with a slap and leapt out of the chair. Aaron shot him a piercing glare as Bill walked off, disappearing into the dark of the warehouse they had chosen earlier.

The Jinn that possessed Martin pressed the plunger from the soap dispenser, squirting a pale blue foam onto his hands. A slow trickle of water hit the back of his shoes and split, continuing its grim expansion past his feet. The body of Martins' previous manager still twitched, its head submerged in water than now poured over from the side of the toilet. The back of its neck was bruised from where Martin had forcibly held him under. Martin stretched out his soap filled palms under the tap. It was an expensive piece of equipment the call centre had installed with much pomp and circumstance. The tap looks like a set of handlebars. The centre poured water when it detected hands beneath whilst each bar contained a drier. He reached under the centre and rather than water pouring out, the driers came on, spraying soapy foam across Martin. He sighed and tried again. Water cascaded across his hands this time. He moved his hands under the bars and the driers came on, until he moved his hands slightly too far for the temperamental machine which poured water again, undoing its own drying efforts. The entity possessing Martin slammed his hands on the counter. It had existed beyond countable time, from beyond the barriers of reality. It had seen civilisations burn and gods cast down. It was a being of much purer essence than these mortals' fragile forms. Magic was it's to command. Yet, it had been defeated by this sink. It turned and left the bathroom, shaking its hands dry instead.

Martin stepped out of the office into the cold air. People walked past, huddled into coats, hands deep in pockets. Small wisps emerged as their breaths hit the cold air. The clouds from Martins mouth were thick and heavy, heat escaping from the primal fire within him. He stood there for a moment, considering just what he wanted to do next, when he felt a pull. Faint and gentle at first, a tiny buzzing in his mind. Slowly moment by moment it grew stronger, the quiet sensation becoming roaring and overpowering. He could feel himself being drawn inextricably. He was being summoned.

"Right, how long do you think it will take?" asked Bill. He and Aaron were stood in the centre of an empty warehouse. A single strip light provided scant illumination, revealing only a portion of the runes they had painted across the floor.

"No idea," admitted Aaron "This is supposed to summon them, maybe it didn't work?"

"Nah, this spell work came to us with the info. Rumour has it the old boss sent it to us. It should work." Bill sat down awkwardly on the floor, his long bandy legs cross awkwardly.

"The old boss huh?" Aaron seemed shocked at this news. "Wow, a lot of people not too happy with how they bowed out. Big risk reaching out like this."

"Makes sense though. If they're right, then this needs to be knocked on the head sharpish. Not too keen on doing Satan's bidding again. They never were one of us really." Bill had pulled his phone out of his pocket and had begun scrolling idly. Aaron paced about impatiently.

"It's been over an hour. If someone summoned me and I took this long I would get a right bollocking," Aaron said, his massive frame shifting awkwardly as he leant on the sill of a large window set into the side of the warehouse. He stared out, his gaze caught by something moving in the night.

"That's the problem, though right?" asked Bill, lifting his attention from his phone. "These Jinn fucks have no sense of proper rules. Just do whatever they want." He peered across at Aaron who had pressed his face as close to the glass as he could. "Hey, you listening to me at all?"

"Shut up idiot," barked Aaron. "They're coming."

Martin stood outside the warehouse. He could feel the pull coming from inside. Its echoing scream filled his mind, driving him onwards. Around him other Jinn had gathered, answering the siren call. Officer workers, mothers, children, vagrants, his brothers and sisters had chosen a wide range of forms. Martin could feel them. An invisible flame shimmering around the other possessed. One girl's fire was a searing inferno. She wore a tattered red dress, her face and body were covered in large burns. Mud was matted in her hair. This was her, the one who had opened the doorway allowing his siblings through. The pain from the beacon had been infuriating, this fragile mortal shell forcing Martin to make his own way slowly here. Slowly, as one, the crowd of Jinn began to walk towards the warehouse.

"How many do you think there are?" asked Bill, trying to steal a peek over Aarons shoulder.

"No idea, hard to see but I think at least thirty? Maybe more." Aaron knocked Bill backwards as he stood up straight. "That's a lot more than we expected."

"Think we need to call for backup?" asked Bill

"I think you arseholes are out of your depth," said a third voice. They turned to see a short man with an athletic build stood under the light. He wore a white tracksuit with white trainers. A grey flat cap covered short blond hair. The man's hands were in his pockets, his elbows bent outwards in a cocksure stance.

"Fucking great a member of the boyband brigade. Going to dance number our problems away?" Aaron puffed up his chest as he spoke.

"God, I fucking wish. Would be a lot easier than dealing with you shitheads." The man pulled a cigarette from his pocket and slipped it into his mouth. It lit on its own, and he took a long drag. "No, I'm here to help you fuckwits deal with this little problem."

"We don't need no help from some fucking birdbrain flyboy," chimed in Bill from behind Aaron, hiding behind the larger man.

"Please, you two used to be big news. Belial and Amon. Real fire and brimstone bigshots. Now you're skulking round in disused buildings playing angry birds and waiting to get your shit kicked in by a crowd of Jinn." The man in white tapped the ash from his cigarette.

"Better watch your mouth feathers or I'll shut you up," said Aaron cracking his knuckles.

"Look you cock wombles, I'm here to help. Names Micky." The man held out his hand. Bill and Aaron stood perfectly still, staring at Micky. "Not hand shakers? That's fine. Look we got as much a horse in this race as you. We need to put aside our differences for now and deal with these bell ends outside. Then we can get back to calling each other all the cunts under the sun. Agreed?"

"Got to be a catch," said Bill. "Never known a fucking flapper to do something without an agenda."

"Yeah he's right," agreed Aaron. "What's the other angle here?"

"Hah! You got me!" laughed Micky. "Look we know your intel and spell work came from someone we have a very keen interest in finding. Thought maybe we could do a deal, tit for tat and all that."

Aaron and Bill looked at each for a moment. "Fine by me," said Aaron.

"Me too," added Bill. "We haven't exactly got much love for them either. You got a deal."

The main entrance to the warehouse was a large metal shutter. Age had worn its mechanism, so it shuddered and groaned as it slowly slid open. Both sides stood facing each other across the slowly rising divide. A large crowd stood on one side, a young girl in red at its head. On the other side two suited men stood either side of a man in a white tracksuit.

"I should have guessed," said Claire. "Just can't leave us be can you?"

"Yeah sorry about that," replied Micky. "But the universe is delicate. We can't have you going around just doing what you want. Things need to be balanced. Even these pit dwellers understand that." He gestured to the men on either side of him with his thumbs. "You're a third party who decides to run up and down the see-saw when it's perfectly level. A nuisance."

"You tell yourselves that. Whatever helps you cope. The universe is chaos. Disorder. Random probabilities colliding with each other spinning off into new events endlessly. That's a kind of beautiful order in its own way," said Claire. She laughed. "You don't even know why you do it do you? This endless back and forth between you tipping the scales one way and the other. It's been so long you've forgotten why you started. There's no time outside this reality you know?" She stepped forward from the crowd, stepping right up to the three men. She leant forward and cupped her hand around her mouth. "I'll let you into a secret, we remember everything. No time means no lost memories. What you do? It's a massive waste of time!" The crowd burst into uproarious laughter.

"We will tell you exactly once," said Aaron, "return to your void or we will make you."

"What you three alone? Didn't think we were worth more effort? Two demons and one angel. You used to rally armies against us!" Claire's voice was raised in contempt. "Armies!" She prodded Aaron in the chest. "You call your little pocket dimension Hell? I'll tell you what's Hell! You would think that nothing exists between realities, but you would be dead wrong. We can slip in here when reality is weakened a little, but that... other place, the same rings true there. The things there can slip into the gap between reality and they are hungry. Long millennia periods of nothingness broken by trying to escape from things I couldn't even begin to describe. Why do you think we come here?" She walked up and down before the men.

"The fuck are you even talking about?" asked Bill. "If that were true you would be throwing yourselves at our mercy, not murdering humans left and right."

"Hey!" said Claire, "Just because we're running doesn't mean we can't have fun. Now are you going to walk away before this chat gets distinctly less friendly?"

"Funny," Micky answered, his voice dripping with sarcasm. "Was going to ask you the same thing." He stretched his neck which let out a loud click. "Ready lads?"

"Guess so," said Aaron raising his fists.

It happened in an instant, between eyeblinks the three men vanished, replaced instead by their true forms. In the centre of their line-up was a mass of overlapping wings, wrapped around a pulsing white light. Before the wings floated a sword and round bronze shield, each of which was engulfed in white flames. To the angels left was a hulking brute. Great horns bent outwards from its forehead, its skin a strange hodgepodge of scales and fur. It stood on cloven hooves, its great muscled torso resting on massive forearms like a gorilla. Aaron shook his horned head, flecks of white foam forming at his mouth. On the right of the angel a humanoid form floated a few inches from the ground. Its limbs were long and oddly shaped, its arms dragging along the ground as it floated slowly. The creature's torso was wrapped in thick black leather straps. It had no bottom jaw, a long lashing tongue thrashing about greedily. Two great metal spikes jutted out from where its eyes should be, trickles of blood running down its face like tears. As Bill hovered slowly forward his body writhed like a snake. With a roar the crowd of Jinn surged forward.

The angel floated in the centre of the warehouse. Its wings tattered and burnt. Blood poured from a wound on Aarons chest, the thick dark liquid matting his scattered fur. Bill held his shoulder, one of his arms torn clean off. New leather straps had grown to cover the stump. Around them lay scattered bodies of dozens of humans. Each one they had slain had released a blast of fire which had vanished into the night sky. Micky's initial beam of searing light had incinerated five alone as they had swarmed towards them. Hubris had been the trio's downfall, assuming that the Jinn's magic would be no threat they had brought nothing to prevent it. Too late they had discovered the flames of the Jinn were anathema to them. The blasts of elemental chaos searing the beings of order. Weakened and tired they had slowly been pushed back deeper into the warehouse.

"I think maybe lads, we misjudged this one," chimed Micky in overlapping voices like a choir.

"You think?" rumbled Aaron. "At least we go down swinging." They had been surrounded, and despite their casualties ten Jinn remained, including the one that seemed to be their leader. The girl grinned, her hands glowing in the dark with blue fire.

"It was a valiant try, I will give you that," said Claire, holding up her hands. The flames in her palms danced excitedly.

"Fuck you bitch!" hissed Bill, spittle flying from his tongue as it lashed about.

"Charming," Claire said as she took a deep breath and blew the fire on her palms. It burst forth in a gout of flame. Micky glowed brightly momentarily and then there was a blinding flash. Claire's mortal body closed its eyes in an instinctive response. They stung, the flash momentarily blinding her. When her vision returned, the trio were gone. Her flames had set the warehouse ablaze and the fire was hungrily spreading throughout it. "Shame," she said.

There was a crash of leaves and a snapping of branches as three men appeared mid-air and crashed through the tree tops. They tumbled between branches before hitting the wet forest ground with a splash of mud. The two men wearing suits lifted themselves to their knees and began vomiting in loud long wretches.

"You're welcome," said Micky trying in vain to wipe mud from his tracksuit.

"Could of fucking warned us," complained Bill, wiping vomit from the corner of his mouth with his sleeve.

"Honestly I didn't even know if it would work. I don't know if an angel has ever done that with demons in tow before. It was a miracle I could do it at all after that fucking shitshow," Micky admitted.

"Well," said Aaron standing to his feet. He twisted his back a few times and then stretched, "at least you know it works. Where the fuck are we?"

"Norway," said Bill without missing a beat. "You only get these kinds of trees growing together like this near the north of the country. What?" He stopped talking as both the other men looked at him puzzled. "I like trees. You guys are ancient immortals and you never picked up a hobby or two?"

"That's fair," agreed Micky. "I got a pretty good home brewery going on in my garage. Think I owe you two a beer at least."

"At least," repeated Aaron. "Why are we in Norway?"

"Didn't really have time to aim." Mickey shrugged. "We better get back to civilisation, let our respective camps know what's going on."

"Ok, well fly us back feathers," said Bill. "Don't think there's anything left in my stomach to throw up.

"Uh, yeah, well," Micky began. He sounded embarrassed. "I'm kind of, out of juice I guess you could say. We'll have to walk."

"Amazing," Aaron rolled his eyes. "Anyone know which way to go?"

Claire stood watching the warehouse burn. Around her were the remaining Jinn. The others would need to find new hosts. She stared at the fire, watching it dance. It was beautiful. Chaos in action.

"You there!" she pointed at one of the other Jinn, a young man in a pale blue shirt who was sitting on the ground, watching the flames grow higher.

"Yes?" replied the Jinn. Claire could see his essence. The invisible flames flickered faintly from his host. Soon they would grow stronger as all that remained of the bodies original owner was purged.

"What is your name?" she demanded.

"This mortal was called Martin," said the Jinn.

"Martin, I would have you gather some things for me. Our enemies close in on us. We will require greater numbers if we are to survive here. Can you do this for me?" Claire asked.

"Of course, consider it done." Martin bowed his head.

"Good, well we cannot sit here and watch these flames forever. We have work to do."

Chapter 16

Lucille hummed to herself as she wiped the bar top with a rag, its cleanliness suspect. She was alone, the hip indie clientele Lucille had cultivated too busy charging large sums of money to tweak corporate logos slightly from an office share to partake in some early morning drinking. She gripped some clean glasses in one hand and placed them on the shelf below the worktop. She looked across at Abbie, who was sweeping a small stage they had installed for what was supposed to be open mic night but had rapidly turned into bad poetry night. Abbie's gaze caught Lucille's and she shook her head. Lucille rolled her eyes.

"This is going to suck," she admitted to herself. She turned and lifted the handset from the old black rotary phone embedded in the wall behind the bar. Tucking the handset between her shoulder and her ear she plucked a business card from the corkboard next to the phone. She peered at it closely carefully dialling the number into the phone. "Hi, yeah, is that Raj Singh? Hi, its Lucille. Yes, I'm phoning you. What did you expect when you left me your card? Figured I send a talking snake or something? Look, I need to talk, can you come by the bar? Awesome, see you soon."

There was a clack as Abbie rested the broom against the bar. "You're going to tell then? That could get us in big trouble." Abbie hopped up onto one of the bar stools as she spoke.

"Probably, but we're all in a lot more trouble if I don't."

Chelsea and Mercedes stood in front of the house. Even in the early morning light it loomed. Mercedes grinned excitedly whilst Chelsea pulled her large pink puffer jacket tighter to herself. The on-off rain of the past few days had stopped, but Pontypridd in the middle of February could be bitterly cold.

"I'm not sure about this," said Chelsea. She shivered briefly in the cold and turned so the house was behind her. "I nearly died last time."

"Of come on, you know it will be fine," replied Mercedes. She was holding her phone up with both hands, trying to get the whole house into shot. "That medium we saw said that she was just trying to talk to you. It was an accident. Said she was drawn to your...what did she call it?"

"Effervescent spirit," Chelsea answered. "I looked it up, I think it means I'm gassy?"

"She got that right!" her sister laughed. "Come on, we go in there, get some videos for YouTube, some pictures for the gram and we are landed." Mercedes turned to match her sister holding up the phone to get a picture of the two of them before the house. "Come on cheer up," she said elbowing her sister playfully. "Milly Jones has two thousand Instagram followers and she thinks she's a model. Someone sent her these weight loss lollies the other day. For free!"

"I pretty sure she paid for those and only pretended to get them for free," said Chelsea. "She only did that to make herself look more important."

"Who cares! We do this, and people won't send us stuff for free, they'll be the ones paying us. The ghost sisters. Ghost hunters, models, influencers!"

Chelsea sighed. She hated her town, its rows of grey worn down terraces, it's boring people, her shitty job in the local Valueways. Some of her friends had left, mostly to Cardiff which was only a single train stop away. As though Pontypridd's grim pull limited people born there to the same postcode most of their lives. Maybe this was a blessing, her way out. "Fine," she said. "Let's do this then." Chelsea pulled her arms from the pockets of her coat. She placed one arm around her sister's waist and pulled her tight to herself.

"Ready," began Mercedes "Three...Two...One..."

"Hey!" they said in unison, dragging out the middle letter to an obnoxious length.

"It's your girls, the ghost sisters!" Mercedes continued. "We are about to enter this house, which we know for a fact, contains a real-life ghost. So, if you want to get the deets on this remember to like, subscribe and smash that bell!" The two girls smiled in the camera with fake exaggerated grins. Behind them the house stood, the morning sun behind it causing it to cast a long shadow. If they had stopped to watch the footage back, they would have seen a pale figure moving very slightly in the top right window of the house.

Mark stood in his hotel bathroom, staring into the mirror. His eyes were sullen from lack of sleep. Behind him the hotel room was still a mess, Mark having left the do not disturb hanger on to keep the maids out. He leant down, dipped his hands into the pool of cold water he had run into the sink and splashed his face. He hadn't been able to sleep, his mind racing over what he and Jess had seen yesterday. Mark felt a sickness in his stomach, a tingling in his fingers, an overwhelming fear that things were spiralling out of control. He filled a glass from the tap and removed a small white tablet from a silver packet he had brought into the bathroom with him, the tablet breaking through the foil with a satisfying pop. He placed the beta-blocker into his mouth and swallowed it with a gulp of water. Mark had suffered panic attacks many times in his life, becoming uncomfortably familiar with the first signs. He stood up straight and pulled the plug from the sink. Tiny needles pricked his feet as he walked back to his bed, the fine layer of iron filings proving to be just as frustrating for a living human as they were to any spirt. He sat down on the edge of his bed and picked up his phone from the bedside table. Still an hour before he was due to meet Jess downstairs. He opened an app on his phone and clicked on the large play icon that filled his screen.

"Guided meditation, track three," said a strange voice from the app. Oddly it was both calming and overeager at the same time. Mark lay on the bed and closed his eyes. "Now, think of a lake. Imagine casting a stone into the lake, its ripples echoing outwards towards the shore."

Lucille sat on one of her barstools. She wore the same look as a child who was sad at being told off, but still convinced what they had done was exceedingly funny.

"You know that's a breach of your protection agreement!" shouted Rajan.

"Well, not technically, I didn't contact anyone from my old life, just left them a tiny package," replied Lucille, holding her forefinger and her thumb close together.

"A package with instructions is contact," Dale chimed in. "Why didn't you give us the same information when we visited the other day?"

"Because you would have been like a toddler in the deep end. Way out of your depth. Jinn are trouble with a capital T. If I had given you what I gave them, you would have some very dead police officers by now." Lucille picked up a glass from the bar and took a long sip through a plastic straw. The drink was bright pink and poured over ice. A small green umbrella sat in the top of the glass.

"We've done alright up until now," Rajan said taking a seat on a stool next to Lucille. "We got you, didn't we?"

"I mean I handed myself in- "

"That's a lie," interrupted Dale.

Lucille shrugged. "I tell a lot of lies. Even to myself. You could say it's a well-developed skill."

"Look, we need to know what you told them. You called us here Lucille, you want to tell us. Can we cut the crap on the tee-hee I'm the devil aren't I so naughty routine." Rajan pressed his index finger onto the bar to stress his point.

"Ok, look. The little information parcel I dropped off contained a note letting my old..." Lucille thought for a moment, trying to find the right word. "Gang. My old gang know that Jinn are back and walking around. I did a little divination to see the rough area the Jinn were in and left instructions on a spell that would draw them in. Moths to a flame. Or I guess flames to moth in their case? Either way I thought getting them all in one place would make them easier to be deal with."

"And?" asked Rajan

"And nothing. My contact never got back to me. Which means they either ignored me or did what I suggested, and it went horribly wrong. If it had gone right they wouldn't have been able to resist rubbing my nose in it."

"How would they have done that? You're supposed to be incognito," enquired Dale.

"I'm still *the prince of darkness*," said Lucille lowering her voice to mock the title. "Leave a prayer at your local satanic church and it's like a royal mail delivery straight to my brain. It's incredibly annoying. You know how many teenagers who think they're cool I get rattling around in here daily?" She tapped the side of her head.

"Know how many Jinn are out there?" Dale said. He had pulled his phone from his pocket and was staring at the screen.

"No idea," Lucille admitted. "Bound to be a bunch though. Like I said last time you start with one and it holds the door open for others to get through. You need to deal with them all or the cycle will just continue."

"I think I know how," said Dale looking up from his screen. He held his phone out in front of Rajan. "This is from Mark and Jess' report. The recipe on the scroll worked."

"What scroll? What recipe?" asked Lucille, spying unsubtly over the phone screen.

"We found instructions on mixing ingredients to make I guess Jinn repellent? Apparently a first dose forced the Jinn from its host body, a second got rid of the Jinn entirely," said Rajan scrolling through the report.

"Well, that is interesting, found that in your famous archives, did you? I need to pay a visit, seems I could learn a few things," Lucille said, taking another sip of her drink.

"Never in a million years. And it's a bit early to be drinking isn't it?" Dale said, disappointment in his voice.

"It doesn't work on me. Need to do more than just buy this girl a drink." Lucille winked at him.

Dale blushed. "I have a plan anyway. We're going to need to know how you do the spell to draw them in."

"No." said Lucille sternly.

"What do you mean no? You broke the rules of your protection, we could toss you out on your arse you know?" Rajan said.

"You won't do that." Lucille rolled her eyes. "We both know I'm way too useful a source to give up. You want that spell you need to make a deal for it."

"You're asking us to make a literal deal with the devil?" Rajan said, his voice weary. He found dealing with Lucille particularly tiresome.

"That is sort of my modus operandi, I will admit. What I want, is a trip away."

"A trip?" replied Rajan, slightly shocked at the request.

"I'm locked in this bar day and night. Never go out, never do anything. I know the delivery guy from the Valueways around the corner by name. I want a holiday. To Blackpool. I've never been to Blackpool, I'd like to see it." Lucille crossed her arms.

"I'm sorry, you want to take a trip to Blackpool. That's it? Nothing nefarious?" asked Rajan.

"What do you take me for? I gave up that life. I just want a week away- "

"Weekend," interrupted Rajan.

"Fine a weekend," conceded Lucille. "You can send someone with me, so I'm supervised at all times."

"We'll check with the boss," said Dale, his head turning to Rajan. "I mean, it's not an unreasonable request I guess?"

Lucille clapped her hands excitedly. "Oh, I'm glad you agree. There is one more stipulation. I want D.S Cooper to be my...supervisor."

Aasif tapped the side of the rental van he had procured. It was old, the paint on the side declaring the rental company had mostly peeled off rendering it unintelligible. Aasif's face beamed with pride. He had been sent in after the company had banned Jess and Mark, upset at the shredded tires of the previous rental they had made.

"She's a beauty, isn't she?" he asked.

"It's a bit beat up. Is this all the rental company had? We gave you our expenses card, couldn't you get something? I don't know? Nicer?" Jess said. She scowled at Aasif.

"My Dad used to have one of these. Tough as old boots it was. The newer Transits are shit in comparison. Last one they had left on the court. Can you imagine that?" Aasif walked to the back of the van as he spoke, opened the rear door.

"I can absolutely believe that," said Mark, his voice thick with sarcasm. "Help me with this trunk." Gripping one end each he and Aasif slid the heavy case into the back of the van.

"Do you really need to carry all this wherever you go?" asked Aasif dusting off his hands.

"Saved your arse when we needed a Quran," Mark answered, tapping the leather fondly.

"We could of just, Googled it? I'm sure I could have found a copy of the Quran online. Hell, a bunch of these books would fit on a tablet pretty easily." Aasif stepped down from the back of the van.

"We tried that once," said Jess. "Mark is very, fussy, about his books."

"Look, what if we're stuck somewhere without a charger, or whatever we're dealing with messes with electronics?" Interjected Mark. "I'm just saying paper copies never fail you."

"I guess," admitted Aasif. "Has either of those things ever come up though?

"Well no," stated Mark. "Doesn't mean it couldn't. We shouldn't rely too much on new technology." He stopped talking as his phone rang. Mark pulled it from his pocket and answered it, the irony lost on him. "Hey Raj. Right. Ok. It's a date." He put his phone back into his pocket. "Raj has a plan. He's going to text us a list of what we need, and he and Dale are going to meet us here this evening."

Chelsea stepped slowly through the house. The last time she had been here was a riot of sound and colour. A rave at a supposedly haunted house had seemed a lot of fun. Now it seemed disrespectful. The signs of the party were still scattered about, lingering reminders of an insult to the dead. In front of her Mercedes strode confidently, phone held outstretched.

"It was here, in this very house my sister encountered a real live ghost!" she said excitedly. "Spirit can you hear us? If you can give us a sign." There was nothing. A pervasive silence that seemed an act of defiance. Mercedes stepped onto the first step of the groaning stairs. "It was up these very stairs, on the second floor that Chelsea first saw her. The ghost of a maid." There was another low groan as she took another step.

"I think we made a mistake Merce, we shouldn't be here." Chelsea zipped her jacket up further, somehow it was colder in the house than outside it.

Mercedes stopped the recording. "Don't baby out on me now. We're already doing this in the day because you were too coward to do it at night. Come on Chel, we need this. I know you're as sick of this shithole town as I am."

"It's just, she clearly doesn't want anyone here. I don't like it. You shouldn't mess with the dead. It's not right."

"The dead shouldn't have messed with you then. It's only fair," Mercedes said, seemingly pleased with her logic. There was another groan from the staircase. Mercedes hadn't moved. "What was that?"

"See, let's get out of here!" pleaded Chelsea.

"When the goings getting good? No way." Mercedes started recording again and excitedly stamped up the staircase.

The two girls stood in the room where it had happened. A barren awful place. Chelsea felt ill, like the peeling wallpaper was the world itself peeling away. The window she had fallen from had been shut, she hoped by the policeman who had come to see her. She wondered what he was doing now. *Probably another case* she thought, *who would believe what happened to me*? Chelsea stood at the centre of the room, almost paralysed as her sister orbited around her eagerly filming the room.

"So, show me where you were standing when it happened Chels." Mercedes prodded Chelsea in the back waking her from her daze.

"Uh I was right here by the window," Chelsea said, trying to keep as much distance between herself and the glass as she could.

"Come on, move in get closer, people can't see you there." Her sister waved her hand beckoning Chelsea into the shot. She nervously slid to the side.

"There's a woman right there." Said Chelsea.

"So that's what happened next?" Mercedes asked, her gaze fixed on the camera.

"No, I mean right now," whispered Chelsea, her body shaking with terror. Mercedes span around to catch a momentarily flash of a dress moving away from the doorway. She ran out through the door, trying desperately to catch a glimpse with her phone. There was a loud bang as a door slammed shut at the other end of the hallway. "Merce no!" cried Chelsea as she ran after her sister desperately trying to stop her.

Mercedes stood in the room whose door had been slammed disappointed, another barren room like the first. Childish graffiti scrawled across it by someone eager to prove their bravery. *Darren was ere 2002*" it read.

"God you're ok," panted Chelsea, as she stepped through the doorway, the great solid door open swung open so far as to be nearly touching the wall. Her eyes streamed with tears. "Don't run off like that, you scared me."

"Nothing in here anyway, couldn't even get a good shot or anything." Mercedes crossed her arms grumpily. She tapped her foot in frustration.

"Look can we go home, I hate it here," begged Chelsea.

"Ok fine, we can- "Chelsea stopped mid-sentence. The door to the room creaked as it slowly swung shut. Behind the door was a woman in a maid's outfit. All colour had been drained from her, a monochrome nightmare. Her face was twisted and stretched, her fingers long talons. She hung from the wall, feet and hands sticking like a spider. She hissed and leapt at the two girls, her talons held outwards.

Chapter 17

The van rattled uneasily as it trundled down the Pontypridd streets. Something clanged from the underside as it stomped over a speed-bump. Mark wobbled uneasily, squeezed into the middle front seat common on older vans but so very rarely actually used. On his knees rested his work issued laptop. It was a tiny ancient thing, the letters worn from its keyboard, the screen scratched from use. Some bright spark had mandated upgrades to the latest operating software, rendering a previously tolerable machine painfully slow. Mark lifted it pushing the screen close to his face to get a decent look at the webpage he had open.

"This list of stuff Raj says we need is pretty out there. I'm not even sure what some of this is!" Mark dropped the laptop down on his lap exasperated. "One of them I can only find on eBay," he said rapping the screen with his knuckle, "and who knows if this is real."

Jess took the computer from his lap and stared at its tiny screen. "A doll possessed by a ghost. Who has one of those and decides that the best course of actions is to sell it?" Either its fake or they're really blasé about the whole thing."

"Possessed doll?" said Aasif. "I know where to get one of those."

"I'm sorry, what?!" exclaimed Jess.

"Yeah, saw one the other week. There was a convention in town that had one on display." Aasif stared forward, his concentration focused on the road.

"A convention? For possessed dolls?" Jess looked visibly confused.

"No, it was for mediums, psychics and that. They come every year, set up in the town hall. Apparently, it's a popular profession around these parts. There's a big union? Association? However, they're organised. They had the doll there on display for the public. Had to pay a few quid to go in and see it. Supposed to have been on the telly and all that." The van shook as Aasif drove over another speed-bump. "I'm surprised you don't keep tabs on them all."

"That's because it's a crock of shit mate," said Mark. "It's all bollocks. People preying on the vulnerable and grieving for a quick buck. Impressive magic trick I'll give them that. Trust me, if a spirit really wants to make itself known there's no mysterious powers required."

"Still we should go see them. We could use that doll. As for why I have no clue," Jess chimed in.

Marks eyes lit up. "Ah see, well the doll is a representative component. The doll is the human form, the spirit possessing it is a stand in for the Jinn. It's actually a kind of sympathetic magic..."

Jess leant forward and turned up the radio. "I wish I never asked."

They had parked the van outside a two-story building, its ground floor dominated by a letting agency. Photographs in the window described the samey boring houses of the town as "rustic" and "charming". The inside was full of people sitting at glass and chrome desks wearing equally shiny suits. The expensive looking agency seemed at odds with the kind of bland terrace properties they were peddling. Around the side from the flashy agency exterior was a small door. A plexiglass sign screwed to the wall. *"British Society of Spiritualists and Mediums"* it was supposed to read, but some enterprising vandal had scratched off the letters, so it actually read *"British society of tits and mums."* Mark felt himself crack a smile at the sheer childishness of it. He reached forward and pressed the button on a small metal intercom that had been haphazardly attached to the wall. Thick white sealant had been slathered on in an attempt to make it stick. It hadn't worked, the intercom slipping before it had set, leaving it permanently at an odd angle.

There was a crackle. "Hello?" A woman's voice croaked through the speaker.

"Yes, can you buzz us up please. It's the police." Mark said, leaning close to the squawking metal box.

"It's the police Gerald, what do they want? What have you done!" scratched the intercom, the person at the other end forgetting to take their finger off the button.

"Nothing ask what they want!" shouted Gerald loud enough for the intercom to pick him up.

"We can't ask them what they want, it's rude and it's the police," said the first voice. She was whispering rather than letting go of the button. "Come right up!". There was a clack as the door before them opened slightly. Mark pushed it, revealing a set of stairs with worn green shag carpet. He walked slowly up the stairs, Aasif and Jess following behind.

The office that lay atop the stairs was the opposite of the glitzy letting agency below. The green shag carpet of the stair way ended bafflingly at pale brown linoleum that covered the entire office floor. There was a handful of desks scattered around, huge lumbering things made of black metal and MDF boards that must have been white originally but had long since faded into a kind of off yellow colour. The desks were taken up with computers Mark had last seen as a pre-teen. Huge CRT monitors and towers, each a uniform beige colour. Along the wall to the right of the offices was a large glass cabinet. Inside were trophy's, plaques, and commemorative silver plates. They glistened polished to shine and completely at odds with the decrepit office that housed them. Mark stepped over and looked through the glass. A large cut glass trophy read *"Gerald Griffiths Medium of the Year."*

"Hello?" shouted Jess. The office was oddly empty of people. "Hello?"

Two people emerged from behind a pale green partition. A man and a woman both in their late fifties. The woman wore a power suit last available sometime in the mid-eighties. It was bright pink with a purple blouse, it shoulder pads puffing her up like an angry cobra. The man was portly, his gut exposed through his shirt which was much too tight. His hair had long since lost the battle with his bald patch, the few defiant strands brushed over into could only be called a comb over if you were willing to except an exceptionally tiny comb. The man barrelled at them hand outstretched.

"Gerald Griffiths," he said, shaking first Marks hand then Aasif's. His missing Jess did not go unnoticed by her. "Head of the British Society of Spiritualists and Mediums. BSSM for short. This is my wife Carol."

"That your name on the trophies in the cabinet then?" asked Marked gesturing to the glass with his thumb.

"Sure is, I've won the BSSM Medium of the Year contest six years in a row." Gerald grinned proudly.

"Isn't that your own organisation though?" Jess asked puzzled.

"Beat out a lot of competition to win that," Gerald continued ignoring her. "Very proud."

"Uh huh I bet. I'm D.C Holden, this is my partner D.C Curren." Jess flashed her I.D "We're here to ask a few questions about your," Jess pulled out her notebook and flipped a page open for dramatic effect. "Haunted doll."

"Oh Isabella?" Said Carol. "What do the police want with her?"

"We're here to confiscate her sadly. A doll matching her description was reported stolen," Mark said. He shrugged trying to sell the lie.

Gerald's friendly demeanour dropped, his face swapping to a scowl in a moment. "That's not true. I know you're lying. This is about the paranormal stuff that's been going on around town isn't it."

"I'm not sure what you me- "Mark began to reply.

"Oh please. I know your type." Gerald took two steps towards the nearest desk and sat down on the desktop. "You think this is all nonsense, I could tell from the moment you came in. I can read you like an open book if you'll excuse the cliché."

"Cold reading is an impressive skill," Mark admitted, holding his hands up as if to say he had been caught. "There's nothing supernatural about it though."

"True enough, and I've made a long but not exactly lucrative career out of it. But that's not how I started. Been able to speak with spirits since I was a kid. Scared me at first but I soon got used to it. Decided when I was younger to give the medium thing a go and very quickly learnt that being truthful is not what people want." Gerald sighed. "People want to hear their gran is in a nice place, or that their kids love them. They don't want to hear uncle Jim beat aunt Mable and now she's an angry ghost who won't move on."

"I'm the same," said Carol taking a seat beside Gerald. "Well not exactly the same, Gerald can hear spirits, I can sense auras. It's how we found each other."

"It's funny. You never reacted to me asking about the paranormal, like its everyday for you. What are you some kind of ghost police?" he joked.

Jess laughed. "Close enough."

"Well you caught us packing out stuff to leave. Carol says she senses a nasty aura and its growing worse. And there's a ghost I can hear wailing in my dreams on the old house up the valley. We weren't keen on sticking around. Isabella is packed up in a box. Was trying to sell her on eBay but no one wants to buy a haunted doll." Gerald hopped down from the desk. "Come on. What do you need her for?"

"We need it to try and stop what's happening around here. What do you know about it?" Mark asked as he followed him. Jess and Aasif staying behind to question Carol.

"Nothing specific. I know those two murders have something to do with it, and I know there's a bunch more deaths you're covering up. Those spirits are particularly pissed. If my wife feels something she thinks is dangerous enough we need to leave, I know enough to listen to her." Gerald thought for a moment. "I mean, I do what she tells me to ninety percent of the time anyway. Women eh?" Mark nodded awkwardly. He followed Gerald to a small store cupboard at the far end of the office. Gerald reached up and pulled a small wooden box from a shelf. He slid off the lid and offered it to Mark. Laying within the box on a bed of shredded paper was a porcelain doll. Its face was heavily painted, its woven pigtails frayed. It wore a pale blue plaid dress. It was the very epitome of what people expect when you describe something as a haunted doll. "We picked her up from the old owner, paid a pretty penny at the time. It's a famous doll. Worked out well as a fundraiser for the Society."

"It always amazes me what people will pay to see," said Mark. He reached into his pocket and produced the divining crystal he had searched for the onryo with. He held it over the doll and it span slowly in a wide circle.

"You know your stuff," Gerald said, evidently impressed. "Don't worry, its only slightly haunted. Head turning on its own, whispering in the night. That kind of thing. Take it, if it helps stop whatever is happening around here you're welcome to it."

The trunk shut with a clunk, followed by the metal slam of the van door being shut. The doll had been sealed inside its box and placed amongst the stashed occult objects in the back of the van. Mark had tried to assure Aasif that the warding on the case would keep the doll under wraps without much success. Aasif had seen cannibalism, corpses, possessed people and whatever the thing at the care home was but the doll was the one thing that had really creeped him out so far.

"I just don't like it," he said as he started the Van and began towards their next stop.

"It's just a harmless doll, what are you scared of," mocked Jess.

"You don't find it creepy, those beady little dead eyes?"

"I checked it, it's not a particularly strong spirit. We'll be fine," said Mark.

"Really? I thought you said that the ghost at that house is much stronger than it should be, that it turned vicious suddenly. What's not to say the same won't be true of that doll? Can't be a coincidence right, this Jinn turns up around the time a ghost goes nuts? Must be a link there." Aasif checked his mirror as he turned the van on a junction.

"That's... that's an excellent point," agreed Mark. He turned to Jess who had drawn the middle seat short straw this time. "You think maybe the Jinn being around is what made our ghost friend go all Fatal Attraction? Jinn apparently get in through weakened barriers between worlds. Maybe that's letting the ghost manifest more solidly?"

"Maybe, maybe it's the other way around though, the ghost getting angrier is what weakened the barrier in the first place." Jess slipped a notebook from her jacket pocket, draw a short pencil from the metal rings at the top and scrawled the word barrier on the page. "Could be that something else weakened the barrier and it both bumped the ghost up a tier and let the Jinn in. It is a bit too convenient timing wise."

"Good thinking that man," praised Mark. "I think I'll just shut this divider." Mark pulled the small metal window between the back of the van and the cabin shut. "Can't be too careful."

Jess sat at a large round table, paperwork scattered all over it. Around her the libraries shelves seemed to swallow her, as though the forests worth of paper had reanimated into a thick dark wood. She looked up from the files she had checked out and groaned. Aasif was resting both hands on his chin. Jess was sure he was sleeping. The silence of the library was broken by the tapping shoes as Mark walked the aisles towards them.

"I put a bunch more warding up inside the Van, just you know, in case of killer doll," he said taking a seat at the table. His voice was lowered to a whisper. "I let Raj and Dale know we got that particular ingredient, so we don't double up. That would be our luck wouldn't it, two scary dolls. Hey that might be a good horror film, two haunted dolls trying to get each other. Find anything?"

"Too much. It seems like this town is half abandoned buildings with all this lot." Jess gestured across the table at the sea of news articles and deeds. "I kind of went off horror films when I started doing this. Put me off a little."

"I know what you mean. I watch them, but its more to find what's wrong more than anything. Is he asleep?" Mark asked.

"I think so, leave him be. It's been a rough couple of days for him." Jess picked up another building plan, looked at it for a moment and then tossed it onto a pile which tipped over spilling paper across the floor.

"You know I had to mention him in the report after the care home business. The boss heard him over the phone. That's it for him, he's one of us now." Mark picked up one of the plans, stared at it for a moment, turned it around. He looked at it some more before turning back the original way he had it.

"I know." Jess held her head down solemnly. "I thought maybe we could shield him from this. Sort it all out and send him back to his old life. It's rough doing this Mark. All the darkness, the violence. I wouldn't wish this on my worst enemy."

"And yet you do it every day."

"What does that say about my opinion of myself. I don't know how you're so cool and collected with it all yourself." Jess leant back in her chair stretching out her limbs.

"Hah, the answer there is plenty of medication and unhealthy coping methods." He tapped the plan he was holding.

"I'm sorry, I had no idea, you never talk about yourself that much." Jess brought her chair back to the seated position with a loud clack that echoed through the library.

"It's not a big deal. Beta blockers for panic attacks mainly. Plenty of people are on tablets like me. Not so different than taking insulin or heart medication. You're sick so you take your medicine, right? Here look at this." Mark handed her the plans he had been examining.

Jess took the paper and stared the plans over. She thought for a minute. "You are a right pain in the arse you know that? You walk in and find it on the first try. Maybe our luck is turning. This is perfect, it has everything."

Mark nodded. "I know right." He stood up from his chair. "I'll go phone London, let them know we found a site. Wake sleeping beauty up and hand all this stuff back in."

Chapter 18

The crossing button clicked as Rajan impatiently pressed it, his childhood belief that the more presses the faster the crossing lights would change lingering well into adulthood as a habit. He stood staring at the London traffic, thick vehicular cholesterol in the arteries of the city. He stood directly across from a tall three-story building, a thin spindly thing jutting from the Islington streets squeezed between two much larger structures, a thorn between toes. It was a Georgian building, white stone and doorways flanked by columns. Long ago it had been converted from a home to an antiques shop. Each window blocked entirely by roughly stacked furniture and precarious bric-a-brac. There was a beeping and the crossing lights went green. Rajan jogged across quickly followed by Dale, each trying to clear the road in the short pedestrian unfriendly time given. Above the doorway was a hand painted sign, declaring in an elaborate cursive they had arrived at *"Johnsons' Emporium of Antiquities."*

The inside of the shop was a maze of mahogany and china. A confusing mess of blocked walkways and imposing cabinets. The two men edged their way through like explorers, ducking through a collection of low hanging glass lampshades, bursting forth from the tinkling foliage victorious. After a few minutes of meandering they arrived at a clearing in the jungle, a large desk centred within. From here the rows of objects splintered off, as though this were the centre of a spider's web. Sat behind the desk was a small elderly man. A thin ring of white hair circled his otherwise bald head, rough stalks of darker hair erupting from his ears. He wore a moth-eaten red cardigan that seemed older than some of the antiques he sold. He smiled as Rajan and Dale approached.

"George," said Rajan as he approached, he nodded at the man behind the desk.

"Detective! Such a pleasure to see you again. How can I help our fine constabulary today," said George, his voice was faint and gravely, as though his breath was dust.

"I need to procure some...objects. I was hoping you might have them." Rajan unfolded a sheet of paper he had slid from his trouser pockets. He handed it over to an eager wrinkled hand.

"Let's see, oh, well ok I most certainly can help with these," scratched Georges voice as he slipped a pair of glasses onto his face, the bridge held together with what looked to Rajan to be a medical plaster.

"That's great, we need them pretty urgently," interjected Dale. Rajan rolled his eyes.

"Oh urgently! Well why didn't you say!" exclaimed George, sensing an opportunity to squeeze some extra money from the transaction. "Some of these items, ooh, very rare, very pricey."

"Do you have them, or do we need to go see someone else?" asked Rajan. He had dealt with George before and knew the greedy little man would try and squeeze as much as he could out of the transaction.

"I have them, I think there is a transaction that could be made here to benefit both of us. Right follow me then, we'll see what we can do." George hopped out of his chair with a sprightliness that defied his age and wandered between two book cases. "Come on then, you did say urgent right?"

The shopkeeper led the two policemen across the cluttered room to a flight of stairs. The stairway filled a thin corridor its tight walls squeezing at their shoulders uncomfortably as the stairway climbed to the second floor. The second floor was much like the first, a dense collection of objects that seemed to fill every corner of the room. George navigated the stacks of chairs, wobbling vases and lacklustre art like a cat, twisting and turning to avoid baroque carvings jutting from Victorian furniture. They crossed the room slowly, the route across a circuitous nightmare. When they finally reached the other side of the room there was a large heavyset solid wood door, years of thick paint peeling away like skin. George reached inside his worn cardigan and pulled out a small brass key on a chain. He lifted the chain over his head and placed the key into the door turned it with a satisfying click. Happy, he placed the chain back over his head and slipped the key back inside his shirt.

The doorway led to another cramped staircase. Beckoning that they follow him, George led Dale and Rajan up the second stairway. When he got to the top, he stopped for a moment, made the sign of the cross over his heart and stepped across a threshold onto the third floor. Dale followed behind him.

"Jesus Christ!" he shouted. Stood immediately beside the doorway was a glass case. Within it was a desiccated corpse. Its mummified face leering at him.

"Not quite," laughed George. "That's just old Saint Edmund. Cost me a fair bit he did."

"Why do you have the remains of a saint?" asked Dale, "Where would you even get those?"

"This gentleman is one of the best wards you can get. Real power in someone like this." George tapped the glass with his knuckles. "Helps keep out...unwanted...clientele. And you don't want to know where I got him. Right, shall we get working on this list."

The third floor couldn't have been any more different from the rest of the shop. Each item placed carefully in its own glass case. A macabre collection of strange weapons, misshapen bones and unsettling carvings. It was as though a curator had gone mad and run through a museum's archives picking objects at random. A roman Gladius shared a display cabinet with a set of broken ornately carved nun chucks. Two stone tablets rested against each other, one with what Dale recognised as Egyptian hieroglyphs, the other covered in symbols he had never seen before. It was hard to imagine a more esoteric collection. In one corner of the room was a large counter, behind which were rows of jars filled with various herbs. It looked like an apothecary's had been transplanted into the building. George lifted part of the counter on its hinge and dropped it behind him. He leant on the worktop, the list Rajan had given him clutched in his hands.

"Ok so, so first thing is a haunted doll?" he asked, peering over his glasses.

"Oh, scratch that off," replied Rajan, "We managed to get one of those."

"Really? I have a cupboard full of the bloody things. Ok well, next up here is some Jagdiga. Right here we go." George grabbed a jar from the shelves, it was filled with bright purple petals. He opened the jar sprinkling some onto a large set of brass scales that rested at the far end of the counter. Pleased with the amount, he tipped the flowers into a small brown paper bag. He walked back over to the two men and set it before them. "Right that's one lot of Tibetan flowers. Ok the next thing…"

D.C.I Weston picked up a small bronze dagger form the table and turned it over in her hands. It was roughly made, its blade dulled by age, a small crack running through its misshapen hilt. She set it back down amongst the seemingly random assortment of objects that her detectives had brought back from the supplier.

"Honestly gentlemen it looks like you got taken for a ride," she said. The assembled components had cost more than the departments Christmas party budget.

"I know it doesn't look like much Ma'am," Dale admitted, carefully placing a glass jar filled with soil into an open wheeled suitcase. "This is soil from mount Sinai, that dagger is genuine Babylonian, those pebbles are Norse scrying runes the- "

"Yes, yes I get it, all very rare and apparently very expensive," she interrupted. "Still, there is bound to be some dubious legalities to some of this. We could have just confiscated the entire lot."

"We would have lost a valuable contact and supplier then though Ma'am," pointed out Dale. "That's the problem. What we deal with sometimes means we must deal with some unscrupulous characters. I mean, look who gave us the list of these items in the first place."

Florence nodded. She could remember when she was just Constable Weston, walking the streets of her local

Brighton. Things had always been so black and white since then. As she had risen in rank things had gotten noticeably greyer. Undercover stings, informants, plea deals. She chuckled to herself. Those all seemed small compared to buying probably stolen goods at the behest of the Devil. "You're right Cooper. The day it sits right with me I think is the day I need to move on I think."

"I think I agree Ma'am." Dale continued placing the items from the table into the suitcase. "You still think me, and Raj need to head down ourselves?"

"Too right I do. This whole thing has been a complete shitshow. It's getting harder and harder to spin it each day. I've had both the commissioner and the home secretary on the phone this morning. We need to get this sorted." She started at Dale, her arms crossed. He nodded nervously and began to zip up the suitcase. He knew better than to disagree with her. "I'm not thrilled with the arrangement you made either. I don't like the idea of her walking around unsupervised."

"I agreed to supervise her Ma'am, she won't be alone."

"She asked specifically for you Cooper," barked Florence. "You made a literal deal with the devil. I hate how that is the lesser of two evils right now."

"Ok, just got off the phone and they say we have a location, seems like we are good to go," declared Rajan as he stepped into the small store room he and Dale had unofficially requisitioned to store the reagents they had purchased. "Afternoon Ma'am."

"D.S Singh," said Florence, returning his reply. "All ready to go?"

"Yes Ma'am, just come to collect D.S Cooper and then we're off to the station. Curren and Holden will meet us off the train and take us to the site they have chosen."

"This needs to work Singh. These things have been loose a few days and have already racked up a shocking body count. We need to get a lid on this as quickly as possible." The tone in Florence's voice intimated that this was not a suggestion.

"Understood Ma'am," said Rajan. "The intel seems good and it's a solid plan."

"Personally Singh, speaking from experience, that any plan described as solid," mused Florence, "often transpires to be considerably wobblier than first imagined."

Claire stood staring at her handywork, proud of the carnage she had wrought. Blood trickled through her sticky fingers, thin strands of viscera splashing around her feet. She held her bloodstained hands above her head.

"Another!" she shouted. At her command another sheep carcass was dragged before her. Claire knelt, gripping the dead animal's skin and tearing it asunder with her hands. Still warm blood poured from the tear. She eagerly dipped her hands the crimson fluid and began to paint.

The building they had found was a gift. The town was full of empty warehouses and factories, casualties of decades of waning industry. Claire had led the other Jinn here after their earlier clash, eager to increase their numbers. It was perfect. Jinn were pure primal fire, creatures of flickering baleful flame. To summon them required this world own flames. A field burnt down in the night. A lighter in a bathtub. Closed, cold, but still functional a large oven had lain resting in a former bakery. Scores of sweet-smelling baked goods had once grown behind its grilled smile. Now it would simply grow the doorway between this world and another. Claire's hands danced as she painted sigils across the ovens metal shell. The runes had begun to spread across the walls. Around her the other Jinn stood silent watching. Eyes watching the body of the young girl furiously daub blood across the exposed brick, hungrily anticipating what would be soon to come.

The train rattled into the station, its brakes screeching like a wounded bird. Dale held onto the hand rail as the overcrowded train shook, finally stopping in the middle of the long platform that seemed to stretch off eternally. Dale was used to the underground, to be jammed into a crowded carriage. Even compared to that the train was packed. A single carriage that seemed to have been last updated sometime in the mid-eighties carrying the two detectives from the much larger Cardiff station. It was early evening and they had gotten caught in the daily commute, office workers dourly cramming themselves through the single double doors into the tiny cabin. Stepping onto the platform, the wheels of the suitcase clattering on the stone behind him, Dale stretched his free arm. Rajan followed, swinging his elbows in a similar attempt to stretch.

"Remind me never to complain about the tube again," said Dale.

"You mad?" spluttered Rajan. "The tube is way worse than that."

"What? No. At least the tube is designed for it. That was meant for like, thirty people tops," argued Dale as they started towards the turnstiles.

"The tube somehow manages to combine the worst of trains," stated Rajan as he slipped his train ticket into the turnstile. It swung open and he stepped through. "With the worst of public transport," he continued, turning to face Dale as he squeezed the case through his own turnstile. "I once took a tube journey where the entire trip a man played a trombone directly into my face. I will take uncomfortable silence pressed up against a stranger to wilful brass instrument abuse any day."

"I like that kind of stuff," Dale said, "it adds character."

"That's what people say when they want to describe something as shit but not outright say it. Trombones in your face is character. Uncle Jerry is really handsy with the girls, oh what a character," mocked Rajan.

"Fine but you have to admit. It is pretty London." Dale slid the extendable handle on the suitcase down and gripped the smaller rubber handle on the top. He lifted and slowly started down the impressive staircase. He took each step carefully, eager not to drop the case.

Rajan followed slowly behind him. "God, I hate London too." Rajan was on a roll. "Everyone is so rush rush. And queues! No-one queues! I tried to grab some food at a salad place and there was a scrum for the counter! In a salad place!" Rajan was clearly enjoying the chance to air his grievances now he was on the other side of the country.

"Oh, hey there they are!" Dale said quickly, eager to avoid one of Rajan's rambling rants. He hopped down the last few steps, care forgotten in an eager attempt to avoid another lecture about traffic or keeping right on the escalators. Mark and Jess were stood at the bottom of the stairs in front of a worryingly shabby looking van. A man Dale didn't recognise was leaning against the van door.

"Dale," Mark said stepping forward and shaking Dales hand. He grabbed Rajan's as he reached the bottom of the steps. "This is Constable Aasif Rhaman, he's a local who's been helping with our investigation."

"Pleased to meet you." Dale placed the suitcase on the ground and shook the man's hand.

"Likewise, want to get that in the van?" Aasif pointed at the suitcase.

"Yeah, that's a good idea," agreed Mark. He grabbed the door and pulled it open, revealing the hastily spray-painted symbols on the back door. "Oh, uh..."

"Uh what?" said Aasif as he lifted the suitcase. "Oh. Uh is right I guess." Atop the still closed trunk was the Isabella doll. It was sat upright as though it had been posed that way. "That was inside the case wasn't it?"

"Inside its own box, inside the case," added Mark.

"We better put it back then," Aasif said, trying to remain as calm as possible.

Mark raised his eyebrows awkwardly. "Agreed."

"This is perfect." Rajan was carrying a cardboard box that had been filled with small jars. It was as much black seed oil as Jess could buy. After buying out the Chinese medicine shops remaining stock she had traipsed around trying to find more before stumbling across a small quantity in a hardware store that the owner was all too eager to part with, it having sat unwanted, covered in a thin layer of dust. Rajan span around, box cradled in his arms as he took in the building they had found. It was an old office building, four floors of open plan areas. The ceiling was thick foam tiles studded with old style metal sprinklers. There were two main entrances in the front and the back meaning which would make what they needed to do easier Rajan set down his box next to the rest of the supplies.

"Yeah it should do the job," agreed Jess. "Can't help but feel that calling all the super dangerous spirits into once place might not be a super chill idea." She pulled a deliberately exaggerated face, her eyes squinting, lips pursed. "But you know, got to try something." She held up her hands, palms pointed at the sky.

"How did you find how to do all this?" asked Aasif as he took a jar of honey from one of the boxes, checked it and placed it back, trying to find the one that was responsible for the small stain on the bottom of the box.

"A contact, she gave us the list of components and instructions on the spell." Rajan leant against a beige wall, a puff of dust being knocked free as his back hit the plasterboard.

"What kind of contacts have you guys got that give you lists with creepy dolls and weird objects on them? What happened to fun contacts like who to buy a slightly used PlayStation off." Aasif found the culprit jar. He removed it from the box and set down on the frayed lilac carpet tiles that filled the building.

"The devil. She's an arse but she knows her stuff," Dale chimed in.

"Come on Dale, that's not something you should go around announcing.!" Jess stood with one hand on her hip, her eyes burning with disapproval.

"He'll find out soon enough. One of us now." Dale swung his arm over Aasif's shoulder. "Better start looking for a flat in London now, that shit is expensive."

"Dale!" Jess shouted.

"No, it's fine, I figured as much." Aasif shrugged his shoulders. "When you described what happened to you it kind of clicked. It's not like you can actively recruit for this sort of thing, right? So, a copper who comes across this stuff is really your best bet."

"He's good this one!" laughed Dale, tapping Aasif hard on the back.

"Yeah he put two and two together," added Rajan, "makes him a better detective than you." He laughed heartily at his own joke.

"It's ok. You know every morning I get up early, go for a run. No-one else is around, the sun is rising. Its serene, almost beautiful. I love it. But really that's all I love. Mum died when I was little, Dad a few years ago. No other close family, I live alone. That run is all I live for. Day after day. Doing this, doing all this weird stuff. It's helping people. I mean really helping people. Not breaking up fighting drunks or removing junkies from the park. Actual real meaningful help. I think, maybe, that's something worth getting up every day for besides the running." Aasif sat there for a moment, the room silent from his stark admission. "So, the devil is a woman?"

"Well," began Mark, "the devil is a powerful primal entity. If she wants to be a woman this millennium that's up to her."

Rajan chuckled. "She would very much like to also be more, shall we say, acquainted with Cooper. You won't believe what we agreed too for all this help."

Chapter 19

Mark held his phone in his hand, torchlight shining down onto the rooftop below him. He was crouched on his knees spray paint can in his other hand. It hissed like a scared cat as he slowly and carefully copied the sigils from the picture on his phone. Opposite him Rajan did the same, the cramped roof becoming increasingly difficult to manoeuvre on. Each man stepped awkwardly, eager to avoid the wet paint, each grateful that for once the skies were clear. The hiss from the can collapsed into a rattle as it began to run dry. Rajan stood up, admiring his work.

"Toss me that can if you're done?" said Mark, shaking his own with a clack to show it was empty. He set it down and caught Rajan's can as it sailed through the air to him.

"I recognise maybe, a quarter of these? If that?" Rajan waved the small pocket torch he had brought over the rooftop. They had been up there for hours, meticulously marking out the spell work as instructed. Four stories up meant the wind chilled them through, its piercing gale meaning they had to cling close to the flat grey concrete roof of the office block to use the spray paint they had bought.

"I know what you mean," Mark replied, finishing the odd jagged spiral he had been painting. "I've only seen some of this stuff in our archive. Specifically, in the kind of books we keep in the vault." Rajan nodded in reply. At the heart of the Special Investigations archive lay a large metal vault door, the kind you normally only saw in heist movies. A firearms officer always stood guard; even getting in required special permission from Weston. Once inside each book was stored in its own safe deposit. Carefully inscribed runes etched into the metal struggling to keep the books contained. More than once a book had ended up in a detective's bag without them realising, as if the books wanted to leave. They had taken to chaining each book to its deposit box.

Rajan shuddered. "I hate going in there, I swear last time I could hear whispering."

"Yeah, it's a little worrying we're using that kind of magic honestly," admitted Mark. "Plus, I know we don't have much choice, but what is the chance that Lucille is double crossing us?"

Rajan laughed. "I am one hundred percent sure she is double crossing us."

"I'm not double crossing them," said Lucille. She was laying half on her bed, legs planted to the ground, arms outstretched.

"Really? You actually gave them the for real spell they needed?" Abbie took a sip of her tea. She placed the small china up back down on the minuscule kitchens worktop and added another spoonful of sugar. "You're becoming a soft touch."

Lucille sighed. "Maybe? I just figured I let our kind try and they clearly ballsed it up. Time to give the humans a chance."

"They don't have much of a chance though. It's real likely they will all die." Abbie leant her elbows on the back of the sofa, cup and saucer held in her hands.

"Always so downbeat. It wouldn't kill you to look on the brighter side of life occasionally." Lucille lifted herself up, perching herself on the edge of the bed.

"Life? We spend all day running a dive bar in some London back alley. We used to be kings." Abbie took a long sip of her tea with a disgusting slurping noise. "I had everything all ready to go, locusts ready to fly. You know how long it takes to train a swarm of locusts? Hundreds of years down the drain because someone bottled it when it came to showtime."

"Hey!" complained Lucille clearly insulted. "I joined your open mic night didn't I. I clearly have no problems with stage fright."

"Nice of you to twist my words."

"And you said I was losing my touch." Lucille stretched out a toothy smile.

"Ha Ha," replied Abbie, her voice a mocking monotone. "I'm not being fair. I made the choice to join you in this. I just imagined my life being more destroyer king, less IPA recommendations."

"You are pretty good at that though. Business has been picking up lately. The open mic nights are helping a ton. We've sold a bunch of tickets for that gig next weekend."

"That's a problem though. We can only really ever stay small. We're supposed to be laying low. I'm amazed you got them to agree to let you run a bar in the first place." Abbie placed her empty teacup in the sink. She opened a cupboard and removed an unopened packet of chocolate covered hob nobs. She peeled open the packet and offered it to Lucille who eagerly took one.

"Well, I was always good at making a deal," said Lucille. She took a bite of the biscuit. "Plus, I've been working on the small things," she continued her voice muffled by the mouthful of biscuit. "If everything works out business should pick up."

Jess placed her phone back into her pocket, a tear running down her cheek. She took a deep breath, making the recording had taken a lot out of her emotionally. She always felt drained recording the messages she did, and always felt like a great weight had been lifted when she deleted them. Every time she thought she might die Jess had taken the time to record a message for her wife and child. She had recorded dozens, and each time it got a little easier to do. That thought terrified her. Composing herself she returned to her part of the plan. Her jacket had been lain carefully on the floor, her shirt sleeves rolled up past the elbow. Jess was within a small maintenance room on the top floor. A web of pipes surrounded her, leading into a large metal tank. The lid of the tank was set aside, leaning up against the wall. Four men and not even one had held a wrench in their lives. Jess was suddenly very grateful for the time in her fathers' workshop as a girl. He had been a great believer in practical skills, his tutelage proving extremely useful when Jess and Hannah had bought their home. She reached down, picking up one of the jars of honey. The lid popped off with a twist, the thick liquid dropping in globs into the water below.

Shauna sat behind the desk. Light from her computer screen danced over her face. "*Top ten most shocking talent show moments*" played on YouTube. A man was swallowing a sword. Shauna was thoroughly unimpressed. Before joining the police, Shauna had briefly considered applying for a major television talent show. As a Ghula she could easily perform feats that most humans considered dangerous. She could push the sword right through herself if she wanted to. She had decided against it after a friend ran afoul of a monster hunter, the resulting investigation convincing her to try and help people with her life. A few months later and she was training to be join the force. She couldn't really complain. She didn't sleep so was able to rack up a considerable amount of overtime, she only ate rotting meat so was able to buy in bulk from her local butcher at frankly criminally low prices, and her dark skin dealt with the normal ghula problem of being a little pale that for most consumed prodigious amounts of makeup. Normally she was happy to take the night shift, but her company was proving frustrating.

"No updates yet Sargent?" Asked Florence. She had been emerging from her office periodically to check, creeping out from the single beacon of light on the far side of the dark.

"Nothing yet Ma'am," said Shauna quickly minimising the video.

"Ok, well, let me know if there is anything." Florence tugged at the collar of her blouse nervously.

Shauna sighed. "Are you ok Ma'am?" She regretted asking immediately.

"Well," Florence grabbed a wheeled desk chair and pulled it over. "Not really. Something about this just doesn't sit right. Too many things could go wrong. I'll tell you this Shauna, woman to woman. You always worry about your friends, and it only gets worse the higher up you get, it becomes more and more your fault then."

Shauna was a little shocked at the word friends. Florence Weston was an efficient boss, but frankly could be cold and was generally regarded as a bit of a battle-axe.

Shauna wasn't sure any of her colleagues would describe Florence as friend. "I would have thought hard choices come with the territory Ma'am?"

"Well of course, that goes without saying." For a moment the stern commanding officer had returned. "Doesn't make it any easier though," Florence admitted, her serious face morphing into one more akin to a worried schoolmarm.

"I think, maybe, we need to just sometimes admit to ourselves we can't control everything. Worry about what you do have control over. Go home, get some sleep, worrying here isn't going to help anyone." Shauna worried she was being a little too candid with her boss.

"I think you're perhaps right," admitted Florence. "Still I'll stay here if it's all the same. What video were you watching?"

"Video Ma'am?" Shauna's denial would have gotten her a middling grade in high school drama.

"Oh, come on, I could see it as I walked over." Florence scooted the desk chair around to the other side of the desk, the awkward motion of pulling herself on her heels more suited to a toddler than a Detective Chief Inspector of the Metropolitan Police.

Shauna clicked on her internet browser to maximise the window again. "It's talent acts."

"Oh!" said Florence excitedly. "I love this show, click play!"

Aasif shut the Quran with a thud. He was standing beside Jess, who had finished placing the last of the honey and black seed oil into the tank. She picked up the metal lid and heaved it onto back atop the tank, a high-pitched squeal of metal on metal.

"Think that will be enough?" asked Aasif, taking a curious peek into the tank before the lid dropped down into place.

"It kind of has to be. This is a pretty all in plan." Jess tapped the lid on the tank, satisfied it had settled closed. "That happens a little too often for my liking."

"Oddly, that fills me with a little bit more confidence." Aasif held the Quran in both hands, staring at the cover.

"Really? I wouldn't of thought that," Jess said rolling down her sleeves.

"Yeah, well you're still around aren't you?" asked Aasif. He slipped the Quran into the inside pocket of the tracksuit jacket he was wearing causing one side to sag with the weight. There was a knocking on the door to the maintenance room. Dale leant halfway through the threshold.

"You guys ready?" he asked. A chain was wrapped around his hand. It jangled as he moved.

"Yeah, sure," said Jess, slipping on her suit jacket. "Time to face the music."

Shauna stood silhouetted against the doorway. The shining light pouring from the doorway of Florence's office striking out into the dark office beyond. Florence sat behind her desk, terrible royalty free music playing from the YouTube video she was watching. Florence had sat with Shauna for a bit, and then retired to her own office suddenly very cognisant of how awkward it must have been.

"Ma'am, I've just head from the guys in the field. Everything is ready, and they are proceeding with their plan," declared Shauna. She held a print out in her hands of the message, but it felt largely pointless, being only a sentence long. She handed it over to Florence, a wasteful slice of police bureaucracy. Florence took it, glanced at it briefly and set it down on her desk.

"I think," she began, "that I could use a drink." There was a clink as she pulled a glass decanter from beneath her desk. She reached back under and pulled out two small matching tumblers. "You know, I keep this stuff here for when the top brass visit." She poured out two small measures of a thin brown liquid. It smelt like wood stain. "Can't much stand it myself. It's a little too old boys club for me. But, right now, it feels like the right thing to do." She lifted one of the glasses and handed it to Shauna who took it politely. To her alcohol tasted overwhelmingly like paint stripper, her poor sense of taste one of the prices she paid being a ghula.

"Thank you, Ma'am. I'm sure they've been in worse situations before." It felt like a lie coming out.

"I'm not sure any life-threatening situation is really worse than another. Ask a man falling off a cliff how he feels, and I don't think it would differ from someone on the firing squad." Florence swirled her glass, staring at the small vortex that had formed in the whisky.

"Thanks for the drink Ma'am." Shauna set the glass back down on the table. "I, uh, better get back to the desk. In case they call."

"Right, right." Florence set her own glass down, the whisky undrunk. "Thank you, Shauna. That will be all."

The five of them stood atop the roof of the derelict office. The wind was starting to pick up, the threat of the towns ever present rain hanging over their heads. Mark held his grey woollen coat tight against him. The air smelt acrid from the still damp spray paint.

"Ok we all know what to do?" asked Jess.

"Yeah, I'll head over to the other side of the street keep watch," replied Rajan. He zipped up his own thin black jacket and headed down the stairs.

"Ok, kiddo, we got gate duties," Dale tapped Aasif on the shoulder, holding out a set of dark brown chains.

"Guess that leaves us with the dangerous part," shrugged Jess.

"Wouldn't have it any other way," smiled Mark.

Slowly and carefully Jess and Mark began the ritual. In the centre of the rooftop was a large stone bowl in which the varied flowers and herbs the spell demanded had been ground by mortar into a fine powder. Shards of bone, their source Mark decided was best left unknown jutted from the green paste, proud towers rising from a mire. The mixture smelt foul, it stank of death and decay, something perverting the normally fragrant ingredients. Jess placed her sleeve over her nose and placed a handful of small stones their surfaces carved with runes into the bowl. They sank slightly in the paste, sitting amongst it like marshmallows in the words worst breakfast cereal.

"Ok, ready for the next step?" Mark asked, grabbing a small wooden box from by the entrance to the stairwell. He placed it down next to the mixture.

"I guess so," Jess said, pulling a small sheathed dagger from her pocket. She slid the blade free from its cover. It was dulled bronze, worn with incalculable age. "Ready when you are."

"Aasif really go inside my head with this thing." Mark opened the box revealing the doll nestled inside. He gripped it, holding it up under its arms like a messy toddler. Jess held the ancient knife in her hands and thrust, stabbing the blade deep into the doll. It screamed, a horrible echoing roar of defiance. The doll began to thrash about, kicking its arms and legs furiously as Mark struggled to hold it. Its motions became less fluid, shifting from rapid rage to slow methodical ticking movements. The dolls head began to list, it coughed, a bubble of dark red blood forming at its lips. As suddenly as it began the wailing screech stopped, and the doll hung lifeless, a simple toy once more. Mark tossed it into the bowl gingerly, like a new parent disposing of a used nappy.

"Well, that was fucking terrifying. This whole case has been a cavalcade of nightmare material," Jess said, leaning over the bowl, carefully watching for more movement from the doll.

"You know what's scarier? That it probably won't give me nightmares, that I'm starting to become desensitised to all the darkness we deal with." Mark tipped the shredded paper from the box into the bowl. He pulled a lighter from his trouser pocket, an ornate silver thing with detailed etching on both sides. Mark had never smoked in his life, but a lighter had proved repeatedly useful and he had deliberately purchased an expensive one in a misguided attempt to appear flashy. He flicked open the open and click twice on the wheel. He leant down and touched the flame to the shredded paper. It caught alight easily, joyfully bursting into an eager flame. Thick acrid smoke began to rise from the bowl as the plants within joined the fire, causing it to erupt into an impressive blaze. The head of the doll began to melt, one of its eyes turned to liquid, running down its face to mix with the still wet blood that stained its mouth. "Ok, here," he said tossing the lighter across to Jess. "You're up next. You sure about this?"

"Not really?" she admitted.

Claire smiled as she worked, painting her macabre display. She laughed as she worked, splashing the still warm lambs' blood in great sigils around the imposing oven. Around her the newer Jinn stood and watched admiring the work, taking in the deftly woven primal magics. The murmur started slowly at first, a faint ringing in the ears. Slowly moment by moment it grew, the faint upset in the crowd becoming a loud roar. The ringing grew stronger, its lure becoming overwhelming. It was like the earlier summons, but it felt different, more unstable its magic less refined. Slowly, one by the one the crowd drifted, lured by the siren song. Claire stood up, her hands still sticky with blood. She turned and raised her hands in the air.

"Brothers and sisters. Again, we are summoned. Again, they wish to challenge us. Let's go say hello," Claire shouted. Eagerly, and as one, the crowd began to run. A tidal wave of rage, avarice, of unchecked id made manifest, they surged from the building. They had been summoned, and they would answer.

Chapter 20

Rajan sat across the street from the office building they had chosen. He was sat in a separate office building. It was taller but the way it was constructed wasn't conductive to the plan. This whole area of town was full of three or four-story buildings, built initially to try and bring jobs to the area. It hadn't worked, the nearby Cardiff proving to be just too popular and convenient. Rajan leant back in the creaky office chair he had found left on the empty office floor, a straggler from a mass exodus. In his hands he held a pair of binoculars bought in a hasty trip to a local hardware store. They had proven next to useless, the dark setting in much earlier than Rajan had expected. He lifted them to his eyes, peering out of them anyway, scanning points of light in the dark. There! Movement! A second shadow followed the first, followed by another. Flashing shapes beneath the street lamps. He lifted his walkie talkie from the floor, a loaner from an unhappy station commander. He pressed the switch and there was a short burst of static.

"Raj to everyone, I spot movement. Hard to tell numbers but it's a lot. They're coming in real fast. Get ready everyone. Over." He released the button.

"Got it Raj," buzzed Mark from over the radio. "Looks like the beacon spell is working. We're ready here over."

"Dale here, me and Aasif are in position. Good luck everyone, over," crackled a third voice.

Rajan crouched down, trying to minimise his shadow against the window. The office was dark, but he was eager not to give the game away. They would only get one shot at this.

The Jinn burst out from backstreets, from within shadows and from hidden nooks each eager to reach the keening call in their heads. It pounded at their skulls, the piercing ring threatening to burst forth the closer they got. It was a curious mix of incredible pain and overwhelming ecstasy that called them. At this moment, each Jinn desired only one thing, to be close to the beacon. This one was different, a curious untempered thing, the work of hands not used to crafting such delicate magic. The demon's song was subtle, a gentle invite to attend, a polite request drifting across the winds. This one screamed by contrast, an angry demand bellowed as an order. The Jinn scrambled to enter the building, pushing against each other, almost crushing themselves in the glass doorway to the building. It had swung open, no one questioning the fact it was unlocked. They poured into the building like hungry ants, a wild herd of pure abandon. Except for one. Walking slowly, purposefully behind the swarm was a single Jinn, her long red dress torn, her body battered, bruised, and burnt. She stood, waiting patiently for the crush to end, there was plenty of the night left.

Rajan watched from above, in awe at the frenzy below. A tide of people pressing against each other normally reserved for panic news reports about American black Friday sales. There was one who stood out, a young girl standing calmly waiting for the furore to pass. From the description it could only be Claire, the first Jinn, the seed at the heart of the chaos before her. With a great heave the last of the frenzied Jinn collapsed through the doorway. The majority of the crowd had moved on, scrambling over the buildings security barriers and disappearing inside, heading towards the stairs that formed the spine of the building. Claire followed, running her hand across the glass of the door as she strolled past it. Rajan clicked the button on his radio.

"They're in. Looks like, fifty of them maybe? Perhaps more. Claire is here. Be warned most of the crowd seems pretty crazy but she isn't, something different about her. From how mad they looked I would guess we got them all. They really want to get up to that roof. Over." The walkie clicked as Raj released the button.

"Got it Raj," said Jess, her voice wavering in the static. "Dale, Aasif, you're up boys."

Aasif nodded to Dale and together they leapt out of the back of the van. It had been parked directly in front of the office, the two men sat in the back, hiding ready to pounce. They each held a large iron chain, wrapped around an arm.

"You get the front, I'll get the rear fire exit," whispered Dale, taking off in the opposite direction. He jogged awkwardly, trying not to make noise with the heavy chain.

Aasif, stepped carefully towards the front door. He leant out slowly, trying to get as good look inside the reception of the building. Being spotted now would spoil the whole thing. He waited a moment, and satisfied, tiptoed slowly over to the open glass doors. He stepped deliberately and carefully into the reception. The security barriers hung off, broken by the weight of the Jinn pressing against them. He took a nervous breath and got to work.

He gently closed the doors, one at a time, taking care to not make any more noise than strictly necessary. The chain made it awkward, its weight causing his shoulder to throb. The doors closed, he slipped the chain from his shoulder and began to wind it around the door handles. Pulling the chain tight with a clank, he pulled an iron padlock from his pocket. Aasif had imagined it to be some elaborate Victorian thing with a long thing key. He had been surprised to have been presented with a small lock that looked like a black box with a bar, a set of combination dials running along the bottom. Apparently, they were still common. He slipped the bar through the links of the chain and snapped it shut. He finished his job with a line of iron filings supplied from one of the black pouches stuffed into his pockets. Pleased with his work, he shuddered at the next part. With trepidation, he walked further into the office building, following the path the Jinn had taken.

Aasif let out a sigh of relief as he pulled himself into the store cupboard on the first floor they had designated as his rendezvous with Dale. The tall detective, his short cropped blonde hair dripping with sweat leant against the wall. He pulled out his phone and began to type. He held it up in front of Aasif.

"Everything good?" it read. Aasif pulled out his own phone and typed a reply.

"All done. I set a line of iron in front of it too." Dale gave him a thumbs up, pleased with the initiative the constable had shown. Each man turned to face the doorway to the supply cupboard. Silently waiting, willing their colleagues to succeed.

The horde continued its ascent, trampling up the stairs with a thunderous din. The stairs shook with the weight of their footsteps, a pounding overwhelming beat, like a storm crashing against a window. Onwards and upwards they climbed, pulled inextricably to the beacon burning brightly in their minds. The Jinn wearing Martins meat, thrashed his head, sniffing the air as he clambered up the stairs, his hands gripping the steps as her bounded on all fours. The beacon was filling all his senses, its cry overriding everything else. He pushed his way through the crowd, the younger weaker Jinn giving way as he forced his way through. The crowd rushed past the exit doorways to each floor, determined to climb as high and as close as possible to the beacons source. Reaching the top of the stairway, Martin threw a wooden door open. Human flesh poured from the doorway into the office floor. The barren floor loomed large, an arena of plasterboard and bad carpeting. He stopped his run, trying to hold himself desperately in check. The other Jinn filled in behind him, forming a tight wall of bodies. Their chests heaved with heavy breaths, their bodies crouched ready to pounce into another run. At the other side of the room was a woman. Tall with a thin pointed face, her blazing red hair pulled tight into a ponytail. In one hand she held a clump of rags wrapped tightly around a wooden table leg. It stank of petrol. In the other hand she held a silver lighter, its cap flipped open. She cast a long shadow, a nearby streetlamp filling the floor with a dull light.

The crowd parted, as Claire stepped calmly from within. She took a few steps forward from the throng, taking up a position a few yards from Jess. The teenager's body was broken. Cauterised wounds covered her face and body. Great gashes had been torn from dress, it was different from the one Jess had seen before, a full-length maxi dress, vivid red with deep pockets on each side.

"Fancy seeing you again," Jess said smiling sarcastically.

"It was only a matter of time really, you were never going to let this go, were you?" asked Claire. Jess shook her head.

"That's not what we do. This stops right here, right now." Jess shook her shoulders, readying herself.

"We? So, there's more of you? Is that lovely gentleman you were with the other day here? No, no there's more than that. Bold of you to cast that beacon spell. Where did you learn that by the way?" Claire examined her nails, ignoring the bloodstains that ran to her elbows.

"I got my sources," answered Jess coyly. "I don't suppose if I arrest you that you'll all come quietly?" As one the pack of Jinn burst into a horrible throaty chorus of laughter.

"No, no you're right, we wouldn't. You couldn't even if you wanted. Angels and demons fall before us. Humans are nothing, fleshly little upstarts walking around like they own the place. We were here long before you," said Claire with a sneer.

"And yet you need us to walk around, be your little taxis around town."

"A temporary arrangement," replied Claire, her words filled with venom. "Until I find a more permanent solution. It's so easy by the way, all we need to do is promise to right their wrongs and they just invite us right in." Claire cracked a toothy grin.

"I don't think any of these people would want someone dead. Did you tell them that before you barged your way in?" Jess was shouting, Claire's attitude angering her.

"Well, not everything involved a death, a fixed car here, a finished book there. Your kind do have a unique capacity for hatred though. But no, we just said we would fix things. You know your kind has some legends of us as bumbling blue idiots trapped in lamps granting wishes. I suppose we do grant wishes when you think about it. Be careful what you wish for and all that." Claire let out a deep chuckle.

"I'm going to give you one warning," declared Jess. "Release your hosts and return to your void."

"Or what!? You'll burn us with your little torch?" screamed Claire. "Girl fire is nothing to us, we are fire, the primal heat at the birth of the universe. You are kindling before us!"

"Fire I'll give you, but every bit of lore, everything I've seen declares Jinn to be a smokeless flame."

"So! We are pure, elemental flames of the highest order!"

"Exactly," Jess said. "It's the smoke I want."

With a click Jess flicked the flint wheel, the lighter sparking to life. She touched the tiny flame to the makeshift torch and it roared into life. The flame was hotter than Jess expected, the petrol-soaked rag burning with a violent hunger. Thick black smoke began to rise from the dirty cloth and Jess thrust the torch high above her head, a blazing trophy in the gloom. The smoke wafted upwards, spreading out across the ceiling. In an instant there was the ringing of a bell, a pulsing message bellowed by the fire alarm. Jess waited, the split second for what came next stretching out into an eternity. There was a dull rumble at first as unused valves creaked open, water cascading through pipes that had been dry for years. Like a typhoon the water burst forth, pouring from the sprinklers that dotted the building.

Finding the right kind of building was important. It couldn't have been too old, or it wouldn't have had the sprinklers at all. Too new and it likely wouldn't have a reservoir, newer buildings drawing directly from the mains more efficiently. They also needed to ensure the sprinklers covered every section of the building, so not to miss any Jinn. The idea had been formed once they had the beacon spell. They had the cheese, now they needed the mousetrap.

The water, blessed by the Quran, mixed with blackseed oil and honey poured onto the Jinn. They writhed in agony on the ground, steam rising from their skin as the water splashed down on them. One Jinn screeched, a gout of flame fighting its way free from the host only to meet more water, winking out of existence with a puff of black smoke. Another broke forth, then another. Each now empty host lay on the floor, steam no longer rising from them. It was working, slowly each Jinn was being banished, the torrent of blessed water freeing their captives. All but one. Claire stood perfectly still, her eyes fixed on Jess. Steam poured from her skin, red welts starting to form as the heat began to burn it. She screamed, and ran at Jess, launching into a dive that struck her in the chest, the now sodden torch clattering to the ground.

"I will rip off your skin and wear you like a cape as I kill your friends!" shouted Claire. She had gripped Jess by the shoulders, knees pressed to her chest. She pulled her forward and slammed her into the carpet. "You think this will work on me! There is no girl left in here anymore, I suffocated her soul, slowly, snubbed it out like a cigarette! This body is mine now! No possession to break!" She slammed Jess into the ground again. "Blessed water, how clever. But I too am blessed! Blessed by fire, blessed by the forces of creation itself!" Jess writhed in pain, she was finding it difficult to breath. She strained, reached down towards her pocket. "Struggle woman! It will only make your death more satis- "Claire grunted as Jess struck her in the side of the head with a baton. A thin burn ran alongside her head, another wound for the collection. She turned, coming up to a crouch eager to resume her attack but Jess was too quick, bringing the baton around in a wide arc. The second strike hit Claire in the jaw, the sicking smell of burning flesh filling the air as the impact burnt her again. She tumbled to the floor, rolling herself away before righting herself.

"Iron baton," said Jess. She waved the baton with one hand, the other held her bruised side. "Normally we use these for fairies and the like but seeing as you have an aversion to it too. Never can be too careful."

"Fuck you," spat Claire.

"Now that's not nice. At least this way I get to arrest you. Entity possessing Claire, I am arresting you on suspicion of murder, kidnapping- "stared Jess, removing a set of iron handcuffs from the waist band of her trousers. Claire held up her hands, small balls of blue fire rested on her palms.

"Stop, or I'll incinerate you!" Claire threatened.

"Not likely, there are dispel scrolls stored under the ceiling tiles on this and every floor, plus what I have on my person. Remember last time?"

"You're right," sneered Claire, "I do remember last time." She drew had hands together before her lips and blew.

The blast shook the building across the street, the powerful magic losing its coherency. From his vantage point across the street Rajan watched as the windows on the third floor opposite shattered, the form of a young girl crashing through the glass. Her body struck a streetlamp denting it from the force. She hit the ground awkwardly, her leg twisting around as it did. Bone burst forth from her skin, blood splattering across the pavement. To Rajan's amazement the girl stood up, and began limping away down the street, the bone in her leg sliding up and down as she walked. He stood up from his seated position on the carpet and ran to the lift doors across the floor behind him. He slammed the button over and over, frantically waiting for the lift to slide its way to his floor.

"Holy shit are you ok?" Mark put one hand on Jess' shoulder. She was soaked through from the sprinklers. One arm on her jacket had torn at the shoulder. A bruise peaked out from under her shirt.

"I think so? Bit bruised and battered. Crazy thing deliberately cast a spell to blow out the fucking window. Good thing I had a little distance from her. Fuck. "Jess slid to the floor, holding tight to her side. "She got a good few licks in. Nothings broken. Few days and I'll be good." They were stood at the doorway that led to the small access stairs on the roof. The chain that had sealed it shut lay on the floor.

"You guys...ok?" Aasif panted as he emerged from around the corner. "God, I fucking hate stairs."

"Don't you go running?" laughed Jess.

"Not up and down stairs I don't. You should see dale, he's still a floor down. I notice we have a bunch of sleeping beauties. It worked right?" Like Jess Aasif was soaked through. The sprinklers had stopped for now. The sodden carpet squelched as Aasif took a seat next to Jess.

"We didn't get all of them. Claire, the first one. She seemed immune. Mentioned something about ousting Claire's, the real Claire's soul and owning the body." Jess pulled at the torn sleeve ripping it free from the jacket completely. She tossed it across the room.

"Guess that makes sense," mused Mark. He leant against the doorframe. "If the water frees you from possession, if she owns the body outright, is it still possession?"

"Nine tenths of the law I guess," Jess said, smiling nervously at her own joke. "We better call the locals, get these people to the hospital."

Jess and Dale sat on the small step leading up to the back of the ambulance, their bodies covered with a silver blanket that crackled as they moved. Aasif was leaning on the side of the ambulance, wrapping himself tightly with a similar blanket.

"We're going with the chemical spill cover story. That normally works. The handful that are awake don't seem to remember anything, which is a mercy I guess," said Mark, the cold night starting to get to him even though he was the only one who had remained dry, his final fall-back position meaning he had spent the night on the roof.

"Any sign of Raj?" Dale asked.

"When you say it like that you almost sound worried," answered Rajan, stepping around from the other side of the ambulance.

"Where did you vanish off too?" Dales eyes narrowed at him.

"I saw our girl fall from the third floor and start taking off. When I got to the bottom floor she was gone, can't have gotten far, her leg was all messed up. Thought I might be able to find her."

"I'm guessing you didn't," said Mark.

"You are right, even with that smashed leg she was a nippy little thing."

"That's ok," interjected Jess. "We just need to find my phone."

"Sorry? You and phones never mix," Mark said, turning to face her.

"Ha-ha very funny. No, I noticed something about her. Her dress had pockets," Jess bounced excitedly as she spoke.

"So, pockets?" Mark asked bemused. "What of them."

"My sister is always moaning about pockets. Girls don't get them much apparently," Dale said.

"Dales right, we don't. But her dress had them. I slipped my phone in whilst she was on me. So, we just need to find my phone, you know, with a laptop or something. Use the anti-theft thing to track it." Jess smiled, pleased that losing her phone was on purpose this time.

"Well then," said Rajan. "Thank god for dresses with pockets."

Chapter 21

The pain was near unbearable, even to Claire, the spirit within angrily trying to rewire its hosts brain to block it out. The thigh bone breaching the skin glistened wet with blood under the dim street lamps. She limped onwards, the office block and its shattered window disappearing into the night behind her. Claire cursed under her breath. She had wandered straight into that trap, arrogant of her own power. As she walked she stared down at her hands, a vivid crimson stained bright with blood. She barged off into the night, stamping angrily, blood spurting from her leg in an arc as she moved.

Three detectives squeezed themselves around the tiny outdated laptop. The web browser painstakingly and slowly loading the page. Jess' leg twitched impatiently, bouncing the laptop around. Mark and Rajan sat on either side of her. Mark was holding his phone into the air, desperately trying to get a better signal for the phones Wi-Fi hotspot. Rajan, as impatient as ever, was trying to load the same site on his phone.

"Aha!" said Jess. "We're in. Ok um…"

"Um? What do you mean um?" Mark asked, his eyebrow raised.

"It's nothing, nothing, just need to remember my password for it."

"Can't you just reset it?" added Rajan.

"Uh, no, the email I used I don't use anymore, and the password resets for that go to my other email which I normally access through my phone so..." replied Jess timidly. She made the same awkward half shrug half smile that her daughter had made when she had been caught stealing cookies.

"That would be typical, foiled by you forgetting your own password." Mark shot Jess a disappointed look. "Didn't you write it down in one of your notebooks?"

"No, that's data security one-oh-one. Don't write down your passwords." Jess held the laptop tight to her lap, glaring at Mark over her shoulder.

"Come on everyone writes them down. Most people's phone contacts are ninety percent passwords and pin numbers," Rajan said, placing his own phone into the pocket of his trousers.

"Yeah and you write down everything in your notebooks," continued Mark. "You have loggers in the Amazon sending you thank you letters over the paper you use, and this is the one thing you don't write down?"

"Look, you know I just listened at all those data protection seminars you know," objected Jess. "Anyway, lets at least try. Ok so Lana one two three, there we go! In!"

"You're joking right?" asked Mark.

The old metal double doors of the disused bakery slammed open as Claire hobbled through. The building was dark, the great oven unlit, its metal form looking in the shadows. Through curdled rune and bloodstained sigil Claire stepped, forward towards the towering appliance, its metal grill bared like fangs. Lain before it was a sheep's carcass, its stomach torn open. Its innards spilled across the door, glistening in the faint moonlight creeping through the building's high windows. The corpse lay in a pool of blood, long since dried past the point of usefulness. Holding her side Claire limped over to a large ramp which descended to a metal rolling shutter. It was a remnant of the building's past, the place where lorries would have backed in to be loaded with baked goods. Now it was a charnel house, filled with the bodies of sheep stolen from the surrounding valleys. Claire grunted as she gripped one by the foreleg and dragged it up the concrete ramp to the bakery floor. She knelt, her exposed bone tearing further at her flesh. With a thrust she jabbed her hand into the soft sheep's stomach and began to tear apart its skin.

A tiny green dot flashed on the map, blinking happily as it finally settled on a location. It was shockingly close, a small building that a cursory Google search revealed to be a former bakery. Jess grinned at the screen.

"We got her, she's only a few streets over. Come on let's go." Jess leapt up and immediately regretted it, doubling over and releasing a long hissing noise.

"You aren't going anywhere," said Mark, easing Jess back down onto the ambulances step. "She did a right number on you. Sit this one out."

"Fat fucking chance. I need to see this through, make sure it's over," objected Jess. She set the laptop down next to her and slipped off the silver emergency blanket. "I'm coming with."

"Don't think we're going to convince her otherwise," said Rajan, "we should let her come, as long as she stays in the van."

"Oh, I can stay in the van, can I? Tell me sir, may I also vote? Would you like me to shine your shoes whilst I'm at it?" Jess stared at him, her eyes piercing daggers. Rajan sighed.

"You know I didn't mean that," he said. "Just don't want you to get hurt even worse."

"I agree with Raj. If you come you stay in the Van, be our getaway driver in case we need to make a hasty retreat. You'll be safe but also useful, sound good?" Mark crossed his arms and narrowed his eyes at Jess.

"Christ, I feel like a teenager again, trying to argue curfew with my parents. Fine, I'll stay in the van." Jess stood up and stretched her arms. A sharp pain ran across her side. She winced. "Go get Aasif and Dale, we need to get a move on"

"What's going to happen to all these people?" Aasif asked as he waved off one of the other constables from his station. He turned away, walking back towards the ambulances, Dale locked in step.

"Well that depends," mused Dale. "It's up to the prosecutor really."

"There's a special prosecutor?"

"Oh yeah," replied Dale, twisting past a paramedic. "We have a prosecutor, a handful of judges. Not many, it's going to take a long time to work through all these possible cases."

"Possible?" questioned Aasif.

"Well it depends on what each Jinn did for each person. If it's just doing the garden up nice then that's fine, but we know there's at least a few murders."

"But these people were possessed? It's not their fault!" Aasif protested.

"Isn't it? Each of these people were offered something and they all said yes. That makes them an accessory at the very least." Dale pulled his silver emergency blanket tight, it crackled as he walked. His clothes still felt damp as he moved.

"I suppose. Doesn't feel particularly fair though." Aasif carried his own blanket under his arm, the thin material of his tracksuit drying quickly in the night breeze.

"Fairness and justice aren't always the same thing from my experience," said Dale, striding ahead of Aasif, over to the ambulance where his colleagues waited.

The van wobbled worryingly as it trundled down the streets. It listed to the side as it took the corner, sending the detectives stacked within toppling to one side. Aasif drove whilst Dale sat at the side, arm resting on the open window, cigarette ash trailing off into the night air. Between them Jess was squeezed, giving directions from the open laptop on her lap. In the back Mark had given up trying to balance and had sat in the corner by the door, arms outstretched to stop himself wobbling. Rajan was still defiant, standing up as straight as the vans low roof would let him. His arms braced against the ceiling he looked like a baby learning to walk, grabbing at the walls desperately as his legs failed him. The van hit a speed bump with a metallic clang, causing Rajan to knock his head against the roof.

"Sorry!" came Aasif's cry from the front seat.

"I thought this was close?" shouted an annoyed Rajan back.

"It is! I mean as the crow flies. The streets around here kind of wind around themselves," replied Jess.

"Another minute or two at most!" Aasif added.

"Maybe warn us before the next speed bump!" Rajan stumbled around like a drunk as the van took another corner. Dale turned away from the open window.

"You aren't going to warn him, are you?" he whispered to Aasif.

"Absolutely not," Aasif whispered back.

"Outstanding," Dale said with a smirk.

The smell of blood filled the room, an acrid tang of iron, wet and warm. In the dark moved a figure, a young woman on her knees, her arms moving in sweeping arcs. She muttered beneath her breath as she worked, dark guttural mutterings echoing around the room, which seemed to be growing. Reality flexed as she worked, the empty factory floor stretching, its small windows becoming great gothic arches, the disused oven becoming a mighty furnace. Seemingly pleased the woman stood up and walked towards the towering behemoth. She closed her eyes. She could feel them, her brothers and sisters, circling around her, formless fire, eager to burst forth into this world. She turned a wheel on the oven. Something within hissed, filling her nostrils with the smell of rotting eggs. The sulphurous cloud filled the oven the gas pouring out like a tide. Carefully and calmly Claire slide the metal grill up, revealing the heart of the beast. Rows of huge metal trays once lined with cakes and pastries lay empty in their racks. Claire gripped the first and slid it free, tossing it to the ground beside her. One by one she pulled each try free, each clattering into the growing pile as she worked. Satisfied, Claire smiled. Reaching up to her shoulder she slid the first strap of her dress free.

"Brothers sisters, hear me," she said calmly. "I have need of you." She removed the other strap of her dress. It dropped to the ground and she stepped out of the long since ruined fabric. "I am sorry, but there is no time to find you vessels. Our enemies close in around us." She could feel the spirits around her protesting angrily, denied a long-awaited dream. "I have...adapted the ritual. It's time." Claire walked forward, stepping carefully over the metal lip at the bottom of the oven, clambering inside. There she stood, disrobed, her skin wet with sweat and blood glistening from the pale moonlight. She took a deep breath, inhaling the gas deeply. She lifted her hand, snapped her fingers, and burned alive.

There was nothing at first, the town of Pontypridd sleeping peacefully, a cluster of lights set against the blackness of the valley. People sat in their homes, returned from work shifts and went about their lives blissfully unaware of what had been unfolding in their town. Faintly at first but growing stronger with each passing moment a pounding in their heads bloomed. It drummed against their skulls, a few brief moments of excruciating pain.

Aasif slammed on the brakes, the van juddering to a halt as the detectives within screamed in pain. An overwhelming agony, as though their minds were fighting to escape. Then nothing, the pain was gone, replaced with an overwhelming sense of relief, like a pressure valve had been released.

Mark spoke first. "What the fuck was that?"

The bakery was silent, filled with the smell of burning flesh as Claire burned. There was a moment of true silence, a perfect second of unnatural quiet. The flames flicked with nary a crackle. Then a cacophony, a terrible agonising noise as reality itself screamed, ripped asunder, an invisible wound on the universe gashed into the centre of the bakery. The air shimmered, as though looking through the surface of a pool. The Jinn spirits circled, before diving in, the rift forming a torrent from the sinister otherworld they avoided to earth, a raging rapid of energies they could latch onto pulling themselves free of their formless prison. They dived in eagerly, pouring through the rift, bursting into reality with great gouts of fire. Too intoxicated with the chance of escape the Jinn didn't realise something was wrong until too late. The sigils were wrong, the freshest wettest runes the wrong shape. Rather than flying free to seek their own hosts they were being pulled, drawn inextricably towards the oven. The Jinn fought, their massed forms creating a twisting furious inferno. Slowly, but inevitably they began to lose their fight, the flames drawn into the smouldering black mass that had once been Claire. Desperately holding onto each other, the pull became too strong, the broiling mass pulled into the oven with a snap.

The bakery was quiet, the oven continuing to run with a low hum, its light illuminating the room. The air seemed to shimmer and ripple as a creature scuttled its way through. It was a huge thing, thousands of tiny segmented legs on a long thin body. Its head was a long wolf like snout, great fangs jutting from its jaw. Multifaceted eyes blinked from atop stalks which eagerly scanned the room. It has two sets of long gangly arms each ending in a series of scything blades which twitched like fingers. Its body was covered in thick chitinous plates, matted brown fur burst forth from between the gaps in the insect like armour. It hissed and began to scuttle around the chamber, its upper body writhing like a snake. More bizarre creatures followed. A massive hairless gorilla with tentacles in place of a head. A strange almost formless thing came next, a great blob like mass with huge feathered wings. Its pulsating pink form covered with horrid fanged mouth. It stretched itself like putty to move, the mouths stretching forth like an unborn baby kicking against its mother stomach. The horrid insectoid creature that had emerged first sniffed the air and began to scuttle towards the open doorway.

Shauna knocked on the open door. Florence was sat at her desk, staring at the still undrunk glass of whisky. Florence didn't look up, so Shauna knocked again. Florence looked up from her drink.

"Oh, Sergeant, any news?" she asked.

"Yes Ma'am. The operation was a success. All the Jinn were banished except for one. They are currently in pursuit." Shauna smiled as she spoke. Florence closed her eyes, head titled back towards the ceiling.

"Any casualties?". Florence drummed her fingers on the table nervously. This was the worst part of her job. Every one of her officers knew the risks of their jobs, but it was still her asking them to put themselves in danger. It made her sick to her stomach, a nervous roiling pain.

"Nothing major Ma'am, some like bruising with D.C Holden but," Shauna looked down at the printed copy of the email, "nothing a bag of frozen peas won't fix. D.C Curren's words Ma'am."

"Oh, thank god," Florence said, she picked up her glass and drank it in one. It tasted like wood smoke, of the smell from her father's regular barbecues as a child. It burnt as it poured down her throat. She placed the glass down on the table with a slam. "What about the civilians?"

"Everything seems good there. They will need to be checked over properly at the hospital. Possessing forces don't really look after their hosts. Probably a few broken bones or torn ligaments the Jinn were ignoring. Local forces and ambulance services have picked them up. We're going with the standard chemical spill cover." Shauna held out the paper, which Florence eagerly took.

"Fifty-eight!" shouted Florence as she scanned the document. "Fifty-eight new cases. We are not a well-funded unit Sergeant. We have eight detectives total and a huge portion of our budget goes into protecting that bloody archive. You know how hard it is to convince people to fund your department when your department is a secret? Christ even the people that do know are always on me to tighten the purse strings. You have no idea how much this operation cost alone! You should see the bill for the materials the department had to buy." She sighed, and leant back in her chair, which creaked as she did. "You know on telly a secret department is always flashy computer screens and dashing agents. It's never having to change toilet paper suppliers because its three pence cheaper per roll."

"I find reality rarely lines up with entertainment Ma'am," Shauna said. She chuckled at the thought.

Martin stared up at the roof of the ambulance. He lay on a trolley, a thin silver emergency blanket wrapped around him like leftover meat. He felt awful, as though all the energy had been drained from his body. His muscles ached, his head pounded, and his teeth felt oddly numb. He wondered how he got there. The last thing Martin could remember was taking a strange phone call. The voice knew him somehow. The police were saying that there was a chemical spill of some kind, the fumes causing people to hallucinate. Deep down Martin knew that wasn't true, but he accepted it; a convenient lie being preferable to accepting whatever terrible truth lay behind finding himself in a crowd of other people, laying wet in an empty office building, tiny burn marks covering his skin.

"You doing ok there champ?" asked a Paramedic as he climbed into the back of the ambulance. His head was bald but his face with covered with an uneven beard, its rough hair striking out at odd angles. A faint splatter of dried blood was smeared on his aged wrinkled face. His uniform sat oddly on him, tight in all the wrong places, as though it were meant for a man much smaller.

"Yeah, I think so. Really tired," Martin said, struggling to find the energy to speak. The paramedic leant forward holding on to the top of the ambulance's door frame. He gripped the door with one hand and pulled it shut. He gave a thumbs up to another man in the driver's seat, his back to Martin. The driver returned the gesture. "Am I going to be ok?" Martin asked.

"Oh yes," said the paramedic. He reached inside his jacket and slid out a large dagger. It shone brightly even under the tiny ambulance light overhead. It glistened like no knife Martin had seen before. The blade itself was basic, solid unremarkable craftsmanship, function over form. The handle was something different. It made of two separate strands of metal, each twirling around the other but never touching until they reached the end of the handle. The tip was what appeared to be a coin. The coin was rough, not a perfect circle. Upon its centre was a man's head in profile, a laurel wreath resting atop his hair. Martin had seen similar coins before, many years ago during a school trip to a local Roman museum. "Everything is going to be fine," said the bearded man, before plunging the dagger into Martins chest.

Chapter 22

The van's door slid shut with a low roar, a cry of squealing metal followed by a clunk. The five of them stood around it, checking pockets and readying themselves. They had arrived at where Jess' phone supposedly was. It was a small building, red brick and faded green tin roof. Small windows ran across the top half of the building revealing nothing of what was within. They had parked in a large concrete forecourt, beneath a faded sign declaring the place to be *"Vale Bakery"*. The letters were worn and partly covered by bright pink graffiti, a burst of colour in an otherwise drab place. One side of the courtyard sloped downwards to a set of metal shutters, a loading bay for happier days. From here they could still see the office building they had used for their trap, flashing ambulance lights blinking away from the valleys side. Its hallways once again empty, if sodden, the remnants of the spell hastily removed.

Mark opened the rear door of the van, leaning in an opening the trunk inside with a satisfying creak. He had to admit Aasif had been right to get a van, it made carrying the heavy box much easier, though Mark wished he hadn't picked this van. The thing had smelt faintly of cigarette smoke and sweat, and the smell somehow only gotten more noticeable the longer they used the thing. He unzipped a black cloth tool bag revealing the array of batons within. Held in by black elastic, two loops already empty, was a selection of custom batons. Jess in her fastidiousness had labelled them, silver and iron. Mark slipped out the remaining two iron batons.

"Raj, Dale," he said handing each man a baton. Rajan flicked his wrist, the baton extending out to full size. "Jess, give yours to Aasif, remember you agreed to stay in the van!"

"Yeah I remember!" said Jess. She held out her own baton towards Aasif, stopped for a moment, and then begrudgingly placed it into his open palm. "Keys," she demanded, the fingers on her hand flexing in anticipation. Aasif placed the keys into her eager hands.

"Keep the engine running, just in case," said Dale, testing the weight of his own baton in hand.

"That's real upbeat," chastised Rajan.

"Just being realistic."

"There's a first for everything I guess." Rajan punched Dale lightly on the shoulder. "Right game faces on then. We ready to go end all this?"

Within the darkness of the bakery something chittered to itself, a horrid high-pitched trilling noise. The thing writhed as it slunk about. Its lupine snout sniffed the air, something new was nearby. It slithered carefully, keeping its distance from the still burning oven. The bizarre tentacle creature let out a braying howl though it lacked a visible mouth. The winged sack had taken up residence in the rafters of the building. There was a horrid wet sucking noise as it feasted on a pigeon that had been too slow. Around their many feet scuttled innumerable smaller creatures. A swarm of tiny crab like creatures, miniature human like hands in place of claws. The faint shimmer in the air rippled as a small flying creature halfway between bird and fish burst forth. It let itself glide for a moment before flapping its wings and circling the building in a wide arc. The creature with the wolfs snout stabbed downwards with one of its blades skewering one of the smaller creatures. It hungrily swallowed it, the still whole wriggling creature disappearing down its gullet.

On the side of the bakery, around the corner from the metal shutters was a set of large double doors, off white metal set into the bare read brick. Four men stood before it nervously, shoulders hunched in misplaced bravado.

"On three?" asked Aasif, stepping forward and place his hand on the handle of the left side door.

"On three," agreed Dale, taking the opposite position.

"Three," began Aasif.

"Two," followed Dale.

"One," they said in unison, pulling the doors open.

The swarm burst forth as one, drawn eagerly through the now open door. The flying mouth horror was first, knocking Mark off his feet as it barged through the doorway, taking off into the night air. A tide of smaller creatures washed over him. Mark waved his arms furiously, trying to bat the creatures away from himself. The hairless ape was next, bounding through the door way and leaping over the high outer wall in a single leap.

"Jesus fuck," complained Mark as the swarm dispersed. He grabbed Rajan's outstretched arm and pulled himself to his feet. "What the fuck were those?"

"Your guess is as good as mine," mused Rajan. "Evolutions rejects maybe? I've seen some weird shit in my time."

"Just another thing to add to the shit pile," said Dale. "Let's get this done first and then worry about fucking squid gorillas and flying ball sacks."

"He's right you know," agreed Aasif. "Our element of surprise is gone, so let's get a fucking move on."

They advanced through the doorway into the inside of the bakery. It was dark, the faint moonlight having vanished behind the omnipresent clouds. At the far side was an old industrial over, it burned, the light from the flamer flicking across the otherwise empty room. The smell of death and blood filled the air, the floor and walls were covered with dark crimson runes. The firelight danced over scattered sheep corpses, their guts spilled out across the floor. There was a faint shimmer in the air, a layer of gossamer laid across reality. The room itself felt unnaturally thin, almost intangible.

"What the hell?" whispered Dale. "Somethings really wrong here, I can...feel it I guess."

"I know what you mean, it's like there's less...resistance? I'm not sure how to describe it," came Marks whispered reply. "Anyone got eyes on the Jinn?"

"Hard to see anything in here," admitted Aasif. He was stood slightly behind the detectives, advancing slowly forward, baton in hand. "Hang on, can anyone hear- ". Aasif's words failed as he burst into a roar of agony. He clutched at his elbow, blood pouring from between his fingers. His forearm, still clutching the baton bounced across the ground. Behind him a creature loomed. Its thin arms ended in thin blades, its right set glistening with Aasif's blood. Multifaceted eyes stared at the men, its thin furred snout sniffed deeply, spittle forming at the corner of its fanged maw. Its bladed fingers twitched hungrily. Aasif collapsed to his knees, still screaming in pain. Mark ran, leaping into a dive. He struck Aasif in the chest, the two men rolling across the dust floor. There was a clink as the blades of the creature dug deep into the concrete behind them.

The beast hissed angrily, scuttled about on its many legs, forming a circle around the men with its hairy segmented body.

"Shit, shit, shit, shit," muttered Aasif, his screaming had stopped, replaced by horrified denial. He was getting pale, the blood pouring free from his wound.

"I got you man, hey, hey, look at me!" shouted Mark cradling the panicking Aasif. Mark began to unbuckle his belt.

"Sorry, you're not my type," spluttered Aasif. The creature roared and lashed out Rajan. He twisted to the side evading its blades and brought his baton around bouncing off its armoured hide with a loud ringing noise.

"That's it, keep the British stiff upper lip. Here." Mark looped his belt just below Aasif's elbow pulling the leather tight. "Just need to keep this tight and you'll be as right as rain."

"Ah fuck!" shouted Dale as he narrowly avoided a blow from the creature, its blade drawing a thin cut across his back. "Any ideas?" he cried touching his wound. There was blood on his fingers. A creaking rattle of the metal shutters groaned to life answered him.

"Hey, fucking ugly!" Screamed Jess. She held one of the smaller crab like creatures in her hands. Its shell had been smashed in "Hey look at this, tasty huh!" She tossed the creature onto the bottom of the ramp and ran backwards, ducking under the still rising shutter.

The creature cascaded forward, eager to fill its belly with ready food before resuming its attack. Its centipede body poured down the ramp, tiny legs pounding as it moved. Beyond the shutter and engine revved, its sound a competing roar. The creature cried out in response and leant down, shovelling the crab like creature into its move. It bit through its shell with a loud crunch. There was another rev of an engine then the squealing of tires as the rental van rocketed down the ramp. It launched itself slightly as it sped into the concrete divot, its tires spinning in the air as it struck the creature.

The collision was an explosion of flesh and metal. The front of the van struck the creature pressing it down onto the concrete floor. The pressure shattered its shell, spraying thick red gore outwards like a popping water balloon. The van carried onwards its front end striking the ground, the old metal frame proving no resistance to the ground. The front crunched and buckled, fragments of metal spraying outwards, striking the walls and the twitching form of the dead beast. The van tipped forward its roof rolling off the read of the creature's thin body, coming to a rest on its side. The front half of the creature lay slumped, twitching slightly as its life drained away.

The driver's side door of the van popped open, pointing defiantly upwards to the sky. Jess lifted herself through and sat on the door frame, her legs dangling over the front window.

"Fucking good thing I stayed in the van," she said and let out a long cough. "Fuck thank Christ this old clunker had fucking airbags." She lowered herself down, sliding down the windscreen. She stumbled, uneasy on her feet. Carefully she staggered up the ramp into the bakery proper. "Fuck Aasif!"

"He'll be ok if we can get him to a hospital," said Mark still gripping the makeshift tourniquet tightly. "We need to do something about this fucking, I guess hole?"

"It's a rip," said Rajan. "Remember what Lucille said? Jinn creep in when the gaps between realities are thin. Whatever they were doing has turned that thinness into a gaping hole."

"So how do we fix it?" asked Jess.

"Not a fucking clue," admitted Rajan.

"We ask an expert," replied Dale. "Sorry buddy," he said crouching next to Aasif, "going to need to borrow some of this." He dipped his fingers into the pool of blood below his arm.

Lucille hummed to herself as she swept. It always seemed like either Abbie or herself was sweeping. True hell it seemed was the floor of a bar after a busy night. As it was currently only early evening Lucille was trying to get a jump on it, try a little preventative sweeping. It was proving difficult, a particularly drunk hen party who had described the bar as "*Like such a dive*" had spent most of their time complaining loudly, spilling more than they drank. She felt a tingling in her ear and reached in to scratch it. The itch got worse as it always did.

"Fucking teenagers," she muttered to herself.

"Oh, great and powerful Satan! Master of lies! Lord of shadows!" said the voice in her head. It sounded familiar. "I beseech you with my prayer." She did recognise her voice. For the first time in a very long time, Lucille replied.

"Dale?" she asked bemused. "Laying it on a bit thick, aren't you?"

"I wasn't really sure how to do this, I'm kind of just winging it." His voice was oddly faint, as thought something was interfering.

"What's going on? Did my spell work?" Lucille opened the door to her flat and started up the stairs.

"So yes, it worked, but we have another problem. There's some kind of...hole? Weird shit came pouring through. Rajan reckons it's a tear, that thinness between realities you mentioned."

"What kind of weird shit, like crazy messed up monsters, all kinds of weird limbs and stuff?" she asked, taking a seat on her sofa.

"Yeah exactly."

"He's spot on. Sounds like your Jinn opened the doorway a little too far and this reality and another are bumping metaphorical uglies."

"So how do we fix it?" Dale asked, the octave of his voice shifting, the tear meddling with the prayer.

"You don't. The universe is a tough old broad, it will heal itself over time. As long as you stop whatever opened it in the first place, so it doesn't do it again. The more tears the longer it will take to heal. One is a few hours, two a few days, you get the gist." She shrugged, even though she knew Dale couldn't see her.

Dale sat cross legged on the floor of the bakery, in front of him was a pentagram drawn in Aasif's blood. He had no idea what he was doing, trying to be as cliché as possible, hoping the intent would be enough. Dale was pleased to see he was right.

"Lucille says it will close on its own, in a few hours," he said. He wiped his hands on his coat, smearing it with blood.

"A few hours is a long ass time if shit like that," Mark gestured to the mangled heap of van and creature, "comes through."

"It's fine," said Rajan. "Me and Dale will stay here, watch the rift whilst we wait for the medics to arrive for Aasif, you two track down that last Jinn. She must be nearby. No offense Jess but you're a bit battered, better you go face what we know is out there, let us deal with whatever the hell comes through there next."

"None taken, that's a fair point," Jess crouched down, lifted something from the floor. "Slight issue," she said turning around. A tattered red dress rested in her hands. She reached into the pocket and produced her phone. "Now how do we find her?"

"You don't," came a reply, it was Claire's voice, but quietly behind its dozens of voices, in faint harmony.

The fire in the oven shifted and moved as Claire floated forth. Her skin was perfect, the wounds from her ordeal gone. The flames cloaked her like and aura, flicking around her. Her hair lashed about with the flames, caught in their updraft. She stretched her arms outward, a fresh vivid red dress weaving itself around her as she moved. The rift shuddered violently as she approached, the faint ripple becoming a booming wave. She smiled, and held up her arms, marvelling at her new form.

Chapter 23

Claire floated in place, her light illuminating the chamber with a pale orange glow. They could feel the heat emanating from her. She inched forward slowly, a fiery angel of destruction, tongues of fire erupting from her form, scouring the ground around her. Slowly they edged backwards from her, Mark dragging Aasif as he lapsed in an out of consciousness. The rift shuddered and raged, the room seeming to stretch and bend at Claire's very presence.

"I will burn you all slowly and revel in your ashes! I will burn the ground on which you have walked, the places you have been and the people you have loved!" She screamed, her voice a chorus. "I will consume everything and everyone you know. And why? Because I can." Claire's flames shifted from their orange to an incandescent blue. The heat filled the room, it was oppressive.

"Not bloody likely!" shouted Jess. She stood before the inferno, sweat dripping from her brow, bruised, battered, but defiant.

"You most of all. You who have hounded me at every turn. I will so enjoy killing you woman. Then I will kill your friends, whoever taught you these magics, and then finally I will kill any family you have, and I will savour all of it. The power of a hundred Jinn fills this vessel, and you dare to stand before me!" Claire's face was a sneer, half hidden in the flames.

"A hundred Jinn you say?" replied Jess. She laughed gently to herself and slid her hands inside her jacket pocket.

"Something funny mortal? You mock the brothers and sisters who gave themselves to me. You besmirch their sacrifice."

"Well it's just a thought. You have the power of all those Jinn your strength amplified. The opposite must be true as well?" Quickly and in one movement Jess thrust her right hand from her pocket, the handful of iron filings scattered from her palm. They struck Claire who screamed in agony, green sparks bursting forth as each mote of iron struck her. She dropped onto the floor, her feet stumbling backwards. Jess threw another handful again, erupting in another display of green fireworks. Her fellow detectives caught on dashing forward to add their own handfuls to the barrage. Claire screamed as she was beaten backwards, her flames dying with every step. Finally, she let out an unholy howl and burst into an uproarious blaze, the force knocking the detectives backwards. Jess crashed to the ground and rolled awkwardly, whilst the men, less hurt than her, struggled to keep their footing. The flames became a twisting spiral, a tornado of heat and light. It curved upwards smashing through a bakery window. The vortex pulled itself through and vanished into the night air. Embers of fire remained, scattered across the floor like confetti.

"Good thinking," applauded Mark, helping Jess to her feet. "Problem is now we need to find her again."

"We also need to deal with this rift I guess?" Dale pointed over his shoulder at the bend in reality. Looking directly at it made Jess' eyes throb. It had calmed itself, settling down to how it was before Claire had emerged.

"Yeah also those," Jess added, pointing at the rising forms behind Dale.

The motes of flame pulsed with a growing light. They coalesced into small fires that reached out, stretching and shaping itself into a new form. They grew into pillars at first, before splitting, taking humanoid forms, arms and legs erupting outwards. The figures were made of pure combustion, but controlled and shaped. For a brief scant moment, a bestial visage could be seen, before flicking away in a wash of flames. The figures flexed, a grotesque mockery of human behaviours.

Mark crouched down beside Aasif, the tourniquet had come loose so he pulled it tight. He was paler, drifting in and out of consciousness. Mark grabbed him under the shoulders and began dragging him towards the door, away from the advancing figures.

"What the fuck is this now?" Marks words were strained as he pulled his unconscious colleague.

"Jinn," replied Rajan. "I think this is what they look like naturally, it's like the pictures I saw during research, but with more actual fire." The Jinn advanced, twelve in all, a wall of coming flames. The front two burst into a run, rushing at the detectives. Jess ducked below a lashing burning claw, rolling across the ground to avoid the strike. Dale leant backwards, the Jinn's thrust tearing his shirt. It smoked where the flame had raked it. Rajan swivelled on one foot circling his attacker. He lashed out instinctively in retaliation, striking the Jinn with an overhand swing of his baton. The dark metal carved through the Jinn's fiery form easily, the lack of resistance causing Rajan to stumble. He caught his footing and righted himself to see the Jinn he had stuck evaporate into tiny specks of fire. They rose slightly in the air before falling gently, like burning snow. "Iron!" he shouted. "That's why they need hosts! It banishes them completely in their natural form!"

He needn't have shouted, his colleagues seeing the results of his strike emulated him. Jess jabbed her baton at her attacker like a dagger, plunging it deep into its chest. It exploded into its own flaming dust. The Jinn that had struck Dale lunged at him again and he raised his baton, a hand at both ends to block the strike. The Jinn's outstretched hand disintegrated as it struck, causing it to fall forwards, the hot shards pelting Dale. His jacket smouldered slightly, and he patted it down. The remaining Jinn, seeing how easily the first three had been dispatched rushed together, counting on their numbers to overwhelm their prey.

"Duck!" Mark shouted, throwing the last of his iron filings over the now crouching body of Jess. It struck the mass of flame, the four lead Jinn exploding, whilst the others stumbled. Stunned momentarily the detectives swung wildly, Jinn bursting apart around them. Then none remained. They stood, batons in hand, breathing heavily within a blizzard of fire and ash.

"Ok? Are we good now?" Dale said, flicking burning dust from his face.

The bakery burned, smoke and fire rising into the night. Mark sat on his trunk watching as Aasif was loaded into the back of the ambulance. His tanned face had turned white, the paramedics attaching a more permanent tourniquet. He turned away, his gaze drifting to the burning building. It was ironic that even after triumphing over creatures of literal primal flame that the detectives had burnt it themselves. It had seemed the easiest way to cover evidence of the nightmare creature within whilst also keeping people out whilst the rift sealed.

"I know that face," Jess said as she sat down beside him.

"What face?" he asked, still staring at the fire.

"That's your thinking face, the one you get when your mulling over an idea." Jess pulled a notebook from her pocket, flipped it open to a blank page and held her pencil ready. It had snapped at some point in the night, and she held the front half poised to write. "Come on then, do tell."

"I was just thinking, we're just back where we started. All the other Jinn are gone but Claire is loose again. She'll summon more. Hell, she might even open more of those rifts, letting god knows what come through. Think what was in the care home came through something like this?" The fire danced in his eyes as he watched the bakery burn. It was oddly beautiful.

"No, it was more like it was being made there, all those hands." Jess shook herself, trying to lose the image from her mind. "I get what you mean though, same kind of feeling too it. I think Jinn just being around weaken space around them, allowing for weird magic and rifts and stuff."

"It's a chicken and the egg thing, right? Did the Claire-Jinn get through because reality around here was thin? Or was the Jinn being here doing that? I think that's maybe why that ghost went from being a harmless thing to an onryo, it got riled up, empowered."

"Well the ghost appeared before we think the Claire-Jinn was around right? So, the chicken came first? Or whatever reality being weak first is in this metaphor," said Jess. She wrote "*jinn*", followed by a question mark in the centre of the notepads page and surrounded it with a cloud

shape. She drew a line from the cloud and atop the line wrote
"*what came first?*"

"It doesn't sit right. Raj reckons Lucille says some
places are just naturally like this, but Pontypridd isn't exactly a
supernatural hotspot. Something or someone did this."

"Another problem for another time." Jess rested the
notepad on her knee and placed her hand on his shoulder.
"Let's sort out this mess first."

"I have an idea about that," Mark admitted.

"I told you so." Jess smiled and picked up her notebook
and pencil again. "Let's hear it."

"I hope this doesn't become a recurring thing," wished
Lucille. She was sat on the toilet, her jeans around her ankles.
He liked her thumb and leant forward, rubbing against graffiti
on the cubicle door.

"Last time, scouts honour!" said Dale.

"Well, what do you need then? I'm kinda...busy at the
moment." The graffiti wouldn't budge, scrawled in permanent
marker. Lucille frowned at it.

"Is there another way to cast a beacon spell? It doesn't
have to be as strong as before, enough for just one Jinn." Dales
voice was clearer than before, less distorted by interference.

"Not really no," Lucille thought for a moment. "Do you
have the stuff left from the first one? The ashes?"

"Yeah, we scooped it into evidence bags before we left."

"Ok good, there might be enough juice left for a second
attempt. If you only need so summon one it should be ok. I

think. Never done it myself." She leant back against the toilet, the cistern rattling behind her.

"You mean you gave us a spell you didn't know would work?" barked Dale.

"I knew it would work, just never had cause to do it myself. There's a subtle difference." Lucille pouted, annoyed at the insinuation of carelessness.

"The devil is in the details huh?"

"Something like that." Lucille smiled at the joke. "Ok, draw all the same runes as before. Set something, anything really that's on fire in the pile of ashes. Bit of paper, wood, doesn't matter. That should be enough to have one last shot. It won't be strong and won't last more than a minute or two mind you."

"Thanks Luce, I'll tell the guys. That was a big help," Dale said, his words drifting into her mind.

"Oh well, you're welcome." Lucille could feel her cheeks blushing. She grinned like a schoolgirl. Luce. It felt very informal. "Oh, and I was kidding before, you're welcome to call me anytime!" There was no reply, D.C Cooper was already gone. "Shit," said Lucille.

"Ok seems pretty straightforward then," Mark said, motioning for Jess to stand up off the trunk. He opened the lid and reached in, producing a clear plastic bag filled with ash.

"She said it wouldn't last long," Dale said, continuing his information rely from Lucille. Behind him the bakery's fire still burnt but the fine mist like rain had returned, adding itself to the hoses from the fire engines that had pulled into the forecourt. Mark slipped the bag into the pocket of his grey woollen coat, it bulged out, too large to be easily stuffed in.

"That's fine, she flew out of here like the fucking human torch, I'm guessing she'll be there sharpish. Speaking of sharpish, we should. No, they spotted us." Mark closed his eyes for a moment, and then reopened them, his face now all friendliness and smiles. Across the courtyard Chief Inspector White had seen then and was power walking over his face twisted with rage.

"I don't care how super special your department is, or how many papers you have from the home office," he began, screaming at them over the roar of the water pumping from the fire engines, "I want you gone." His face was beetroot purple, a mix of anger and breathlessness from his stomp across the courtyard. "Everywhere you go you cause chaos. Now your burning buildings down and getting limbs removed from my officers! I want you out of here. Preferably you can fuck off back to England."

"We're nearly done her Sir," Jess said, stepping between the furious Inspector and the three men. "Then well be more than happy to get out of your hair."

"I certainly fucking hope so. We should have handled this ourselves." The Inspector pointed angrily at her. Jess couldn't help but turn her gaze to the ambulance, which was pulling out of the courtyard. She dreaded to think what would have happened had the locals tried to deal with the problem. There would be a lot more like Aasif she thought.

"Well, we do need to requisition a car, if at all possible?" Jess winced as she made the request.

"Anything take anything!" shouted White, exasperated. "The quicker it gets you lot the fuck away from here the better."

The passenger side door of the police car slammed shut, its bright yellow and blue standing out strikingly against the dour grey stone of the house. Jess rested her arms on the car roof staring at it. It occurred to her that through everything that had happened, this was her first time coming here, to the house that had started their ill-fated trip across county. Mark straightened his coat and adjusted his collar.

"Ok ready?" he said. "Follow my lead and we should be fine."

Chapter 24

Rhiannon stared in the mirror, having polished it to a gleam, the light dancing across the room. She adjusted her pinafore, and straightened her hem, taking care to conceal her growing stomach, new life coalescing within. She lifted her chin. Maid she may have been, but Rhiannon took pride in her appearance, though it fostered rumours around the town that she had ideas above her station. She had brushed them off. She was a maid for now, but Merfyn was a gentleman of some renown, he had promised her marriage and he was bound to follow through any day now. To not keep his word would be unthinkable.

Rhiannon held her skirt up slightly as she trotted down the stairs. She turned a sharp corner at the bottom and wandered into the kitchen. It was warm, a gentle fire crackling within the oven. The flames danced before her eyes, growing stronger, more violent. She stared, her vision narrowing to a figure within the fire, it looked like a young girl, she screamed in agony.

"Morning Rhiannon!" said Gareth, the houses cook. Money from the mine hadn't been what it used to recently, the entire staff having been reduced to just Rhiannon and Gareth. He startled her with his welcome, causing Rhiannon's gaze to drift away from the oven. When she turned back it was a simple welcoming flame again.

"Morning Gareth," she said half-heartedly. "Breakfast ready?"

"Nearly, just get those eggs boiling and then we're good to go. Sleep well?" Gareth prodded at an egg submerged in a saucepan. It listed gently across the bottom. Rhiannon looked puzzled, it was an odd and possibly inappropriate question.

"I'm sorry?" she asked incredulously. "Whatever do you mean?"

"One of the lads in the fields stopped me as I walked up, had some tale about a woman wailing through the night. Claims it was a ghost but seeing as this is the only house for some ways and you're the only woman in the house..." Gareth trailed off, his voice a mixture of embarrassment and concern.

"I was fine," Rhiannon asserted. "Mr. Davies and I were in the house all night and heard, nor made, nary a peep." She reached down and opened one of the cupboards that ran around the kitchen. From within she pulled out a white china plate, delicate blue patterning running around the rim. She sighed. "I'm sorry, I didn't mean to be so terse. I know you mean well." Gareth nodded, he and Rhiannon had both lived in and around Pontypridd their whole lives and had known each other as children. Rhiannon had gotten him the job as cook, saving him from a lifetime of darkness and lung problems. She placed the plate on a silver tray Gareth had already laid out. "Those eggs done yet?"

Merfyn Davies sat in his parlour, newspaper open wide across his lap. Though it were only early morning he had dressed fully. A fine cut dark grey suit clung to him. It suited his face, which was ruggedly handsome. He turned the page, the paper rustling as he did.

"Any chance of some breakfast soon? Some of us have work to do today!" His voice was stern, the tone of a man so used to having his way that anything else was unfathomable. He folded the paper and set it down on the small side table next to him. He leant back in his chair scowling at the doorway, the tall sides of the green leather armchair covering him in shadow. A moment passed, and Rhiannon bounced in through the doorway, moving as quickly as her unwieldy dress would allow. "Breakfast is to be served at seven A.M. sharp! I have appointments to keep."

"I am sorry sir, but to be fair it is only five past the hour." Rhiannon placed the tray onto his lap, two egg cups sat on the china plate, a boiled egg in each. A row of thin sliced and toasted bread ran around the outside of the plate.

"And yet now I am expected to rush my morning meal so that I may keep my appointments. If you are ever to be lady of this house, you must learn to keep an orderly schedule." Merfyn tapped a spoon atop one of his eggs angrily, the shell cracking from the blow. "Go gather your things, I would have you accompany me into the town."

"Yes sir," answered Rhiannon. She curtsied, then back out of the room. Once she was past the doorway she smiled giddily to herself and excitedly bounced up the stairs.

Rhiannon walked behind Merfyn, keeping as respectful distance as he led her through the town. What was once a tiny village had exploded in population over the last few decades, growing fat on the proceeds of coal. The newly built station dominated the town, its vast stonework carved into the hills themselves, the power of man over nature writ large. It seemed to stretch forever, trains of a length Rhiannon could scarce believe being filled with black stone, their empty wagons waiting hungrily. She stopped and watched. Spending all her time at the house meant she very seldom saw the fruits of Merfyn's labour, the fuel of industry plucked from the ground. Industrialist. She liked that title, it seemed very modern.

"Keep up woman, we don't have all day to be dawdling," barked Merfyn clapping his hands together.

"Sorry sir, I was just admiring the station. It's very impressive." She trotted over to, being carefully to remain ladylike despite the increased speed. "I just find it so interesting, the trains coming and going."

"Yes well, it's not so impressive when you have to pay to use it. The charges are exorbitant. Anyway, come along, we have meetings to keep."

Rhiannon followed across town, from one meeting to the next. She was made to wait outside for each, although from what she could tell Merfyn's meetings involved him walking into a room, hat in hand, to be shouted at. His face reminded her of her fathers, begging for work on doorsteps. He had refused to work in the mines like everyone else. It terrified him, the thought of dying underground, to be forgotten by everyone. Rhiannon understood the thought, it was unsettling.

"Gods forsaken imbeciles," muttered Mefryn as he slammed the door behind him. He stamped down the small stairway, the huge house behind him looming ominously, its heavy wooden black door a void in the white stonework. "There's a new vein, I know it!" He stormed off down the street, seemingly forgetting Rhiannon was there. She walked briskly after him as he ranted to himself. "I just need funds to expand the mine! Idiots, do they not see a worthwhile investment when they see it."

"Sir is everything ok?" She asked as she caught up behind him.

"What, oh, yes I'm fine," replied Merfyn, adjusting his hat slightly. His face was bright red. "Come, let's return home. I have had my fill of business for today."

The rest of the week the cycle continued. Merfyn would leave the house in the morning, only to return by midday, red faced and furious. He had stopped taking Rhiannon after the first day, leaving her to tend to the home on her own. Whilst the house was large, and she was the only maid, Merfyn rarely ventured out from his parlour so she often found herself with nothing to do. Consequently, the house gleamed. Every wooden, glass or metal object buffed to an overpowering shine by Rhiannon simply for something to do. Her pride was her mirror. It was a gift from Merfyn, full length and mounted on a baroque wooden frame. Rhiannon loved it, every morning she stood there, staring at herself in the mirror, watching the bump on her stomach slowly get bigger.

"Marriage!" she shouted, her voice trembling.

"Yes, that is what I said," Merfyn said, his voice quiet and calm. "I am to be wed to the daughter of Dai Jones, he has a respectable business making coaches and their sundry attachments, for the horses and so on. Smart man, there will always be call for those. He is willing to invest in the mine, in exchange for marrying his daughter. Very shrewd of him." Merfyn lifted the small teacup Rhiannon had brought in for him to his lips and took a sip.

"But you promised to marry me!" Rhiannon shook, her world shattering before her eyes. "What about our child? You promised!" Tears streamed down her face, her hands gripped tight into fists.

"You will be well... taken care of." He placed the cup back onto the saucer, the delicate china rattling as he did. "I suggest you begin packing some things, it would be inappropriate to keep you on as a maid after this." He lifted the broadsheet that was resting on his knees and opened it.

Gareth struck hard with the cleaver, severing flesh with a single strike.

"I'll kill him," he growled, throwing the strip of beef into a boiling pot. "You just say the word Rhi and I will, I swear." He struck again with the cleaver, it sliced through the meat, sticking into the chopping board.

"No, no, don't do anything..." she said, fighting through cascading tears. "You don't want to lose your job too." She wiped at her eyes with her sleeve.

"My Job?" Gareth asked baffled. He threw another strip of meat into the pot. "If you think I'm working for him after pulling something like this, you're as mad as he is. This is for me to take home." He pointed at the bubbling pot. "I suggest you do the same, grab what you can and get out of here."

"I can't," she stopped, trying to compose herself. "I can't do that, he said he would make sure I'm looked after. If I left now I can't imagine he would follow through."

"Yeah like he followed through with promising to marry you?" Gareth stared at her, hands resting on the wooden table that dominated the kitchen. "He's a different class to us Rhi, they're all like this. Money first, even over love. You think he'll suffer an expense like that."

"It's his child, how couldn't he..." she trailed off, staring down at the table.

"Listen to me Rhi, leave. Walk out that door and don't come back."

Rhiannon awoke, earlier than usual. She slipped on her uniform, not bothering to examine herself in the mirror. She had stopped doing it weeks ago, it was too painful a reminder. She stepped over the large bag that held all her personal things. She had packed it, ready to leave, and yet every morning she got up, put on that uniform and went to work. The days were harder and longer now Gareth was gone, the cooking tasks adding to her workload which had grown considerably larger with the upcoming wedding. Everything was being replaced, the carpets, the furniture, the paint on the walls with some invention called wallpaper. Change was all around her, a swirling maelstrom of chaos in what had been a stable reliable life. Rhiannon stood in the kitchen, waiting for an egg to boil, watching one of the decorators stripping paint from the kitchen wall with a metal scraping tool. She watched as the grimy mint green paint peeled away. It had been there for as long as Rhiannon had worked at the house, it felt like her own life was being scrapped out of the place, the stones being shaken free of any trace of her.

"Seven A.M. what is so hard about that? It is not a difficult ask. It's now quarter past the hour, I have been waiting fifteen minutes. Unacceptable. Me and my guest will now be late for our appointments. Again." Merfyn stared at her, arms crossed.

"I am sorry sir, won't happen again sir." Rhiannon set the tray down on the brand-new table which sat in the centre of the parlour. The tray wobbled as she lowered it, heavy from the two plates, each with their own egg cups and toast.

"Apologise to my fiancé too," he demanded.

"I am sorry my lady," Rhiannon curtsied as she apologised.

"No need, I keep telling Merfyn he should replace the cook," said the woman. She was short but thin, her face softly curved. She had long flowing black hair, which curled at the ends. She was beautiful, and a perfect match for Merfyn's rough handsome features.

"As I said Myfanwy, I am replacing all of the staff at the same time. It will be easier to bring in a staff who have worked together already at another household. Rhiannon here shall be leaving us soon."

"Is that true Rhiannon? A shame, I do so like you." Myfanwy smiled, it felt fake, only the pretence of niceness.

"Yes, my lady. It's fine, Sir had already lined up a new job for me at another house. He did promise to look after me." She shot Merfyn a glare.

"Really! Well that's so considerate Merfyn, how nice of you."

"Gather your things." Merfyn's shadow stood in the doorway, moonlight from the landing illuminating him in a pale glow. Rhiannon stirred, sitting up in her bed. She blinked slightly confused.

"Sir?" she said, her voice hoarse.

"I said gather your things, you leave tonight, I have made arrangements." His shadow moved oddly in the light, as though he wasn't fully there.

"But it's the middle of the night? Can it not wait?" Rhiannon asked, rubbing her eyes.

"No." Merfyn stated. His voice was serious but quiet. It was sinister. He stepped forward into the room, out from the shadow. He was dressed oddly, wearing a set of rough-hewn woollen trousers and an ill-fitting shirt. They did not suit Merfyn. "Is this your bag?" he asked, pointing to Rhiannon's prepacked clothes.

"Yes," she said, still groggy. She turned, slipping her feet into a pair of slippers, their pale blue matching her nightgown.

Merfyn followed her down the stairs, his hand on her back, almost pushing her. He carried her case in the other hand, holding it up to his chest to not knock the walls and wake the house. He marched her out into the night air, its cold chilling her through the thin gown. He motioned for her to follow and walked around the house to its rear. Rhiannon followed, confused as to what arrangements he had made, to require a night-time flight. It had been raining, the wet mud squeezing between her toes.

As she rounded the corner she saw Merfyn, he stood with one of the cellar doors in hand, the ground a monstrous void before him. He motioned down at the all-consuming black with his head.

"The cellar? What's going on?" Rhiannon shivered, holding her arms close to herself, trying but failing to ward out the cold.

"I've been taking money from, well everywhere. The mine profits, part of the investment, the money Jones has given me for the renovation. I've been storing it here. I promised I would look after you. We need to collect this before the carriage arrives to take you to your new home." Merfyn unhooked the oil lantern they keep on the outer wall by the cellar and struck a match, using it to ignite the lantern. Its dull fire casting and orange glow, shadows rising over Mefryn's face. "Come on, down you go, we haven't much time." Carefully, Rhiannon stepped down, into the blackness. There was an odd smell, sharp to the nose, like bad liquor. It smelt like the clear watery substance the decorators had been using to strip the paint from the walls. "For what It's worth, I am sorry Rhiannon."

Merfyn swung the case aiming to throw it down the stairs. It was weightier than he expected, and it pulled him forward. The trousers he had borrowed from one of the decorators were too long for him and he tripped. Losing his footing in the wet mud he tumbled head first into the cellars stone stairs, his nose breaking as he struck them. The force of him falling shook the cellars doorframe, causing the door he had left only balanced open to slam shut behind him. As he fell the lantern came loose from his hand smashing onto the cellar floor. The turpentine burst into flames as he had planned. Rhiannon screamed, the noise muffled by the thick stone walls of the cellar. The fire spread outwards, Merfyn having been thorough in his planning. Slowly, painfully, they both burned.

Chapter 25

Mark stood before the house, Jess by his side staring at the doorway. The wind had picked up, the omnipresent fine mist transitioning to a full downpour. It soaked the ground, turning the dirt into a thick mud. They were alone, Dale and Rajan staying behind at the bakery to watch over the rift. The house seemed almost pathetic, its dull worn stone, thick with graffiti, its broken windows and door which hung agape. It was a shadow, the failed promise of shelter clinging helplessly to the hillside. Leading the way Mark stepped across the threshold and began to climb the stairs.

"Hello?" he shouted as he crested over the top of the stairs. "Anyone home? Jesus Christ!" At the end of the landing were too bodies. Mark thought he recognised them as the girl who got pushed through the window and her sister, though it was difficult to tell. Their bodies had been slashed, faces shredded, stomachs torn open. The hallway carpet was stained with blood, a great smear of it running along the wall as though one of the bodies had been thrown against it. One of the girl's hands clutched her phone tightly. "I'm sorry girls," Mark said crouching next to their bodies. "I should have warned you not to come back here."

"Interlopers in my house," croaked a voice behind his ear. He could feel a chill in the air, the figure behind him casting a long unnatural shadow. He spun around and came face to face with a young woman in an old Victorian maids' outfit. It was the same one who had come to his hotel room.

"Hi, uh, remember me?" Mark waved nervously.

"Why of course I do. Welcome home dear." The ghost smiled, revealing rows of needle like fangs hidden behind her otherwise sweet face.

"I need to borrow the uh, parlour I guess? Whatever the largest room is. It's for...business." The woman nodded as he spoke.

"That would indeed be the parlour, downstairs, first left from the doorway. The former master of the house used to host business matters in there regularly. Will be you requiring tea?" The spectral figure bounced on her heels excitedly.

"Uh yes, actually, tea for two. My associate is downstairs, she'll take it with two sugars, I'll have it with none," answered Mark.

"She?" asked the spirit, her face stretching as she spoke, her eyes beckoning sunken.

"A work associate only, a policewoman actually, she's married," Mark explained, "strictly business relationship." The onryo seemed driven by a vindictive jealousy, Mark hoped he could convince her that Jess was not a threat. His plan relied on it.

"Married you say?" replied the spirit, her face snapping back to normal. "And a police*woman*," her voice stressing the gendered syllables, "well I never. Personally, I was never one for the suffrage movement myself. I shall get the tea." Between blinks she vanished, taking her leave of them.

"Tea?" Jess asked, still stood in the doorway as Mark trotted down the stairs. She took a step into the hallway, now she seemingly had leave to enter.

"It keeps her occupied for a minute or two. We'll set up in the parlour here, start by opening those windows wide." Mark stepped into the large room, its furniture long gone, any semblance of once being a home stripped away. The walls were mostly bare aside from decades of scrawled graffiti. In a few spots tattered wallpaper remained, scant remnants of a once room encompassing pattern. The floor was covered with litter, glass bottles and plastic cups mixed with leaves blown in from outside. "Once that's done we'll get the spray paint from the car and start I guess."

The door swung open, knocking a bell which tinkled gently. It was an old thing but shined brightly catching the light. The bell had been there since Clive's great-great grandfather had opened it, and he proudly kept it in peak condition, just as his father had done so. Slowly, over the last two hundred years the shop had morphed from a grocer into the sort of everything shop people tended to label as hardware stores. It had proven necessary to compete with the out of town supermarkets. The new Valueways had proven especially detrimental to business. A young woman stepped through the doorway. Clive was always excited to see young people in his store. His clientele was loyal, but they were older and came in more to chat than to buy. Recently a young woman with bright red hair had come in and purchased his entire supply of black seed oil. Maybe she had spread the good word to her friends. Clive's wife had sneered when he had bought some alternative medicine goods to add to the already over stocked and eclectic store.

"Can I help you Miss?" he asked, waving from behind the counter.

"Ah yes, tea please, I seem to be all out, and I have company." As she approached Clive realised she was dressed oddly, like an old Victorian maid. Something seemed off about her, like she was somehow faded. He found it difficult to keep his gaze on her.

"Oh tea, yes we have some somewhere, what kind? Round or pyramid bags?"

"Bags? I'm not sure why what kind of bag it comes in matters. Round I suppose?" The woman looked genuinely puzzled. Clive turned around, scanning the haphazardly stacked shelf behind him. After a moment he spotted what he was after, pulling a blue box for the shelf. He blew dust from the top and placed it on the counter.

"One box of tea. That will be two pounds please." He smiled, opening his cash draw ready.

"Two pounds? Are you mad, that's more than a month of my wages. I suppose I have little choice, place it on the Davies account please."

"I'm sorry Davies account? We don't do tabs. Cash only, tried to convince the wife to get a card machine but she doesn't trust them. Do you want the tea or not love?" He tapped the top of the box.

"Where is Llewelyn? He'll know about the Davies account. Where is the owner sir?" The woman seemed to grow slightly taller, her skin a little paler.

"I'm the owner. Is this a joke? Who put you up to this?" Clive pointed his finger accusingly. The woman sneered. She pointed behind Clive at an old photograph behind him. It was of the opening of the store. He turned his head to look at it. When he turned it back the woman loomed tall, her limbs thin, her colour faded to be almost white. He face stretched and contorted, her fingers dripping talons. "D-D-Davies account was it?" he stammered. "Of course, please, take them." Like elastic snapping back into place the woman shrunk back her initial appearance.

"Thank you, sir, good day," she said cheerily, picking up the tea and wander out through the doorway, bell chiming as she did.

Jess drew her spray can around in a circle, completing the rune. Mark was crouched on the floor painting his own. A stacked pile of debris sat at one side of the room where they had cleared the floor, revealing the solid wood floorboards below. Jess had spent many evenings curled up with Hannah watching one of the many home improvement shows her wife recorded. She often spoke about her dream of one day buying a house in the country, to strip its floors and repaint its walls, to breathe new life into an unloved building. Jess was sure she wouldn't approve of defacing the building in this manner.

"Tea is served!" came a voice from the doorway. Jess looked up, getting her first glimpse of the onryo. She looked like a normal young woman, though slightly ephemeral, as though her existence didn't sit right with Jess' vision. She was carrying a wooden tray, one which two teacups and a teapot rested. "I am sorry it isn't the finest china, that seems to be missing. I had to get one of the older sets from the attic." She held out the tray, offering a cup to Jess. "The tea may not be the best, I had to pop out special and what I got isn't the best quality. It came in these little cloth bags for some reason. Not sure how your supposed to make a proper pot with those." Jess took the cup, it was cold, a horrid looking pale brown water swirling with.

"Oh, thank you," she said, trying to remain polite.

"Merfyn tells me you're a policewoman," the ghost looked impressed, "I wasn't even aware such a thing was possible."

"Yes well, you would be surprised," replied Jess, holding the teacup close to her chest. "Me and Mar- Merfyn, are nearly ready here. Could we get some privacy when our guest arrives. We'll call you if we need you. I'm sorry I didn't catch you name."

"Rhiannon" answered the phantom. "Are you sure you don't need me?"

"Not yet," said Mark stepping over and taking the tray from her hands. "Like Jess said, we'll call you when we need you."

Dale sat on the ground, his back leaning against the wall of the bakery. He took a long drag of his cigarette before offering it to Rajan.

"You know I don't smoke," Rajan said. He was sat next to Dale, coat pulled over his head to try and protect from the rain. "How is that even alight?"

"Cosmic benevolence, the universe understands that after today, a cigarette is well earned." Dale placed it back to his lips and too another drag. The ruins of the bakery smouldered, the building collapsing under its own weight during the fire leaving only a blackened skeleton. The air above the building shimmered slightly. It could be heat form the fire, but it could be that other, darker thing. Dale and Rajan knew to take no chances and so sat in the rain and waited, two sodden sentinels.

A tiny orange flame danced in the parlour as Mark sparked his lighter. He knelt to the bowl before them, ashes poured into it. In the centre was a flyer, *"Rave at the haunted house!* it read. He had thought it ironically appropriate. He held the lighter to the edge of the flyer which caught aflame slowly burning down to the ash like a candle wick. There was a brilliant flash of bright blue flames as the ashes burnt for a brief moment, before all that was left was a foul-smelling smoke. Together, facing the windows, they waited.

Claire sat on the hillside, the grass from the fields surrounding her. She stared down at the tiny pathetic town. Its people sleeping despite the events of the night. From here she could see everything. Claire's home, the house she took refuge in when that accursed woman had first found her. The warehouse where she had scuffled with demons. The office block where humans had stripped her of her allies. The bakery where she had been reborn. She was sick of running. From humans, from angels, from the nightmare things that hunted in the gap between worlds. She had poked and prodded at the crack in reality until she had slipped through and found her host. A sad lonely girl twisted by betrayal. She was an easy target, all too eager to say yes to something offering to take all her pain away. She was gone now, her soul squeezed out from her flesh shell. Claire was surprised to find she missed her a little.

She sat there, the rain bouncing off her body, tiny jets of steam erupting as they hit her when she felt it. Just for a moment, a brief fleeting second. The same cry as before, but faint, the last drops of magic to be squeezed from it. Across the valley, just outside the town. She stood up. Running, that was all she had done. Run from the void, run from that woman, ran from the bakery. No more. Fire swirled around her, scorching the field, the grass being swept up into the twirling inferno. The first rocketed into the air, over the sleeping town of Pontypridd, a spear of flame jetting from one side of the valley to the next.

The pillar of fire crashed down into a courtyard. Claire took stock of her surroundings. She stood before an old farmhouse that had been expanded until it sprawled outwards, a stitched together corpse of a home. A police car sat in the driveway. Claire snarled and began to walk forwards towards the house, steam rising from the footprints her bare fear left in the mud, her heat cutting a path through the pouring rain.

"Here she comes," said Jess, more from nervousness than any kind of warning. "I hope this works." She patted Mark on the shoulder. "Showtime old boy."

"Right ok. Hello? Rhiannon? Can you come to the parlour please," he shouted, cupping his mouth as he did.

Rhiannon stood where her mirror had been. It was there this morning. Where was it now? She frowned, adjusted her uniform and began to walk out of the room when it hit her. Rage and jealously pounded in her head. It filled her, as it had filled her on the night she had thrown a harlot through a window. It was stronger this time, the emotion spilling out from inside her, warping her body. She grew stretching outwards as she had done before, but further now. Her limbs became long spindly bone, her fingers and toes stretching into long stiletto like talons. Her eyes sunk until they were pools of black, her fair flowed freely as though it were submerged in water. Her skin become ashen grey, her outfit fading until were completely white. She grasped the doorway with her claws, pulling her now massive form through the doorway, squeezing through with a wet squelching noise. She dropped onto the landing and began crawling down the stairway on all fours, hissing as she went.

"This is the last time. You will not survive this night," said Claire, a smell of burning wood filling the room, burn marks running across the floorboards where she had stepped in through the window and walked across the room.

"Dear, you came!" shouted Mark, stepping forward. The heat radiating from the Jinn was almost overpowering. "I am so glad you accepted, we are to be married within the month!"

"What are you blathering about? Have you finally gone mad human, has this all been a bit too much?" Claire sneered at him, as he continued his advance.

"Mad with love for you my dear! I couldn't be happier!" He grabbed Claire's hand, holding it with both of his own. Mark winced as his hands began to burn. "Oh Rhiannon," he said as a loud scratching noise got closer. "I would love for you to meet the love of my life."

A massive creature extended its head into the doorway, its neck stretching through into the room. It snarled and bared its fangs, a woman's face stretched across a beast of unbridled frenzy. It squeezed through the doorframe, cracking it as it pulled itself through, talons dug deep into the floorboards.

"What is this? Stay back beast." Claire thrust her hand forward, a jet of white-hot flame erupting from her palm. Mark dropped to the ground, rolling across the floor as the blast struck Rhiannon's grotesque body. It struck her in the torso, which rippled, the flame vanishing inside her.

"I have lived worse infernos," croaked the creature, it had a voice like a creaking door. It lunged forward with its talon hand, grabbing the Jinn tightly in her fist. She thrashed in defiance, small jets of flame escaping from between the onryo's fingers. "You come to take everything from me! Again! Harlot!"

"You are deceived, this is a- "Claire began, her words cut off as she began to gag. The onryo's other hand was melting into a fine mist, which was filling Claire's nose and mouth. Panic filled her eyes, then rolled back in her head as the mist continued the fill her. Rhiannon placed her onto the floor, because collapsing completely into a roiling cloud, which force its way inside the twitching girl. She shook for a moment, then stopped, lying motionless on the floor.

"Holy shit, did, did that work?" exclaimed Jess. She ran over to the prone girl, touching her hand to her neck. "She's cold, well normal human cold, there is a pulse, I think she's alive."

"Call an ambulance, well one for each of us," Mark held up his hands, which were red with welts. His shirt was soaked through with sweat.

The doors to the ward swung open as Jess rolled the wheelchair onwards. Aasif sat in it, his one arm bandaged at the elbow, the forearm missing.

"I brought you a visitor," she said. Mark looked up from him the paper he had been trying and failing to read, his hands wrapped tightly in bandages.

"The burn unit huh? And I thought I had it bad," joked Aasif.

"You lost an arm," Mark replied, shifting himself more upright in the hospital bed.

"At least I have one usable hand, which is more than you do right now. Push me a little close please Jess?" he asked, looking over his shoulder.

"Can do." She pushed the chair further forward. "Thought you might like to know Claire is alive, but still in a coma, they're not sure she will ever wake up. Her father has woken up himself but has no memory of anything. That was a ballsy move we pulled."

"How did you know that would work?" Aasif asked, "I'm not sure I follow it one hundred percent."

"Rhiannon, that was the ghosts name, went from a normal, well normal being relative. A normal ghost to an onryo because the weakness between this world and the other was affecting her, it empowered her. Or I guessed so. That's how Claire, well Jinn-Claire got in, through that weakness. It seemed like when she super charged herself she was affecting that weakness just by being here. I guessed that's what caused the rift. I also guessed that being near Rhiannon it would have a similar effect."

"That's a lot of guesses," Aasif said. "A lot could have gone wrong there."

"We didn't have many other options left," Jess added. "I do feel bad, we manipulated her to get what we wanted, and it seems to have destroyed the both. She didn't deserve that."

"Either way, I want to apologise Aasif," said Mark. "It's our fault what happened to you, we should never have gotten you involved.

"I could have walked away at any point, it's not your fault. Plus, the doctors say you saved my life cutting the blood flow like you did. There's no hard feelings on my end. Gives me plenty of time to study up anyway. Already had transfer papers to move to London for a D.C.I Weston I think? She seemed nice on the phone. Better get used to my face buddy," Aasif said, holding out his hand. Mark took it and shook. "I always wanted to be a detective."

Epilogue

They burst from the tree line, greenery showing the roadside as they sprinted happily to the roadside.

"Blessed civilisation!" shouted Bill, twirling excitedly. "Finally. Don't get me wrong, I love a good spruce, but I've had enough Norwegian wilderness for a while." His suit was torn, green stains across his shirt. He was accompanied by a tall stocky man whose suit was in a similar state of disarray.

"I know the feeling. I just need to sit at home for a few weeks. Watch a lot of Netflix. Stay as far away from green for as long as possible." Aaron brushed off a sprig of pine that had gotten caught in his jacket. "There's some documentaries I've been saving, seems like a good time to start working through them."

"Oh, there's a real good one on beautiful undersea reefs!" said Micky as he emerged from the tree line behind them. His white tracksuit was still perfect, untouched by the ravages of the wilderness. He had been annoyingly chipper the whole time. Micky adjusted his flat cap, pulling a cigarette from under the brim, he placed it between his lips.

"Not really my style," said Aaron. "More into the serial killer documentaries myself. Just find them fascinating. What's it like in their heads, you know?" Micky stared at him slightly puzzled.

"I would of thought that would have been easy for… your kind?" he asked.

"Hey not cool Micky, your kind? I thought you were better than that." Bill closed his eyes and shook his head, disappointed at the angel.

"Not what I meant, and you know that." Micky rolled his eyes. "Getting humans to kill each other is like step number one in your playbook that's all."

"The how of getting humans to kill each other is easy," began Aaron as he began walking towards a large metal roadside. Its yellow metal emblazoned with the names of nearby towns. "It's honestly easy. The bit that gets me is why? Why do it? You whisper in someone's ear about a neighbour spying on them and suddenly boom, there they are with an ice-pick giving them an ear exam with the pointy end. Says here Oslo is pretty close."

"Well, enjoy the walk gentlemen, I shall be seeing you around," Said Micky. He tapped Bill on the back enthusiastically.

"What?" Bill asked.

"Well, I'm all recharged ready to go, so I'm off. I hear Oslo is lovely this time of year." Micky grinned, taking two steps backwards, arms outstretched.

"You're not going to take us with you?" Shouted Aaron from in front of the sign.

"No, only got enough juice for one, and well whilst it's been a real blast, I'm going home to enjoy a nice long bath and some relaxing whale song." He tapped the cigarette in his mouth with his finger, the end of it sparked to life. "Laters." There was a blinding flash and then he was gone.

"Arsehole," said Billy, as he began the walk over to Aaron.

The sun blazed down onto Blackpool, a suspiciously bright and warm day for late March. People were taking advantage of the unseasonal weather, sitting along the beach or walking the pier. For Dale it was too warm, he could feel the sweat pooling under his arms. He had insisted on staying at least semi-professional the shirt and trousers combo he had chosen being woefully ill-suited for the heat. Lucille had at least dressed appropriately, she was wearing a red summer dress covered in white spots. Her hair was tied with a matching cloth, which she had topped off with a wide brimmed black straw hat. She was currently making an order at the counter across the pier. Dale spread his arms out across the top of the bench. He had never been one for trips to the beach as a child. It always seemed his parents decided to go at the same time as every other set of parents, so Dale had always associated it with being stuck in traffic for hours, slowly roasting in a hot car. The brief hour or two or lukewarm sea water and overpriced chips seemed like a poor exchange. He had to admit though, he was secretly enjoying this assignment. He was coming around on beaches as a concept.

"Here, got one for you too sourpuss, you going to lighten up a little?" Said Lucille, she was carrying an ice-cream cone in each hand, a rod of flaky chocolate impaled in each.

"I'm not supposed to lighten up. I'm here to supervise you. It's not a holiday," he retorted. "This is serious work for me."

"What and work can't be fun? Go on. Take an ice cream. You know you want too. Don't make me tempt you, you'll know I win." Lucille winked. "Take the ice cream man, live a little."

"What is it apple flavour?" said Dale.

"Yes, funny. Never heard that before, totally original joke. Its vanilla, you know, plain." She deadpanned. She passed him the ice cream, Dale taking it from her begrudgingly. She took a seat beside him on the bench, crossing her legs and adjusting her dress. She took a lick from the ice cream and then looked at the sky for a moment, thinking. "Its funny right, we think of vanilla flavour being plain when vanilla is a famously strong flavour? What's up with that?"

Dale laughed gently. "Big vanilla I guess. Good marketing. You ever drop one of those little bottles of vanilla essence?"

"Oh, that's the worst, I did it making cupcakes once and the bar stank for weeks!"

Gregg knocked back a shot, his friends chanting him on he took another from the bar. He blew out the flame and drank it, before moving on to the next. Olympus wasn't the best nightclub, but it was all Broadstairs had and on buy one get one free shot night Gregg was Zeus himself, lord of the club. He had that stupid boring slideshow the police had made him sit through to thank. It had been one particularly dull slide about not using his abilities that had given him the idea. His trade in fake trainers having fallen by the wayside, Gregg had taken to making outrageous claims about his drinking ability. An eager line of brazen young men turned up the Olympus shot night every Wednesday for the last four weeks, cash in hand to try and win a bet against him. He laughed heartily as he slid the forty pounds from the bar, his opponent collapsed on the floor. Free drinks and easy money! Why hadn't he thought of this sooner.

"Fucking hell you know how to put them back. Fucking aces mate!" said a young man in a gaudy tracksuit, its colours fading from dark blue to bright pink in a gradient. It looked truly awful. He wore a matching a hat, the label still stuck in the brim. "I wish you had started doing this months ago, you're my star attraction!" Gregg took a seat next to him, ducking under a rope that separated to booth from the club floor proper. "Need to tell me your secret someday."

"No secret, I just have a medical condition means I can process booze. Just goes right through me without getting me drunk. I tried to do that TV talent show but it's not family friendly is what they said." Gregg looked up at the ceiling wistfully. "Would been nice to be on TV Dave, you know?"

"I don't think it's all that. Aim too high and you just fail, need to aim for the middle, easier to slide right on in. Look at me, I could have moved to London, tried to open a club there. Would have probably seen me on my arse trying to scrape a living as a club promoter. Never do that by the way, it's just ninety percent giving out flyers and twenty five percent being an arsehole," said Dave.

"That's more than a hundred percent"

"You ever meet a promotor?" asked Dave. "They are absolutely bringing extra arsehole to the mix."

"Fair point"

"Either way, I decided to open a club in my hometown instead. Now I have the biggest club in town, premium trackies, and all the ladies are lining up. Aim for the middle. Speaking of ladies, hey girls!" Dave waved down two young women from across the bar. "I got someone who was real keen to meet you."

Gregg tumbled through the door to his flat, his keys slipping from his hand, his lips locked with the young woman's. She wore a short strapless dress, its cheap PVC material shimmering in the light. Her long hair was bleached blonde, her dark foundation stopping abruptly on her pale neck. She released her kiss and giggled.

"Where's the bedroom handsome?" she asked, her arms draped around Greggs neck. He reached his hands up, taking hers and leading her deeper into the flat, past stacks of takeaway containers and dirty plates. She trotted behind him excitedly, her high heels clicking on the laminate. Gregg pushed his way through a beaded curtain, revealing his room beyond. It had a worrying number of topless posters tacked alongside football posters. The girl pushed Gregg backwards onto the bed, crawling over him, holding her body close.

"What's next?" asked Gregg.

"You get what you deserve," said the girl. Gregg felt a searing agonising pain as she stabbed deeply into his stomach. His wound burnt, sizzling angrily as she stabbed again and again. Each thrust of the blade tore through him, blood erupting from him like a fountain. Gregg lay still, life draining from his body and the girl still stabbed, a seal inside her broken, pouring vengeance into the world. She finally stopped, leant back, and pulled the blade from Greggs body. Its silver edge gleamed in the faint light creeping through the beaded doorway. Its handle was a twisted helix, topped with a Roman coin.

Aasif stared out of his window at the London skyline. Everything felt so cramped and close compared to Pontypridd, like he had moved into an ant's nest. People stacked on top of each other, houses, offices and shops forced together by centuries of pressure coalescing into unmovable diamond buildings stuck firmly into the ancient ground. His first week here had been almost oppressive, Aasif having spent all his life in a place where you could always see at least some green, no matter where you stood. Everything seemed to loom around him, like the shadows in his nightmares, judging him silently.

"Ok, this is the last of them," said Rajan, placed a cardboard box onto a stack of similar boxes.

"Thanks Raj," said Aasif, "I really needed the..." he thought for a moment. "Well, you know what I mean." Aasif walked over to the box Rajan had brought it an opened it, pulling out a cheap white plastic kettle. "Cup of tea?"

"Yeah that would be great. It's a good place you found. Not too bad."

"Are you serious? This place is tiny, it's like living in a box. My Ponty flat was twice the size and one third the price. Why anyone would actively choose to live here I have no idea." Aasif walked back over to the box and pulled out two mugs. "Sugar?"

"Yeah two please. Milk as well. You'll get used to it, London's not as bad as it first seems," said Rajan.

Aasif turned to face him, seriousness turning his face to stone. "I hate it, and it's awful."

"Oh, thank god," laughed Rajan, "everyone else who moves here spends the first few months talking like this was the land of rainbows and honey. I normally try and let them work it out on their own."

"Can we talk about the fucking tubes? Who decided to combine trains and buses and keep the worst parts of both? And no-one says sorry! For anything! If I was this rude back home I would get a black eye and some bruised ribs. You know they made me stand on the tube coming here my first day. No-one offered me their seat. Trying to keep a suitcase from rolling away and hold onto those fucking tiny hand grips with only one arm was a fucking challenge. I had to grip the damn thing between my legs like I was riding one of those mechanical bulls." Aasif poured the kettle which had clicked off mid-rant. "Plus trying to find anything is impossible. I tried to go into a corner shop for milk before the truck arrived for my stuff and I swear that there was one at the end of this very street that has just up and vanished. It took me twenty minutes to find one and somehow thirty minutes to walk home."

"Ah, you just found out about London time, it's a bit wonky around here, if something is supposed to take ten minutes its half hour. Thirty minutes its two hours." Rajan tapped his watch for emphasis.

"Please tell me that's not some supernatural thing."

"Nah just shit traffic and two thousand years of just sticking streets wherever the felt like that morning." He grasped the mug Aasif offered him and took an eager gulp. "How's it going studying for the exam?"

"Not too bad, I think. I would love to pick your brains about some aspects of it, from you. Mark, Jess and Dale too. Where is Dale by the way?"

"You will not believe this," said Rajan, taking another sip, "work paid for him to go on holiday."

"No, I'm not doing it," said Dale. He crossed his arms like a petulant child and turned his back to the stall.

"Come on, it's just throwing the ball," pleaded Lucille, "look at the prize, you know I need that!" She pointed excitedly. Hanging at the back of the coconut shy was a large stuffed toy in the shape of a cartoon devil.

"You have all the subtly of a hammer sometimes you know that," Dale said. "The sign for your bar for example."

"It's just a bit of fun. Come on, try and win me a prize. Loosen up a little." Lucille gripped his arm and look up at him, batting her eyelids in an exaggerated fashion.

"Ok fine. But because I want to try it, no other reason." Dale reached into his pocket and produced a pound coin. He placed it into the palm of the stall attendant who passed him three white plastic balls. The first two he threw went wide, the third one struck a coconut, but bounced off, the hard-hairy fruit stubbornly unmoving. Dale grumbled to himself and produced another pound coin. "I'll get it this time," he whispered to himself.

Jess opened the driver side car door and sat down, resting the plastic bag onto her lap. It smelt of vinegar, salt and oil. She shut the door and began digging eagerly into the thin white plastic, the bags rustling as she did. She produced a white paper bag, which she placed into Marks lap.

"Did you remember the curry this time?" he asked. He began to unwrap the paper, his bandaged hands making it slow and difficult.

"Ah shit, no, I forgot. Sorry." Jess pulled how own portion of chips from the bag.

"See, this is why I normally make the chip run. The sooner I lose these the better," Mark said, shaking his hands over dramatically. "I can't wait to carry things again. You know that might be the saddest thing I ever said."

"It might very well be," Jess laughed. She removed small brown paper bag from inside the plastic carrier and dropped it ceremoniously onto Marks chips. "Of course, I remembered. I wrote it down."

"Finally, a use for all those notebooks you carry." Mark carefully removed the carton from its wrapper, holding it delicately between his forefinger and thumb, his palms still too painful to put pressure on. With his other hand he slowly peeled off the lid, his hands like pincers, like a bomb disposal robot opening a yoghurt.

Jess excitedly tapped his shoulder with the back of her hand. "Hey there he is, we're up." She pointed at the creature as it trotted into the light from the streetlamp. A strange hairless ape, its writhing tentacles peeling open a black rubbish bag. It began to dig through the rubbish eagerly.

Mark stared down at the now open carton in his hands, his chips rapidly cooling in his lap. "One day," he said, "I will get to eat these when they're still hot."

A MESSAGE FROM THE AUTHOR

Firstly, a huge thank you for reading this. If you liked it, please do consider leaving a review. Every single review makes a huge difference to an independent author. Jess and Mark, as well as the concept of the Special Investigations team, sprang from the pages of a short story collection I wrote, Horrorscopes. You can find two of their canonically earlier adventures there, along with ten other short stories. A sample story can be found after this message.

To be as up to date as possible on upcoming works, please check out the links below or send me an email at contact@pwhillard.co.uk

- **Website – www.pwhillard.co.uk**
- **Facebook – www.facebook.com/pwhillard**
- **Twitter – www.twitter.com/evidar**
- **Discord - https://discord.gg/A7HS73A**

Libra- A Short story from the Horroscopes collection

Today's your day! A new job role awaits. With Mercury in ascendant, remember to treat others the way you wish to be treated.

Charlie checked her phone again. The address read "275 Olympia street", but the building she was stood in front of didn't list ThemisCorp as an occupant on the board outside. A great steel and glass behemoth it loomed over her. She shrugged, maybe the signage was out of date. She put her phone away and walked into the reception.

"Hi," Charlie greeted the receptionist. "I've got an interview at this address for a ThemisCorp? It's not on the sign outside"

The receptionist let out a slow audible sigh. "They really need to correct that address, happens all the time. You want 275A. Really annoying." The young man spoke with a level of contempt, like Charlie had purposely gone to the wrong address. "Go out the main doors. Take a left, then a left again past this building." He had taken his gaze off Charlie and was now far more concerned with something on his computer.

Charlie stomped angrily out of the building. The sheer rudeness of the man. She took a left as he said, and then turned left again. She closed her eyes dejectedly and lifted her head, letting out a frustrated moan as she did. The second left was an alleyway. Something had gotten into one of the rubbish bags that had been tossed here and now rotten food had been dragged all over. It was typical. Finally, an interview with a seemingly big company with a swanky office building and it was really in some disgusting back alley. Interview practice is valuable she reminded herself as she tiptoed past some kind of slime that seemed equal parts white and green. At the end of the alley a sign had been screwed to bare brick. It read *"ThemisCorp"* above a large red arrow instructing people to follow the alley around to the left. "Oh, come on." complained Charlie aloud.

She followed the alley around its corner. Charlie was behind the big office building now, but the walls around her were brick with a thick layer of dirt and grime. She guessed they must have gone cheap with the back of the building. Typical corporate bluster she thought, show a good impression but cheap out where you can. She weaved past a large American style dumpster emblazoned with one of the company logos she had seen on the board, some gaudy cartoon bull. Another sign the same as before was again screwed to the wall. ThemisCorp to the left it indicated. Strange, she didn't think she had walked the whole length of the office building, that thing seemed huge. Charlie felt like she had barely gone anywhere. She turned to follow the sign and walked off down the alley it indicated. At the end of this one was another sign for a left turn. This didn't make sense, she had gone around in a circle, she had to be at the front again. Yet there it was, another alleyway. Maybe she had walked past a turn? Conscious that her interview was in twenty minutes she moved her handbag to her other shoulder and continued onwards. Everyone knew that they expected you at least ten minutes before the interview time. Judging on how eager you are before it even began.

This time the alley ended with a large metal staircase, the kind of American style fire escape you rarely saw in Colchester. "You've got to be fucking kidding!" shouted Charlie as she saw the sign. *"ThemisCorp, please take the stairs,"* it read. Still muttering profanity, she bent down to remove her heels. Last thing she needed was to get caught in the metal grate. The dark green metal of the stairs was cold and harsh even through her tights. At the top of the staircase was a red wooden door. A small plexiglass block screwed to it at eye level stated that this was the right place. She slipped her heels back on and stepped through the door.

The reception was pristine. Everything was a pale grey or chrome. The placed seemed to almost gleam. It was oddly bright. A young woman sat behind a large curved desk in a white pressed suit, with a white shirt and a plain black tie. She gestured to Charlie. Maybe this wouldn't be so bad after all she thought.

"Hello dear, here for an interview?" She asked.

"Yes, I'm Charlie Sutton, its scheduled for two," replied Charlie

"Ok well, you're a little early. Eager to leave a good impression." The woman winked at Charlie. "I'll let your interviewer know you're here. Please take a seat," she said gesturing to a set of large white leather chairs. Charlie could have sworn they weren't there when she came in. "My names Nikki. I'll be back in a moment if you need anything." Nikki stood up and walked down the corridor. Charlie could see she was wearing trainers with her suit. Her heart dropped. That was hardly professional.

Charlie looked frustratingly at her watch. It was now twenty minutes past two. Her overall impression of the company was getting worse by the minute. She browsed through Instagram idly as she waited. She scrolled through the stream of celebrities advertising weight loss products and of models promoting poorly planned festivals. All so vapid she thought. Charlie let out an audible tut. Never a day worked between any of these people.

"Ready to go?" Said Nikki. Charlie nearly dropped her phone she was so startled. Was she there a minute ago? "Room eighteen, just down the hall and to the right."

"Right, ok, thanks." Charlie grabbed her handbag, slipped her phone into it and stood up. "Any advice?" she asked Nikki.

"Try not to be too judgmental of how we do things." Nikki replied, waving at Charlie as she walked off down the corridor.

"Room eighteen. Room eighteen," Charlie repeated it to herself, so she didn't forget. She counted the doors off as she walked past them. Sixteen, seventeen, eighteen. She gripped the handle, opened the door and stepped through. Charlie suddenly felt like she was falling for a brief second, that sharp sickness of a drop. She stumbled slightly and righted herself. She looked around in disbelief. Charlie was stood in another identical corridor. She turned around to go back the way she came and bashed her nose on a very solid wall, dropping her handbag in shock "What the hell?" she muttered rubbing her nose. Ahead of her was another door like the one she had come through. It was labelled "One". To her right was a large set of fire doors. To the left the corridor continued onwards. There was no door at the other end, so Charlie pushed open the fire doors and stepped through into another identical corridor. On the floor in front of her sat her bag. "What the fuck is going on?" She turned to investigate her original corridor. Her bag was also sat there, perfectly mirrored. She tried the door marked "One" in her panic. Locked. Same with the next door labelled "*Two*". She scooped up her bag and began to run as best she could in her heels. When she reached the end, she leant against the end wall. Charlie heaved against it hoping it was in some way fake. "Ok, very funny, you can come out now!" she shouted, hoping it was a cruel YouTube prank. There was no answer, so she tried the doors nearest her. Seventeen. Locked. She gripped the handle for eighteen and turned it. The door creaked open. The room beyond was pitch black. The light from the corridor seemed to stop at the threshold. Charlie tested the ground beyond with some trepidation. It felt solid enough. She stepped through. She stood still for a second. The blackness seemed to envelop her, a thick shroud of inexistence. The room felt strangely warm, like she was wrapped in a thick blanket. Then, the blackness became searing unbearable light. Charlie closed her eyes, they still burnt. She screamed.

When she opened her eyes, she was sat in an office chair behind a desk. She was in a reception. A young woman in a black skirt suit and light pink blouse was stood before her. She carried a large black handbag over one shoulder. The woman had her blonde hair in a ponytail. Bottled, thought Charlie, and her contouring wasn't very good either.

"Hi," She said "I've got an interview at this address for a ThemisCorp? It's not on the sign outside?"

Charlie's mouth moved on its own. She couldn't keep herself from letting out a loud sigh. This was the fifth time today alone. "They really need to correct that address, happens all the time" why was she saying this? "You want 275A. Really annoying." She could feel the annoyance at having to repeat herself. She felt anger towards ThemisCorp for not correcting it. "Go out the main doors. Take a left, then a left again past this building." Her gaze was caught by the computer screen in front of her. The image had begun to flicker and distort. The screen went totally black except for large white letters. They read "JUDGEMENT". Everything went white again.

When her version came back she was laying in an ally way next to some ripped rubbish bags. She tried to move but her side screamed in pain. She could feel blood soaking into her thick mottled coat. It felt like her stiches had split. She adjusted herself on the sleeping bag she lay on. Charlie pulled her coat closed to try and keep out the cold. A woman in a black skirt suit walked past, trying to gingerly step past spilt rubbish. She paid Charlie no attention. Charlie pulled out a day-old newspaper from under her sleeping bag and began pulling out pages from the centre to stuff into her coat. The headline on the front page read "JUDGMENT". Then the white returned.

Charlie was sat in a tiny bedsit. It was cold, but she knew she couldn't afford to put on the heating. She had spent her last on getting the most recent pictures taken. She clicked the button to upload them to Instagram. It was draining, constantly trying to promote herself all day every day. The few advertising deals she had paid so little she had almost considered stopping, but her entire life for the past few years had been about presenting herself in a particular way. How could she change all that? She typed into the text box. "#JUDGEMENT" it read.

When Charlie opened her eyes, she was relieved to see she was herself again. She was sat in front of a desk. She was in someone's office. Across from her was a tall older woman. She had short blonde hair and like Nikki was wearing an all-white suit. There was a large set of bronze scales to one side of her desk.

"Are you alright Miss Sutton? You seem to have spaced out a little bit there?" The woman asked in a thick Greek accent. In front of her was a name plate that read "*Dike Astraea*"

"What? Sorry? I'm not sur- "stuttered Charlie.

"I'll repeat the question then. Name a time you worked well in team in a target driven environment." Dike said, holding a pen expectedly.

"I'm sorry, I'm not sure what's going on here?" asked Charlie.

Dike wrote something down "We'll move on then. What's your biggest weakness?" she asked.

"Look I don't know what's going on, but please just let me leave," Charlie begged.

"Not that one either? Ok, next question. Did you ever consider stopping when you ran over that little girl?" Dike tapped the pen impatiently as she spoke.

"How do you know? What? What is this?" Charlie was breaking into tears as she spoke.

"Ok well, don't worry, next up is the tour, I do hope you enjoy it!" Dike stood up and motioned to the door.

Charlie felt an overwhelming urge to stand up and walk out the door. She stepped across the threshold and found herself standing on a large open plan office area. Rows of desks lined the office, each with several people sat in a row staring at computers and wearing headsets. They looked like slaves on a rowing ship. Several of the people were crying, others were staring directly ahead, with cold dead stares.

"Oh, hello dear!" Charlie had expected to see Nikki, but instead there was a young woman about Charlies age. She was wearing a suit the same style as the others, but it was black with a white tie. She was flanked by two other women each identical to her. "I'm Lachesis, but every just calls me Lacey, these are my sisters." The other women nodded. "Now come dear let's take the tour!"

"I'm sorry," sobbed Charlie "I just want to go home."

"Nonsense! Getting the tour is a good sign! Never known someone get the tour and not get the job!" Aren't that right sisters?" The other two women nodded in response to Lacey. "Now come along." She put an arm around Charlie and pulled her forward. "This is the call floor. This is where out agents make decisions that for some customers could be life and death! This is what you'll be doing if you get the job!" As they walked past one of the phone operators slumped onto his desk. "Oh, I hope that gentleman's alright" said Lacey as they walked past. Someone else had walked over and was lifting the man from his seat. "We do have an err... high turnover here"

"I don't understand. I thought this was for loss adjusting. What's going on here?" asked Charlie through the tears.

"Loss adjusting? Is that what they're calling it now?" Lacey laughed. "I suppose you could call it that. We used to do this all ourselves, me and my sisters. We worked for our cousins, you've met Dike yes? Her mother named this company you know? Anyway, we couldn't do it ourselves anymore, too many clients you see. Right that's the call floor. Not a long tour I'm afraid." They were stood in front of an office door. "Right through you go dear, final interviews in there." Lacey opened the door and pushed Charlie through with a shove.

Charlie was sat on a bike. It was bright pink and had tassels on the handlebars. She rang the bell excitedly. It was a Peppa Pig one and she had begged her father for it. She set off along the pavement, wobbling as she went, her stabilisers stopping her from falling over. Her helmet sat uncomfortably on her head. Across the street, her friend Sandy was waving. She looked left, then right and then started to pedal across. She didn't see the slight tatty Ford KA come careening around the corner too quickly. Charlie felt the impact. She could feel her ribs shatter, shredding her lungs. She felt her legs turn to fragments, held together by the twisted metal of her bike. The crunch of her spine as she hit the ground head first. Charlie tried to scream in pain but couldn't breathe to do it. She watched through blood stained vision as the car stopped, waited a moment, and then begin to drive away. She could hear Sandy screaming as she closed her eyes and felt the same warm blackness from earlier.

"Congratulations!" Dike was sitting on the edge of one of the desks on the call floor. Charlie was sat in a chair facing a computer screen. "You got the job! Immediate start. Let's get you going". Dike picked up a headset and placed it Charlies head. She sat motionless completely numb. "It's on the job training sadly! You'll pick it up though. You're good at judging people. Not so good as sticking around to be judged for your own mistakes though. Never mind! Here comes your first call."

There was a loud beeping tone in Charlies ear. A faint voice came through the headset. "Hello? Where am I? What's happening?" It was almost a whisper.

"He-Hello," stuttered Charlie. The computer screen had brought up a whole host of information. It had a name, John Austin, forty-eight from Swansea. "Is that John?" Asked Charlie.

"Yes, yes that's me! Where am I? I can't see anything? I remember falling, then I was here." John was frantic. The screen stated *"Fell from a second-floor balcony. Potentially fatal."* John had started to cry "Please, I've never done anything to anyone!" The computer screen updated again. It read. *"Stole three Mars bars aged six. Cheated on maths exam aged sixteen. Refused his brother a kidney aged thirty-five."* Underneath in bold black text was the word judgement. Then two icons. One of a solid thread. The other one featured a thread that had been cut.

"Well?" asked Dike? "What do you think? Yes or No?"

*The full Horrorscopes collection, by P.W Hillard, can be found on **Amazon**.*

Printed in Poland
by Amazon Fulfillment
Poland Sp. z o.o., Wrocław